Kode-X ©

Rise of the Twin Flames

Written by:
Hanif Burt

Story by:
Hanif Burt, Fatah Freeman, Leonidas B. Thomas Jr.

Hanif Burt

ISBN-13: 978-1514723074

DEDICATION

Unknown to us, this story had been subconsciously brewing in our minds for well over 30 years. Then, one day, what started out as a simple Madlib session between three cousins resulted in the decision to combine our imaginations into one incredible tale.

It has been an amazing journey for all of us. We've dreamed, cried, laughed and learned while writing this story. As children we had incredible imagination that we let society bleed out of us. Never again. If we've gained only one thing from writing this story, it is that we've reasserted a portion of our imagination. Never stop dreaming—it is an essential part of life.

This book is dedicated to consciousness and the pursuit of raising one's spiritual understanding. The purpose of this book is to have fun with the imagination while exploring principles that may be unfamiliar to much of Western society. Hopefully, after reading this book, a jolt in your imagination can spark the journey to increase your spiritual understanding. This is our story. Hope you enjoy.

Hanif Burt

ACKNOWLEDGMENTS

The greatest things accomplished are done with a woman's love. In this world, what else is greater? To the woman who makes me great. I love you, honor you, and thank you for teaching me what love is. Through you I met God.

-Hanif Burt

Chapter 1

Adam walked, wounded and tired, dragging his feet under the hot African sun. He was shackled and chained to a string of others from his village. His wrists and ankles were bloody and singed from the heat of the metal cuffs. His legs wobbled from the long, miserable journey. His face was worn and cracked from the hot sand blowing against it. His dark chocolate skin beaded with sweat, reflecting the torrid, scorching glare of the sun's piercing rays upon his muscular physique. His normally handsome and peaceful face was ragged and stressed from the arduous journey. Exhausted, he could barely lift his feet off the hot, dusty ground. His swollen and thirsty tongue made it next to impossible to swallow. Even if there was water to drink, his throat muscles would find it difficult to contract enough to allow passage. He occasionally licked the salty sweat off his burning arms to wet his parched tongue.

I am a Zulu warrior. May my death come quick and honorable, rather than continue to suffer this hell, Adam thought.

Adam, being one of the great Zulu warriors, would gladly take death over living with defeat. Emotionally dazed, he barely noticed he was staggering up a large silver ramp. He conjured up enough energy to slowly lift his weary head.

"By the gods," said Adam with a raspy voice as he noticed he was now entering a large, silver, oval wheel.

The wheel was four times the size of his village and hovered effortlessly in the sky.

What is this thing? This cannot be real. I must be suffering from the thirst, thought Adam.

It was rumored across the land that his enemies had a powerful wheel that could take to the skies. But Adam had no idea how they could control such a powerful weapon. That being said, it was clear from the previous battle that his enemies weren't invincible. Adam saw the bloodstained fields with their strange looking corpses sprinkled amongst the fallen Zulu.

His tribesmen weren't the only ones who gave the invaders a good fight. His master teacher told him the Zulus in the east managed to bring one of the wheels down with one of their secret weapons: the merkaba.

As Adam walked into the wheel, there were no signs of his enemies—another confirmation of their power. Since their defeat, Adam hadn't seen the enemy. Yet they could capture him and his villagers and walk them many miles without ever being detected. This was by far the Zulus' greatest defeat.

Further into the wheel, he heard loud clashing sounds and screams of terror. With every scream, Adam felt his heart plummet. He looked about the wheel as the despair gripped his body.

After passing a dimly lit room, he saw her through a small barred opening. It was the love of his life. She was being held captive in a room crammed with dreary villagers all reeking of pain and misery. Once she spotted Adam, she screamed for him. She fought her way through the rancid, packed room to get to him.

While reaching through the barred door, she cried for Adam, begging him to do something to save her and their unborn child. "Adam help me, help me please, help me please," she implored.

He feared for her and what could come next to their unborn child. Her panic-stricken voice and face made him forget about his long, laborious journey and defeat. The fear on her face filled him with emotional strife, rage, and anger. He madly pulled and tugged against the line of chained villagers trying to save her. He tried to resist by gripping his bloody feet into the metal ridges on the floor. Despite all of his efforts, the chained line continued to pull him along, giving him no chance at rescuing her. He wasn't sure what was causing the line to pull him ahead. But whatever it was, he wasn't strong enough to stop it. The further away he was pulled from her, the more hysterical she became. He jumped and threw himself wildly around, yet Adam's outburst was ignored by the chained villagers. Breaking a Zulu spirit was an immense task, but the toll of the journey was far too great on their souls. Adam's failed attempt at saving her left hopelessness in his heart.

The further Adam was forcibly pulled away, the more Nia sobbed; her eyes dimmed with sorrow as all hope faded. Just inside of earshot, Adam heard her scream with terror. He had never heard a scream like that before. The sheer horror in her voice tore through his soul. He bucked like a newly caught mustang in his last attempt to free her. It was pointless; he didn't have enough strength to overcome the shackles binding his hands and feet. As her screams faded away, Adam fell to his knees— weeping, knowing what her silence meant. He let her down. He ached for her with all of his heart. Before Adam could get himself together, he started to vomit. His distressed body was in complete shock. With no mercy, the line of chained villagers continued, dragging him in his own vomit. He was dragged into a room packed with more villagers that reeked with the vile stench of suffering. He realized he was in the same kind of room that his love was in before her gruesome death. His eyes swelled with panic as it dawned on him what was about to happen. Adam had had enough. He re-established his Zulu pride and desperately tried to rally the others. But with most of the Zulu warriors dead, he'd have to rely on the might of the villagers. Still paralyzed by their defeat, the villagers hardly reacted to Adam's rally. Their stunned faces just stared hopelessly back at him. Suddenly, a large door slid open. Out came large, metal wheels, spinning with razor-sharp blades. The villagers shrieked with panic. Their cries were eventually drowned out by the high-pitched sound of the metal wheels. The first group of villagers were sliced, diced and torn apart. Screams of horror filled the room as villagers' flesh flew, blood sprayed, and bones were shredded. The villagers scrambled away from the blades, scampering as far as they could to the back of the room. Those closest to the powerful blades were immediately blended and liquefied. The smell of shredded flesh polluted Adam's nostrils. The liquefied remains swirled down a drain in the floor like a thick bloody soup. With his body drenched in blood and his heart pounding, Adam still tried to save the others. He shuttered at the horrid thought of his body being ripped, shredded, and flung about the walls, to eventually ooze down a drain. In the midst of the gruesome scene, Adam noticed cold, dark eyes peering down at him from a window above. The face was difficult to make out, but the eyes glared with soul-shattering evil. They seemed to enjoy the anguish, the agony, the despair, and they especially seemed anxious for his death. Eventually the wheels were upon him. Adam pressed his back as far as he could against the wall to avoid the instruments of death. As the wheels began to grind into his chest, he heard a sweet, calming female voice. "Wake up Adam, wake up."

Chapter 2

Adam woke up haunted by his nightmare, gasping for air. His heart pounded while sweat poured down his face. He looked up at his ceiling while wiping the tears out of his eyes. He took a moment to settle his heart beat. While lying in his sweat-soaked pillow, he was relieved that this was all a dream. Yet he was irritated that he'd had such a graphic, painful re-enactment of his death. Adam had been having similar dreams his entire life, dreams so real that it was hard to separate them from reality. For many of the dreams, he still bared markings similar to birth marks. It was as if he had lived a thousand lives. To a certain degree, Adam felt as though these events had actually happened to him. He felt the pain of the chains, the fatigue in his body, the fear in his heart, and the death of his loved one. Adam looked down at his wrist and ankles, "Ohhh shit!" he murmured.

He examined the front and back of his wrists

and ankles to make sure his eyes weren't deceiving him. Reaching out his arms and rubbing his wrist, he saw that he had light bruises. It was as if he had been actually cuffed, like in his dream. His wrists ached and throbbed as they did in his dream as well. His ankles were swollen with dark bruising that was sensitive to the touch. There was even a long vertical bruise down his chest. The bottoms of his feet were red and worn, with blistering on his pads and heels. His parched tongue was swollen and sticky, begging for hydration. It was like he was re-living his nightmare.

Am I fuckin' still dreaming? Adam pondered. *This can't be real… how can this shit be real?*

He took more time to study his painful bruising.

Adam pinched himself and said aloud, "This … this must have really happened!"

Adam tried to figure out what phenomenon could make his body show physical signs of trauma from a dream.

Putting the nightmare aside for now, Adam slowly pried himself off his pillow. Although he knew the voice was most likely in his head, he frantically looked around for the sweet calming voice that woke him from his dream. He thought maybe this time would be different. He looked to his left, to his right, just hoping that she might surprise him from somewhere in his small studio. But she wasn't there; it was his imagination yet again. Adam flopped back down to his pillow, shaking his head in disgust.

What the hell is happening to me? he thought.

He had so many dreams of her, so many experiences with her, and yet he hadn't physically met her. It seemed as though he lived a thousand lives with this woman. He'd been continuously dreaming about her since he was a small boy. In his dreams, he felt whole and complete while being around her. Outside of his dreams he felt empty, like half a person without her. Upon awakening from each dream, he'd relive the hollow ache the mystery woman gave his heart over and over again.

Out of the thousands of dreams he'd had, her face wasn't always identical, but her eyes, voice and scent remained the same. She often went by different names, but lately the name Nia seemed to fit best. Her voice could always soothe him. He knew more about this mysterious woman than anyone he had ever met. He knew her favorite color, why she was afraid of heights, even her favorite foods. It felt to him like a permanent obsession he had carried over lifetimes. This sticking obsession kept Adam from having any meaningful relationship to date because no woman could ever compare. This Nia, he just couldn't shake. To some degree, the love of this woman had doomed him, an unfair curse of unmated twin flames. This was very embarrassing for Adam… to be in love with a woman he had never met. Despite the oddity, it was this special relationship that gave him comfort; he drew energy from her as much as he could to give his life meaning.

Adam rolled out of bed, realizing that he was off to a late start for work. Despite his tardiness, he still made time for TV. He grabbed the remote and turned on his small television to catch the regular morning news pundits discussing the recent public enemies of the government.

Adam continued getting dressed as he listened to one of the guest analysts on the broadcast, "These guys are more than a menace to society, they are motivated by their radical ideas. We believe this rebellion is led by two brothers who call themselves Kojo and Clutch. We don't know much about them but we believe they are originally from West Africa or Nigeria."

Africa? Let me see what these dudes look like, thought Adam.

He turned to the TV to see head shots of the duo. Kojo appeared to be a man in a small boy's body. His size made him seem non-threatening. He had a wide, flat nose, a clean-shaven five o'clock shadow with a larger than normal bald head. His eyes had a strong, devious glare, like he was pondering his next big scheme. The look on his face was characterized by arrogance, almost as if he thought he was better. He had a cigar to go with his elitist persona. He was neatly attired in a light brown leather jacket, with a collared polo shirt underneath.

"Look at him... he thinks he is the shit. Big head must be the brains of the group," chuckled Adam while ironing his shirt.

Clutch's head shot was shown next. The mere sight of his picture was enough to wipe the grin off Adam's face. Clutch was huge, very muscular, with a broad flat nose and newly grown stubble across his face. His head was bald, his skin was dark brown, and his jaw was pronounced, connecting to strapping muscular chords in his neck. To match his brawny look, he wore a rugged fatigue jacket. The very sight of him was enough to make anyone alone with him feel nervous, intimidated, and threatened. His physical stature alone could dim the confidence of a young Cassius Clay. Clutch's intimidating stare was a direct blow to Adam's manhood, which was an extremely rare occurrence.

Growing up in an orphanage, Adam was no stranger to conflict. His daily fights as a youngster gave him the preparation and heart to face the most daunting of thugs, crooks, and gangsters. He once beat down a rowdy gang of bikers for a simple disagreement over a dice game. Adam lived a hard-knock life, and being a large man himself, found very few men could intimidate him or make him think twice. But with one glance at Clutch's head shot, Adam immediately knew he'd think twice before he would go at it with Clutch.

Adam quickly buried the dent in his pride from Clutch and listened closer to learn more about the terrorists.

"Why are these men so dangerous?" asked the host.

The guest analyst confidently and quickly answered, "Well we believe they are responsible for the banking shutdowns in South Africa and Nigeria in 2008 that caused a run on the market in various economies, which of course they haven't fully recovered from, costing governments billions of dollars. We believe they are looking to do the same here in the States."

The host continued asking questions, "Isn't your position based on conservatism that your party…"

Before the host could finish, the guest analyst

rudely interrupted, yelling, "This is not a time for politics, Hal ....tell that to all the innocent civilians these men have murdered over the years or all the ailing families they have affected by whipping out and stealing their life savings! These men are terrorists and have to be brought to justice. Don't forget about their ties to the Colony..."

"Enough of the negative!" said Adam, talking to himself while cutting off the TV.

"Let's get this day started off on the right foot," he said while thumbing through songs on his mp3 player.

He made light of his reoccurring dreams by playing an ironic song, "Here we go again," by the Isley Brothers. He cranked the music loud, enough to disturb his neighbors. His usual neighbor nemesis, Ms. Williams, was the first to complain. He ignored her wall-banging protest, and continued cranking the music. Adam readied himself for work; all the while Ms. Williams continued her objection with verbal profanities.

"Get over it!" yelled Adam through the walls to his neighbor.

He continued singing and prancing about his small studio, cranking the music louder and louder. Looking at his wrist, he noticed the bruises were starting to fade. He raised his pants and saw the same could be said about the blemishes around his ankles. His chest bruise was also becoming lighter.

"Man, what's happening to me? This is the strangest morning shit ever! I must be goin' crazy. Ain't no telling what my day's gonna be like," he said.

Adam stood just over 6'4", packed with 225 pounds of lean muscle. His physique was so perfect, Greek gods would envy him. Although he was 33, his superb genetics would allow him to pass for 25. He was chiseled with good looks; light brown almond-shaped eyes, a jetting jaw, and perfectly sculpted cheek bones. His skin was like smooth milk chocolate, blemish and wrinkle free. He had a light, un-groomed mustache and goatee that added to his rough demeanor. His hair was wooly and wild like a lion's mane.

Showered and dressed, Adam grabbed his security badge, belt, favorite head phones and headed out the door.

Usually the Phoenix skies were littered with chemtrails, casting the city in a gloomy grey haze. They hung above the city like floating oceans. It had been difficult for the city to live up to its moniker of 'the valley of the sun' since the late nineties. On this day, the skies were clear, not even a cloud in sight. Adam took time to feel the sun's warm, desert radiance on his face. As the toasty Arizona morning sun greeted his skin, he noticed something different inside. The sun's rays spawned thousands of tingles within his body, causing him to feel stronger, faster, and clearer in the mind. He no longer felt his body's nagging aches and pains. He looked at his bruises and watched them completely vanish before his eyes. While in awe of the disappearing blemishes, he was jolted by his neighbor.

"Next time, turn that rap bullshit down, we are trying to sleep over here!" yelled his neighbor through a window.

"First of all it ain't rap, it's the Isley Brothers. You should know about them, they from your era. Second, if you don't like my shit then turn your bullshit music down," defiantly yelled Adam.

The neighbor continued yelling, "You kids are so disrespectful..."

Adam walked off waving his hands in a dismissive manner. Raking his hands through his wooly hair to perfect its lionesque style, he said, "Yeah yeah yeah— whatever, Ms. Williams. You always complaining about somethin'..."

Rocked in mid-sentence, Adam's mouth hung open, his hands slowly dropped from his hair. He was shocked to his core at what he saw. Walking down the street he saw auras around people. It looked like a colorful living energy that radiated outward two feet from each person's body. It was beautiful. Each aura was different, like a fingerprint uniquely filled with amazing colors. He walked down the street in slow motion, head on a swivel, meticulously eyeing every person on the street in amazement. Waiting for the bus on his way to work, he saw the auras of the passersby, driving cars, riding bikes, jogging, and walking. He slowly got on the bus, ruffling a few feathers as he rudely stared and studied passengers' auras.

"Take a picture, dammit! It will last longer, you dirt bag," screamed an elderly lady on the bus. Embarrassed, Adam chuckled and turned away.

"My bad," he pleaded as he settled firmly back against his seat.

He spent the rest of the ride looking down into his lap in deep thought—perplexed, overwhelmed, and confused by his new ability. His mind was racing, searching for some type of explanation for what he was experiencing.

This can't be real... maybe I'm still dreaming. Nah, that's crazy! Maybe I need to chill out on those rum and Cokes. Or go see a doctor or somethin', Adam rationalized silently.

He reached his stop and in a listless daze he lumbered off the bus. For the moment, Adam tried his best to put his thoughts aside in order to prepare for work. He arrived at his job and was rushed at his locker by his good friend, Jolon. They were an odd duo, essentially complete opposites. Jolon, an overweight Native American man, was in his fifties. Adam, nearly half his age, had the body of a NFL linebacker. Jolon was jovial, fun, and engaging. Adam, on the other hand, was introverted and antisocial. Jolon wore his long gray hair slicked back into a long ponytail. He had tanned skin, slanted eyes and a full-figured face. Despite their differences, Adam had allowed Jolon to get close to him. In fact, Jolon may be one of the few who had ever witnessed a smile on Adam's face. Still unsure of what was happening to him, Adam discreetly studied Jolon's aura from the corner of his eye. He was careful to hide his secret from Jolon.

"Adam… Adam… hey man…I need you to do the thing… come on man, this is the last time," begged Jolon with extreme urgency and excitement in his voice.

Still burying his head in his locker so that Jolon wouldn't know he was grinning, Adam said in his usual deep voice, "Jolon, I told you I don't do that anymore."

But Jolon was relentless, "I know but this is the last time. Oh come on man... let me show you a picture of her."

Jolon franticly scrambled through his messy wallet for the picture.

"Here, look... ain't she a doll?" asked Jolon while waving the picture in Adam's face.

Adam wiped the grin off his face. He took his head out of his locker to get a look at Jolon's new lady interest.

"Give me that," he said as he jokingly snatched the picture out of Jolon's hands.

"Ohhhh... she kinda looks like your cousin Eddie. But at least it's an improvement over your last girlfriend," laughed Adam while handing the picture back.

"Very funny mister tall, dark, and lonely," said Jolon, snatching the picture back from Adam.

"Come on, man... this one is different. This is the one... I know it, bro. Okay, I'll make you a deal; I'll do all the security sweeps for a week straight," pleaded Jolon while carefully tucking the picture back in his wallet.

"Hahahaha okay, okay man, don't get ya panties

all bunched up," chuckled Adam as he closed his locker.

"I'll do it, but meet me after break is over. I don't want a bunch of people to see or they'll all start asking me all over again," demanded Adam.

Jolon was relieved. "Thank you, thank you! If you weren't so ugly, I'd kiss you," he said jokingly.

"It's all good, bro, and you know I'm just clownin'. She's pretty cute," said Adam, impressively nodding his head in regards to Jolon's girl.

"Oh, I forgot to ask... how did things go with Monica?" questioned Jolon excitedly.

As close as Adam was to Jolon, he could never let him in on his embarrassing secret that pretty much made women invisible to him. Nia was real to Adam, but Jolon would never understand his dream girlfriend. After all, she'd been with him since he was a boy and she was the only girl he really knew.

Adam winced, "Uh... Ah man well... It didn't. I kinda canceled on her again."

"You what?" yelled Jolon, throwing his hands up in disbelief.

"Dude, what good is it for you to be blessed with the tall, dark and handsome package if you not going to put it to use? You killing me with this bullshit. Are you gay? She is incredibly flexible, owns her own dance studio, and you on the other hand are a security guard, hoping to get promoted to a mall cop one day. Dude, she is a fuckin' ten!" cracked Jolon.

Shaking his finger and taunting Adam, "I never met anyone who'd cancel on a girl like Monica. Yea you might be gay, bro."

"Don't get your day started with a kick in the balls," answered Adam.

Jolon chuckled, "You know it's in the food and water. I'm just saying..."

They both broke into laughter.

"Okay I gotta roll, I'll see you at 10, bro!" said Jolon.

Jolon uncoordinatedly stuttered his pudgy body around the corner and ran off to get back to his work. As he prepared for his shift, Adam smirked and shook his head at Jolon's boy-like excitement.

Chapter 3

Walking to the break room just after 10:00 am to meet Jolon, Adam was customarily greeted by the office single women clamoring to make their acquaintance.

"Good morning, Adam," he heard from a voice down the hall.

"Oh, hey... good morning, Trisha," he casually responded while picking up his stride to meet Jolon.

"Hey, when you're done with your rounds, could you stop by my desk?" asked Trisha.

"Man, this girl is never gonna give up, "Adam sighed and murmured under his breath.

"Trisha, I'll try but I'm real busy today," he said.

Picking up on Adam's hesitation, Trisha

responded quickly, "I'm not going to bite. All work and no play leads to a boring life, big boy."

Adam uncomfortably nodded.

"Okay, Trisha, I'll keep that in mind," he said before heading into the break room.

He grabbed a seat and waited for Jolon in the break room. Outside of the room he heard rising chatter, as if the voices were coming his way. He was shocked when the news station's general manager walked in with the parent company's CEO—Winston Chase of Crow Corp. They were accompanied by crowds of buzzing photographers, reporters, and brown-nosers. Winston Chase was a multi-billionaire who controlled 60% of all media across the world. His empire also covered technology, mining, medical, energy, and transportation sectors, among many others. He came from a long line of philanthropists, entrepreneurs, bankers, and politicians. Simply put, the man and his family owned the world. It was very rare for him to be in the States, let alone in person at one of his companies. Distracted by his dream, Adam forgot about the CEO's visit. The bruises around his wrists and ankles, the haunting images of auras surrounding people on the streets and at work, completely distracted him.

Knowing his reputation around the office, as the local mind reader, Adam tried to put his head down so as to not look inviting. However, he was too late. The GM approached Adam at his table. In an effort to impress Winston Chase, he introduced Adam to the CEO.

"Oh, this is Adam Quinn. He's the station's local mind reader," said the GM, while reaching out and proudly touching Adam's shoulder.

"He is amazingly accurate with his gift. I mean, this guy is incredible. One time he read me and my wife's..."

The CEO was immediately intrigued and rudely interrupted. "Oh really?" he asked as he brushed pass the GM.

"Mr. Quinn, would you like to test your skills on me?"

Before Adam could answer, the CEO boldly took a seat in front of Adam and made himself comfortable. Not taking no for an answer, he put his hands on the table and readied himself for Adam to read his mind.

Adam sighed in his head. Many would love the opportunity to read the mind of the richest man in the world, but not Adam. Reading minds often left him emotionally and mentally drained. The more accurate, the more energy it would take. He had to do it for money in the past, but the emotional toll was just too great. The crowd clamored and hovered around the table to witness the reading. There was no getting out of it. The implied pressure put Adam on the spot. Now he was compelled to follow through with the reading.

Dammit Jolon, he thought.

His first observation was that the CEO didn't have an aura. Even though Adam wasn't sure of exactly what the auras meant, he knew that the minute the sun's rays touched his skin, his gifts were stronger. But now wouldn't be the best time to try to figure out what the aura meant or how to use these new gifts. Truth be told, he still didn't comprehend how or why he had so many other special abilities.

***

Adam was born as an indigo child and raised in an orphanage. Possessing several spiritual gifts, he could routinely see spirits and into the future, and he could often witness other realities. At a very young age he was frequently seen talking to his "imaginary friends." He was even marked as a haunted child because of the paranormal events following him throughout his time at the orphanage.

It was one of those events that ruined his best chance of ever being adopted. When Adam was four years old, his potential parents arrived to see Adam sitting alone in his bed with three toy blocks orbiting him, while all the other beds in the room were neatly stacked in the corner. It was an impossible feat for a four year old to accomplish without help. The blocks were difficult enough to explain, but lifting and stacking the beds was impossible. It was enough to earn Adam the creepy reputation as the possessed kid. The paranormal event ruined Adam's chances of having his own family. He was devastated and closed his heart off—cursing his innate talents. He became an outcast and suppressed his abilities in order to fit in.

As Adam grew older he often wore hoodies, his way of hiding away from the world. He only found refuge in music, a coping mechanism that would remain prevalent throughout his entire life. A downed head, hoodie, and head phones was how Adam rolled. It was only later, once he got older, that he developed the ability to read people's minds. It was the only socially acceptable sixth sense that he willingly disclosed to other people.

Chapter 4

Adam sat for a few seconds, studying the aura-less Winston Chase. He was tall, thin, and neatly dressed in a business suit. He was well into his 60s, with scaly, pale white skin, as if he'd never had any exposure to the sun. His hair was dusty blonde, combed over like a proud banker. His upper lip was very stiff, almost resembling a frown, giving off an elitist vibe. His eyes were squinty, cold, soulless, and void of compassion. They had an eerie similarity to the evil soul-shattering eyes that Adam had seen in his dream that morning—those same eyes that seemed excited to watch his gruesome death. He had a dark stare that reached deep inside Adam's soul, the type of stare that would give a lesser man chills throughout his entire body.

He coldly smiled at Adam, but it was obviously fake and manufactured. Adam usually had a narrow ability to read a person's mind. But on this day it was much stronger, making Adam extremely uncomfortable. Adam hissed and popped a comforting toothpick in his mouth. He shuffled the toothpick from side to side while glaring hard at the CEO. He raked both hands through his wooly fro and hesitantly reached for the CEO's hands. Immediately he felt something intensely different, much more data than he was used to sensing when reading someone's mind. It was as if a computer screen was scrolling in fast forward inside of his head, similar to a TV switching through hundreds of channels per millisecond.

Adam tried to interpret the data in order to impress the CEO and crowd, but when the data came in all at once it was far too overwhelming. He saw pain, misery, evil, anguish, human suffering, lies, deceit, misinformation, disinformation, temptation, and war. The CEO's face began to contort, as if another entity was masked behind the human face, something immensely evil. The CEO's eyes also changed, resembling a twisted demonic beast. His pupils were large, devoid of irises, with reddish-yellow slits dominating the eye. The image drove a bone-deep chill throughout Adam's body. He retracted as if he was touching the hands of a demon.

He lost control, fell from his chair and frantically screamed, "Get away from me... what the fuck are you?"

Adam scooted and scuffled himself as far away from the CEO as possible, completely forgetting he was surrounded by a large crowd. He bowled over a few cameramen and reporters as he back pedaled away from the table.

Again he hysterically shouted, "What are you?"

While frantically looking back and forth into the crowd, Adam asked, "Did anybody see that, did anybody get that on tape?"

The crowd wanted no part of Adam's crazy antics. They shook their heads in pity and shame at Adam, now sure to be deemed the office lunatic. When they distanced themselves from him, Adam realized only he saw Winston Chase's contorted face. Adam tried to plead his case as the CEO's handlers stepped in to subdue the situation and help the CEO to his feet. He firmly straightened and arranged his suit while dishing Adam a sinister look, a lasting glare that tore straight through Adam's soul.

Clearly upset, the CEO laughed off the embarrassment. In an attempt to interject levity into the situation, he remarked in a sarcastic voice, "Now I remember why I never let anyone read my mind."

The crowd chuckled and he half-heartedly smiled

for the cameras and left.

Still crouched against the wall, Adam raked one hand through his afro. His gut told him this was somehow connected to the morning's events. Gnawing on his toothpick, he pondered the familiarity of Winston Chase's eyes.

I know I've seen them before, he thought.

Adam's thoughts were disrupted by the disappointed expression on his general manager's face. Shaking his head in disappointment at Adam, he ran out to catch up with the CEO.

Catching the tail end of the incident, Jolon hustled to Adam's aid. Helping him up, he asked, "What happened, big man, what you see?"

Highly agitated, Adam shrugged off Jolon's help.

"I said 10:00, dude," yelled Adam while angrily tossing one of the break room's chairs.

Mistrustful, Jolon backed away from the agitated Adam, "I'm sorry, man. I got held up. What you see?"

Adam rudely brushed pass Jolon and headed out of the break room. Jolon trotted behind him.

"Bro, what's going on? What you see?" he asked while grabbing Adam's shoulder.

Adam quickly turned around with a raised clenched fist, ready to strike. His eyes narrowed and jaws tightened.

Jolon spotted the fire in Adam's eyes and began to back away while saying, "Dude, it's me."

Still gnawing on his toothpick, Adam sighed and punched through the hallway wall, a punch so powerful that it brought down the lights in the hallway.

Pulling his fist out of the wall, he said, "I saw the devil!"

He then turned away and headed down the hallway.

"Huh, the devil?" asked Jolon.

"What are you talking about... Adam... Adam... My bad, bro! I didn't know this would happen, man," pleaded Jolon.

Adam returned to his security office, sat down at his desk, and began to sort through his thoughts.

I know I'm not crazy, I saw what I saw... I know what I saw, thought Adam.

Moments later, as Adam's back was turned, the CEO glided into Adam's office, softly shutting the door behind him.

"What did you see?" he asked with a relaxed, direct, and intimidating tone.

Startled, Adam quickly turned around, in his chair. Upon seeing the CEO, he immediately frowned and his face became contorted with rage. His heart raced, and his nostrils flared with each increasing breath. Adam peered directly at the CEO, squinting with boiling anger inside. It didn't matter that the cameras didn't catch the CEO's morphed face, Adam's readings were never wrong. In his mind, he was preparing for a duel with something evil.

Adam flew out of his chair with such force it smashed against the desk.

"What are you, some kind of demon?" he blurted.

The CEO ignored Adam's question. He continued, slowly walking closer to Adam, all the while staring with his cold, dead eyes. Adam matched his stare with clenched fists.

"I don't know what you are, but what I do know from reading you...you bleed and can feel pain!" said Adam with thunder in his voice.

Unfazed by Adam's comment, the CEO smirked and continued slowly approaching. With every step, Adam got more and more angry. He prepared himself for what may be the fight of his life. Face to face, both men were deep into a stare-off, studying each other's face. Adam was on full alert, waiting to throw all he had at this unknown evil. The CEO took a large sniff of Adam's scent.

"Mmmmmmhhhhh," he moaned, as if he was trying to feed off of Adam's fear.

He slowly licked his lips, and in a slow, deep monotone voice he said, "Yesssssss...You've apparently seen something."

The CEO's words confirmed Adam's suspicions.

Whatever he is, he isn't human, Adam thought.

This awakened a new jarring feeling inside of Adam. His adrenaline was now pumping. As his breath deepened and his chest grew more broad, his uniform tightened. He felt energy pulsating throughout his body as he trembled with rage, and his face snarled like an attacking wolf. He tensed, as the veins in his arms became enlarged.

The walls began to rumble and shake. Slowly, the office supplies started to rattle and rise off of Adam's desk. He had yet to notice, as he was dead locked on the mysterious CEO. Still showing no fear, the CEO looked at the floating office supplies with minimal interest. Adam's gaze was broken by a floating stapler passing between he and the CEO's face. This startled

Adam enough to break his deadlocked glare with the CEO. As his anger and hostility turned into intrigue and amazement, all the objects suddenly dropped. "BOOM." In awe, Adam looked stunned at what had just happened. The CEO casually watched as the objects fell, hitting the ground. He squinted his eyes and took an even deeper look at Adam, as a scientist studies his caged specimen. A muscle under his eye began to twitch, and a bit of his top lip tightened and quivered. That twitch in the CEO's eye gave Adam the eerie sensation that this wasn't their first encounter. Adam's brow ruffled at the thought. Both men were speechless as the standoff continued. The CEO cracked another evil smile, broke his stare with Adam, turned, and walked out. Before he did, he paused at the door.

"Have a good day, Mr. Quinn."

With a condescending smirk, he chuckled and left. Adam was in complete shock. He plopped back into his chair and let go a heavy sigh.

Raking both hands through his afro, he thought to himself, *What... the... fuck... just happened!*

He shook his head in perplexity, pondering if he was somehow still trapped in the same dream. He had ignored many strange coincidences in his life, but this was something that just couldn't be ignored.

***

An hour later, Adam's supervisor came in and showed him some paperwork that pointed to Adam committing company fraud.

"I didn't do any of this, John. You know me! We even have the cameras to prove it!" plead Adam.

John slowly shook his head while throwing his hands up, "I'm sorry, Adam, it's done. I'll give you a few moments to grab your stuff."

Pounding his fist on the desk, Adam yelled, "Don't tell me this has something to do with Winston Chase!" John took a step back.

Adam calmed himself at the sight of John's fear. "John, look, something is weird with him, I saw..."

John didn't give Adam a chance to finish his sentence.

He interrupted, shouting, "Adam... Adam...get your stuff! It's done! My hands are tied. And you tied them with that stunt you pulled today, not to mention what you did to the wall!"

Two more security guards appeared outside of

the office. Adam shook his head in astonishment and began to gather his things frantically.

Before Adam was ushered out by guards, he paused and blurted to John, "My stunt, huh? Well... I guess I'll keep to myself what I learned that Winston has planned for you!"

John stumbled back wide-eyed and glared hard at Adam.

He waved his hand to the guards surrounding Adam, "Get him out of here!"

With each step toward the exit, Adam got more and more angry. By the time he left the building, he was fuming with anger and frustration, and haunted with so many questions.

Chapter 5

The bus stop was just a block away, too close of a walk for Adam to get his thoughts together. Still fuming with rage, anger, and confusion, he hopped back on the bus to head home. He plopped down hard, slouching in his seat. He decided to drown himself in the ironic sounds of Public Enemy's *Fight the Power*. The Bose QuietComfort headphones partly hiding in his afro helped take him to his own unique sulking zone. With his arms folded and face balled up in anger, his head knocked back and forth to the tunes. In a dazed and zombie-like stare, he rethought the day's events. He was now certain that something significant was happening to him, but he was still unsure of what to make of it. He thought of his dream, the shackle bruises on his ankles and wrists, the new energy sensations, the auras, the CEO and floating office supplies.

These gotta be connected... but how? he thought to himself.

Massaging his eyes with his thumbs and index fingers, Adam stayed deep in thought on the subject while the sounds of Public Enemy continued to up the ante. His bitter daze was interrupted by a new face on the bus. The face didn't fit. It was different from the typical bus riders Adam was accustomed to seeing on his route. Most of the people he saw riding the bus were blue collared folks. This individual was instinctively different, sticking out like a sore thumb. He was a white male in his 30s, about 6 feet tall and 200 pounds of well-kept muscle, dressed in an all black suit, a thin black tie, dark shades, and a corded ear piece. Very little emotion could be read on the man's face.

Adam noticed the dark-suited man had no aura, similar to the CEO. It immediately put him on red alert. Adam began to study the man, pondering if he was somehow connected to Winston Chase. The bus stopped and two more men dressed identical to the first passenger got on—black suits, thin black ties, and dark shades. The men's faces, ages, and builds were all identical, like carbon copies.

They took their seats on the bus, splitting up. Adam was stunned and caught off guard when he realized their seating positions; one man sat a few seats to the left of him, the other sat a few seats behind him. They were cornering him, and the only way off the bus was through one of these men. Adam slowly shifted deeper into his seat, mouth gapped open in bewilderment. Minutes later, another man with a black suit and no aura got on the bus. Adam tried to figure out his next move. Before he could get a plan together, he noticed the newest passenger took a seat directly across from him. Adam knew from his hard-knock life that they may be surrounding him and preparing for an attack—Hood Science 101. His mind wandered into all kinds of conspiracy theories.

Then he gathered himself. *Stop trippin! You are clean as a whistle; you have no reason to worry. They are probably auditing the bus route for the city or somethin'*, he said to himself.

That shaky logic was enough to calm him until the very next stop. The bus door opened and another man in an all-black suit got on. Adam whipped his head to the front of the bus to eye the new passenger. Another carbon copy. Deep in his consciousness, he knew this wasn't a coincidence.

Suits don't ride on this bus. Now all of a sudden five get on... in the same day, all looking identical... Yea, it's goin' down! he thought.

This rattled Adam's nerves to a new level. He studied the new passenger. He caught a brief glimpse of a gun on the inside hip of the man's suit jacket as he paid for his bus fair.

City workers don't carry guns, he thought to himself.

Adam's heart began to flutter while going through different strategies in his head.

I gotta get off this bus. If they get off with me, it's definitely going down, thought Adam.

As he turned around to press the tape to signal the bus to stop, Adam felt a cold sharp pain in his chest. It slowly ran throughout his body, making his muscles tense. All of a sudden, he was stuck in his seat, frozen and unable to move with the exception of his eyes. His dilated pupils franticly swiveled, looking for understanding. His eyes locked in on the man across from him putting something shiny away inside his suit jacket.

Adam immediately zoomed in on his enemy, thinking to himself, h*im, he did this*!

He had been hit by some sort of weapon that paralyzed his muscles. His eyes continued dashing around his eye sockets in a paranoid manner, fearful of what may happen next. His heart was beating so hard it seemed to want out of his chest. Adam panicked and tried to yell for help, but couldn't summon enough energy to break free from the paralyzed state. Adam's eyes followed the newest passenger like a hawk, as he took a seat next to Adam. His eyes continued flickering back and forth between the men, trying to figure out who was going to make the next move. The newest suited man began speaking into a device under his sleeve.

He calmly said in a low tone voice, "Target subdued. We will finish him off by the river bottom."

Upon hearing the message, Adam's eyes became even wider, more terror-stricken, flicking back and forth in their sockets.

Oh shit! These are hit men...oh shit... oh shit... this is a professional hit, panicked Adam.

The bus stopped and Adam's 225 pound muscular frame was effortlessly whisked off the bus by the men in suits.

Fuck fuck fuck fuck, he panicked in his mind as he strained to break free. *They tryin' to smoke me... this is really goin' down. Dude, you gotta fight.*

Adam was terrified; he had no idea what he had done to deserve this. His life was beginning to flash before his eyes, and his pulse raced at a speed he had never felt. He saw beautiful Nia's face flash before his mind. Adam attempted to summon whatever dormant internal strength he may have.

It's now or never, bruh, he thought.

Adam willed all his might to overcome his muscular paralysis. He closed his eyes and flexed every muscle in his body, as if he were lifting a thousand pound weight. A black SUV skid to the scene with a man jumping out holding the doors open. Frantically peering into the truck, Adam saw the stoic faced CEO, Winston Chase. He was sitting calmly inside the SUV, carefully observing the scene with his cold soulless eyes. Pure, untapped rage overcame Adam. The closer he got to the vehicle, the more he strained to free himself. His eye lids crinkled up like the folds on the back of knuckles. From deep inside of himself, he felt the ability to slowly take back his body. Just as he was about to be put into the SUV, he broke free from the paralyzed state and rammed the heads of the two men carrying him. The sheer force of Adam's blow produced a crackling sound as their skulls collided. As they collapsed, Adam reached for their weapons. When he reached inside the jacket of one of the downed men, he was hit yet again by the same paralyzing weapon. He fell to his knees and froze in a prayer-like position, head bowed. He heard slow footsteps approaching him. He first noticed slick, high-end, well crafted black loafers walk into his frame of vision, followed by tan, creased slacks. Winston Chase was upon him. The CEO took a slight squat in front of Adam. He viscously grabbed a lock of Adam's afro and slowly lifted Adam's head enough to be eye to eye.

Looking at Adam with his cold, dead eyes, he whispered, "Nice try, Mr. Quinn, but the longer this takes, and the more you struggle, the more I'm going to enjoy this!"

This muthafucka! screamed Adam in his head as the anger and frustration started to set in deeper.

Those are the eyes from my dream, he said louder and louder in his head.

This amplified the fury inside of him. His heart started to beat harder; he could feel his body generating powerful energy deep within. He closed his eyes again to summon the energy that had freed him before.

Adam attempted to pump himself up with words—words only he could hear: *Fight, Adam, fight dammit... You have to fight... Fuck this punk shit.*"

He grabbed at the momentous idea that something was so unique about him that it was worth someone trying to kill him. This new realization brought more energy than he had ever known. He now recognized that he had a bigger reason to fight than he had ever realized. He was something exceptional. A familiar feeling swept over him. It was similar to the energy he felt with the CEO in his office. Even in his frozen state, Adam's veins pulsed more quickly with blood. Suddenly the ground started to shake and rumble beneath him as it had before back in his office with the CEO. Within 50 feet of Adam, every loose bit of gravel and debris began to slowly rise.

It's happening again, I can feel it, thought Adam.

In his paralyzed state, Adam mustered up a slight frown as the rocks started to slowly rise. The veins in his neck became enlarged and slowly climbed to his face. A spot on his forehead, just between his eyebrows, started to pulsate.

Yeah… I feel it…I must've did that at the office, and I'm doing this now, Adam realized.

He sensed for the first time a strange relationship he had with the earth that made this possible. He couldn't explain it in his mind, but in his soul it all made sense. They froze his body but not his mind. Adam's psyche was somehow summoning the power to move the earth.

The CEO and his henchmen looked about in apprehensive awe. A few cars slowed to observe the scene. As the rocks rose to eye level, the men scurried back toward their SUVs. The CEO stood defiantly in the midst of the rising stones until his handlers attempted to pull him to safety. As they retreated backwards, Adam sent the gravel and rock toward the men with the speed of a javelin. A thunderous roar was heard as the wall of earth thrashed toward them. The earth struck the men and the SUV with such force that it ripped through their flesh like paper and flipped the vehicle to the other side of the road. Car alarms began to ring up and down the street from the thunderous roar of the earth and tumbling SUV.

Adam broke free of the paralysis and came back to his feet. He surveyed his work in amazement and in awe. Two of the men were dead for sure. Their corpses lied mangled in the street with gapping fist-sized holes. Adam wiped a stream of blood that trickled from his nostrils as his street skills kicked in and urged him to dodge the scene.

As Adam steadied himself on his legs, Winston Chase's head emerged from the wreckage of his SUV. He wiped the shredded flesh of his men from his face while his eyes remained fixated on his prey. He gave Adam a look of bitter hatred, as if he wanted to put his body in a mulcher. Adam met his pestilent gaze for a moment only, but he knew from the hunger in Chase's eyes that they would meet again.

Chapter 6

From observing the scene of mangled flesh and metal, it was obvious to Adam his life would never be the same.

Now what? he thought to himself as he heard the distant sounds of police sirens.

Adam snapped his fingers as an idea popped into his head—I'll grab what I can from home and wait at Jolon's. Hopefully no one will think to look for me there and that way I can at least get my head together and figure this all out.

Adam knew it was a matter of time before the authorities raided his home. It was about a 45 minute jog to his house. If he hurried and luck was on his side, he might beat the cops. Adam dashed away from the scene, jumping over fences and cutting through yards. He took all available short cuts while the adrenaline surged through his body. He continuously mulled over the dustup while running. The sun's strengthening rays on his body pushed him to run at accelerated speeds. Adam didn't notice the five mile journey was done in fifteen minutes, a feat that could only be rivaled by the tossing of an SUV with the mind. Still in deep thought, sweating, and panting, Adam burst through his apartment door with the objective to swiftly get in and out.

Panicked and preoccupied, Adam sprinted toward his bedroom when he was startled by a low-toned voice, "That was quite a show you put on there, Mr. Quinn."

Seated comfortably in one of Adam's fake leather chairs was a small man, contently sitting with one leg folded over the other. He was well dressed in a dark grey suit, similar to what a politician would wear. He had slicked, sandy hair and appeared to Adam as if he was in his early 40s. His olive skin bared years of smoking; the crow's feet around his eyes confirmed it.

Startled, Adam jolted back against the living room wall and said with a thunderous voice, "What the fuck you doin' in my house?"

"Uhh... first of all, this is an apartment," the man said nonchalantly while cleaning his glasses.

Before he could get another word out, Adam flew across the room, clenching the man's collar with both of his large hands, as if he was about to throw him through the nearest window.

"Oh you got jokes! Don't play with me, I'll make your face touch everything up in this bitch. Who are you and what the fuck you doing here?" roared Adam.

"Nice... I guess one more assault today won't hurt. It's not like things can get any worse for you. Relax thunder cat, I'm here to help you, and from the looks of it—two murders and seven aggravated assaults—you need my help," retorted the arrogant man as he positioned his glasses.

Adam relaxed his kung fu-like grip around the man's collar and slowly backed away, shaking his head back and forth.

"I didn't assault anybody. I was attacked... they came at me," Adam countered as sweat continued to bead on his forehead.

"Sure, that is what they all say," cracked the man.

He then pulled out a thin, clear plastic device that was a bit larger than a typical smart phone. He tapped the device and cued up a surveillance-quality video replay of Adam's encounter from the store's perspective across the street.

"How long have you been playing in the sand?" the man said sarcastically as he handed the strange new piece of technology to Adam.

"I'm 'bout tired of your jokes, little man. Now is not the fuckin' time," Adam touted as he glanced with bewilderment at the device playing his video.

"Sorry, I just couldn't resist that one. Look, my name is Agent Parker, Miles Parker. I represent a private organization that works with people like you."

"People like me?" questioned Adam.

"Yes, gifted individuals like yourself who seem to have nascent abilities, or some sort of control over the earth's elements," said Miles.

Adam involuntarily shuffled backward, speechless, bumping the table behind him while raking his hands through his Afro.

"You're baffled, I see. Yes, I shall continue," scoffed Miles as he took control of the conversation.

"So, like I said, I'm here to help, offer you a job of sorts, a way out per se, and it seems you are in a bit of a pickle."

While looking at his watch and motioning to the faint sounds of police sirens coming their way in the distance, Miles said passively, "In fact, the police will be here in a bit to greet you for your wondrous display of sand castle building today."

"A job... Come work with you and do what?" Adam fired back.

This Miles man spoke the truth, Adam knew the police would be a serious issue.

"We work with many individuals that are indigo children, better known as remote viewers, clairvoyants, psychics, telepaths, jumpers, dreamers, and the like. You are clearly one of the most powerful we've seen thus far. We can help you understand your powers as we have done for many like you. We have a special project, specifically for a person of your talents. With proper training you could pull it off," said Miles.

"I'm not ya guinea pig for your black ops projects. Go find another rat and get the fuck outta my spot," shouted Adam while pointing to the door.

Miles paused, leaving a conversational gap long enough for the police sirens to bleed into the conversation.

Tidying with his suit tie, Miles continued, "Okay, suit yourself, Mr. Quinn. It's your life. Anyway, it sounds like this party is going to get a bit more crowded."

"Let them come, I have proof," countered Adam while holding up Miles's device with the surveillance video.

Miles chuckled, "Hahaha! Don't be naïve, Mr. Quinn, you just hurled thousands of pounds of earth at a man that possesses well over half the world's wealth. The end result of that little spectacle is two butchered dead bodies, seven hospitalized, and a large SUV lodged in a store front window. Do you really believe any evidence will make it to court to help you? And if it did, with his money, power, and influence, do you think he'll just leave you alone? Surely you are brighter than that."

Weighing his options, Adam aggressively rubbed the nap of his neck and bit his bottom lip.

"Fuuuuck!" he yelled as he looked away and knocked over shelves.

Miles sat calmly, unfazed by Adam's roar. This rock-and-a-hard-place predicament rested heavy on his shoulders. Adam had plenty of prior run-ins with the law and he knew where that road would end. Deep in his heart, he knew Miles was right—that demon of a CEO would never let him go free. Miles was probably his only way out.

"How do I know I can trust you?"

"You don't," Miles said nonchalantly.

"Look, Adam... May I call you Adam? If I wanted you dead, you'd be dead already."

"No, muthafucka, if I wanted you dead, you'd be dead. Don't get it twisted!" Adam fired back.

"Touché, Mr. Quinn. Touché. So, does that mean we have a deal?"

Adam tilted his head slightly, mulling over the offer while probing his cheeks with his tongue, all the while glaring back at Miles.

"I presume that is a yes," Miles said expectantly.

Suddenly the sound of the sirens blared directly outside of Adam's apartment. Four police cruisers screeched onto the scene and innumerable officers surrounded Adam's door with weapons drawn.

"Wait here, let me take care of this. Go ahead and finish packing. You are going away for a while," Miles said confidently.

He sprung out of the chair, buttoned his suit, and cruised to the door.

Adam took a golf ball-sized swallow as he watched Miles casually stroll out the door. Adam ran to the window to see what was happening. Miles walked out and flashed some sort of badge to the weapon-drawn officers. The cops seemed to be a bit annoyed, but made no effort to come close to Adam's door. In fact, no cop ever stepped beyond Miles. After about 10 minutes of discussion with the lead cop, Miles pulled out his phone and made a call. Five minutes into the call, he handed the phone to the lead officer. The whole time, Miles was as cool as a poised samurai waiting to do battle. The officer snatched the phone from his ear and handed it back to Miles. The lead officer signaled the other officers and they rallied and left the scene. It was an impressive feat, even to a man who had recently discovered he could move thousands of pounds of earth with his mind.

Miles quickly trotted back up the steps, entering Adam's apartment, lit another cigarette and offered one to Adam.

He plopped back down in the seat, filled his lungs with smoke, then muttered, "Looks like we are good to go... pack up!"

Adam raised his hands shoulder high and shook them franticly with a skeptical stare at Miles and retorted, "I'm not gonna just jump in the car and ride off with you. I don't know you like that, homeboy! You might try to take me out to the desert and off me!"

Miles let out a long, frustrated sigh, and said, "Adam, really, are we back here again? I mean, what choices do you really have?"

Adam countered back, "Well, give me something else besides this Humphrey Bogart bullshit."

"Look, Adam, here is what I can tell you: The human body's DNA is evolving, mutating if you will, and birthing super talents such as yourself. We believe you may have been born this way. But, of course, we won't know for sure until we get you back to our labs and get a look at your DNA. This evolution has been happening for centuries all over the globe. But like I said, we have seen it increasing in alarming numbers as of late. It's no question that humans are evolving, Mr. Quinn, but into what is the question. That is where you come in—we need you to help us figure this out."

That was just what Adam needed to hear, he was hooked. He knew deep in his gut that he had to follow this journey and find out where it would take him. Perhaps this would explain this Nia woman that he couldn't seem to get out of his mind.

"That's all good and dandy, but it don't solve my problem with Winston Chase," Adam fired back, hoping he could bluff more out of the deal.

Miles settled himself into the chair, knocked a few ashes of his cigarette onto the floor, and said, "Yes, Mr. Quinn, that is a bit of a conundrum. Nonetheless, it's your conundrum. However, in our program you will become a new person; you'll have a new identity, a new name and a new social security number. Your old identity will be completely wiped from the system and with our training I'm sure you will be properly equipped and ready to deal with any transgressions against you. That is all I can promise you."

Adam bit his bottom lip again and nodded while putting a toothpick in his mouth.

He pushed out a long sigh, "Okay... so what now?"

"Very good, Mr. Quinn. Very good. We are going to be heading to our top-secret facility up north, where we will begin a series of tests, followed by intense training to hone your skills. Upon completion of your training, you will be given a special project that you must complete. After this project is complete, you will be free to go with no reason to ever look back over your shoulder again... as a new man... as a free man."

Sucking his teeth and gnawing down on his toothpick, Adam nodded in approval of the terms. He turned and walked into his bedroom to begin packing. Without a handshake, it was clear that the two men had struck a deal.

Chapter 7

The desert's scorching rays were temporarily put on pause by the massive haboob crawling over the city. The great cloud of dust rolled in over the Phoenix horizon, slowly dwarfing and engulfing the mountainous landscape. Lying under the cloud of tumbling dust rested a small, inconspicuous bar along the southern edges of Phoenix.

Up pulled a dark SUV with tinted windows. From the driver's side, Clutch pried his large 7-foot-4 muscular frame out of the seat. The SUV creaked and sprung up with new life from the relief of Clutch's hefty physique. Dressed in military fatigues and well armed, he swiveled his bald head about the scene with caution, inspecting the premises with his watchful eye.

From the passenger's side, out jumped his

older brother Kojo. Standing just over 4-foot-9, he was dressed in loose fitting fatigues with black combat boots. His head was bald and unusually big for a man his size. His face was smug, with an arrogant expression, and his eyes carried a plotting, scheming, devious look. Kojo lit his Cohiba Toro cigar against the darkening city and studied the coming dust storm as the wind breezed through his long-haired unibrow.

Clutch's thunderous steps pounded the desert earth as he walked over to open the bar door for Kojo. He patiently held the door. Kojo took his time letting the warm desert breeze tickle the nerves of his face before walking into the bar. After a few more pulls on his favorite brand of cigar, Kojo headed in while Clutch maintained his normal security detail outside the bar.

The bar was relatively empty, less one bartender and one drunken patron at the far end. At the center of the bar sat a mysterious man with his cowboy hat pulled down against his brow. Kojo strolled over to take a seat next to the mysterious. He was Native American, with dark olive skin, dark eyes, raised cheekbones, and a strong ridged brow. His face was creased by hard wrinkles with a large scar stretched from his left eye down to his chin. His upper lip was drawn and firm against his teeth.

Kojo pulled an ashtray close, and nodded at the bartender.

"Rum and Coke," he said while dropping ashes into the tray. "Sure thing, Kojo," said the bartender as he scrambled to make the drink. Kojo took a few more strong pulls on his Cohiba while holding the smoke in his mouth for a bit. He let the spicy, peppery, earthy taste percolate around his mouth while taking a warm glance at the cigar before exhaling.

Expelling the smoke, he nodded at the fellow next to him and said, "Happy birthday, old man."

The man continued to stare forward, stone-faced. In a deep, robotic voice, the man calmly said, "You know, you never experience your birthday again. You are rotating around the sun, inside a solar system that is orbiting around a galactic core, all which of course is moving through space at speeds well over 500,000 miles per hour. You never see the same birthday again, so why do your people celebrate it?"

Kojo sighed and scoffed at the comment, "Scar, stop being so theoretical, it's a blessing to get older and wiser."

"These gifts you give—does that mean people are excited you are getting closer to death?"

The bartender chuckled as he slid in Kojo's drink.

"On the house," he said.

Kojo nodded at the bartender and turned back to Scar as he took a sip and another pull from his cigar.

"This is hilarious for me, seeing you still struggling with these benign issues. Scar, you're putting way too much thought into it again. Take sports, for example—we do it because it is fun, it makes us feel good."

Turning back to Kojo, Scar said, "One wins, and the other loses. Is that fun? How can that be fun for the loser? Why would anyone subject themselves to such an experience for fun and then try to convince themselves otherwise? This one is the least of your customs I understand."

"Never mind, Scar. Just continue to leave the humans to me," sighed Kojo while tapping his chest.

"I am forever thankful for your intricate understanding of human emotions and affairs... which brings me to why I need you for the last ingredient," said Scar.

Kojo took another nod at the bartender. He quickly scrambled from behind the bar, grabbed the drunken patron, and disappeared from the scene.

Kojo and Scar patiently watched as the bar cleared out. Puffing his Cohiba with an attentive look about his face, Kojo turned to Scar, "So, what's the last ingredient we need for the counter agent?"

"It's called C-47. It's a synthesized derivative of ibogaine, a compound found in the iboga tree from central Africa. The compound will help synthesize the change in the DNA quality control cells we need to disrupt the Kode-X," said Scar.

Shrugging his shoulders, Kojo said, "Okay, simple enough since it grows naturally."

"No, if it was that easy I'd have done it myself. This one is going to take a bit more finesse, which is why I need you. I can engineer the counter agent, but with my current limited resources I'm unable to retrieve enough of the compound to fully synthesize it. The ibogaine derivative is highly rare, difficult to get, incredibly expensive to synthesize, and it's on your government's list of banned substances. CrowCorp Pharmaceutical is the only corporation allowed to handle it. They have a chemical shipment of the compound scheduled to arrive by armored truck to their western branch in Los Angeles in three weeks. I need you and Clutch to figure out a way to get that C-47. Can you handle that?"

"Can I handle it? Is that rhetorical or do you really want me to answer that?" asked Kojo.

He paused and with a smirk jumped in before

Scar answered, "Never mind, Scar. It's just an expression. We'll gladly take care of it."

Unaffected by Kojo's humor, Scar continued, "Once we get the C-47, we can start to synthesize the counter agent. We will begin with the Colony members first, then they will go on to infect the larger population. We will be less than a year away from disrupting the American BioGrid. From there, we move to infecting those around the world."

"How long will it take to affect the whole world?" asked Kojo.

"After the first group of infections, it will spread rather quickly. It will plunge the current culture into an aggressive revolution. Of course, the government will vilify the counter agent. But I predict we will have the entire world infected in just over five years," responded Scar.

Kojo nodded, finished his drink, and knocked a few more ashes off his cigar.

His normally smug expression transformed into a look of satisfaction, "Okay then, I'll see you in three weeks."

He jumped down from his stool and headed to the door.

"Oh and, Kojo, can you tell Clutch to cut down on

his body count this time?" said Scar.

"Easier said than done, Scar... Easier said than done," said Kojo while heading out the door.

Kojo walked pass Clutch as he secured the premises.

Clutch stood unfazed by the wall of dust blowing against him. "Scar says hello," Kojo related sarcastically.

"Yeah, I heard," grunted Clutch in his customarily deep monotone voice.

They both jumped back into their all black SUV and headed out, disappearing into the cloud of dust.

Chapter 8

Adam and Nia spent the night holding each other, caressing, making passionate love, telling stories, reminiscing and stargazing. Gazing at the stars was one of Nia's favorite past times. It was her own way of connecting with her ancestors. During the night, she shed tears of joy with Adam while peering at the night sky. Adam loved her tears of elation. Throughout the night, he'd kiss at them to show his gratitude.

They lied in the greenest part of the South African bush. All things green were a favorite of Nia's; greenish ponds, green trees, green bushes, and grasses were all things she marveled at. Simply put, green was her most adored color.

It was early in the morning now, the sun just waking to bless the Zulu land with its presence. Adam and Nia still lied with each other, sun gazing and taking in the sun's energy as the land's day creatures became busy with life. The weather was perfect—not cold, and not too hot. The rumble of the nearby stream creaked and crawled its way throughout the land, adding to the beautiful atmosphere for the couple. They lied as close to each other as possible in order to further imprint their presence on one another's souls. While Adam glanced into the morning sky, Nia turned to him and slowly began to caress his face, coiling her fingers about his brow. She circled and twirled her fingers along his masculine jaw line. The rush of dancing butterflies throughout his body temporarily brushed away his normally hard, masculine nature. Once again, he completely gave in to the moment. He loved her touch and proved it by etching a new smirk across his face while still sun gazing. Nia moved to his hair, as Adam closed his eyes and purred like one of the big cats on the African Serengeti. He rolled his chew stick back and forth in his mouth while his tingling scalp converted his smirk into a smile.

"Why do you always have a chew stick?" Nia asked.

"It calms me," smiled Adam.

"Well, I'd kiss you more if it wasn't in my way."

Taking the chew stick out of his mouth, Adam turned to Nia, "Kisses calm me more."

Chuckling like a school girl having her first crush, Nia took the opportunity and pelted Adam with the morning's first kiss.

While still toiling with his hair, Nia inquired, "So what did you learn with Master Zulu yesterday?"

Adam sighed, "Nia, you know I'm not supposed to share what was revealed to me by Master Zulu."

Nia scolded Adam with a sour glance, showing her displeasure.

"Nia, please don't look at me with those eyes. This knowledge is only supposed to be given out once a certain level of understanding is reached," Adam responded, already showing signs of giving in.

Turning back to the morning sky and folding her arms, Nia said, "Are you suggesting I don't have the same understanding as you?"

Catering to Nia, "Of course not, I know you understand the sciences far better than I do. I'm just in keeping with the tradition."

Nia continued staring at the skyline, deep in thought. After being cuddled and coiled, Adam wouldn't dare risk ruining the mood. After all, he knew he'd have to come to her eventually to get the true understanding about Master Zulu's teaching. Nia had an incredible knack for understanding the body, mind, and sciences. If it weren't for her, he wouldn't be as far as he was in his training with Master Zulu.

"Okay okay, but don't tell anybody," Adam finally said, breaking the silence.

Nia rolled from her back to her stomach and propped her head up with both arms while lightly twirling her feet in the air. Her smile and big, beautiful eyes impaled Adam's soul once more.

Adam whispered, "He told me about the merkaba."

"The what?" she asked.

"The mer-kah-bah—it means space-time-dimension vehicle."

Nia didn't blink. Her eyes continued to lock in full attention to Adam.

He continued, "He said that according to Zulu legend the seeds of our great elders came from the stars using the merkaba."

With a scrunched brow, Nia asked, "So, what exactly is it?"

"It is a chariot of immense power that the great creator allows us to have when we are in tune with higher consciousness and spirituality. It's our own personal vehicle that we can use to travel the universe and visit other worlds. One day you and I will travel together," smiled Adam.

"Wow, that is incredible. So, it's our own personal star traveler?"

"Yes, but that's not all. He said when it's activated it surrounds you with a protective shield that is more powerful than 1000 active volcanoes. He said the Zulus in the east used it to bring down the flying wheels of the invaders from the skies."

Wide-eyed, Nia asked, "Did he teach you how to activate it?"

"He said you have to channel immense emotions up your chakras, but I don't know what he meant," Adam responded while lowering his eyes, ashamed of his ignorance.

With a sympathetic mother's giggle toward her child, Nia said, "He is talking about your spiritual gateway, the energy centers along your spine."

Embarrassed, Adam rolled to his back. "How can I ever become an ascended master if I don't understand the teachings?"

"You can because you have me—I will help you. We will do it together."

She grabbed his chin, and turned his face to hers.

She glanced at him for a few seconds before lightly kissing his lips, making sure to keep her eyes open to see into his soul. After the light kiss, she held her gaze, giving Adam the chance to peer back into her soul.

"Adam, I am with life inside."

A slow grin grew across Adam's face.

"Nia, this is most wonderful news for us," he said as he rolled her on top of him.

Adam wrapped his massive arms around her to secure his new family and gave her his best kiss of reassurance.

After spending a few moments daydreaming of his new family, Adam uttered, "My business just got easier."

Adam liked to remind Nia regularly that it was his business to love her, adore her, take care of her, and provide for her. Growing up in nearby villages, Adam would always come to Nia's rescue as a kid and remind her of his business to love her. This was the perfect time to remind her of it again. These words, his actions, the birds, and the stream in the background all helped echo the magnitude of the moment.

They'd been with each other all night and it was

time to get back to the village to begin the day. Holding hands and skipping back to spread the good news, they were disrupted by the thundering sounds of the village war drums. Alerted and now rushing back, they could see smoke billowing out near their village. The closer they got, the louder the screams, cries, and panic from familiar voices they heard.

They arrived to chaos—huts on fire, charred remains, and mangled bodies throughout. Adam and Nia froze to the sight of their village being ambushed by large, silver, oval wheels in the sky. Adam took action by holding tight to Nia's hand and running to grab his double-sided spear to begin the defense of his Zulu village. As he ran, he was nailed by a white flash that hit him in his chest. It was a cold, sharp pain and before he knew it he and Nia lied paralyzed, staring right into each other's eyes.

Her eyes were no longer calm and inviting, they were filled with a glassy stare of terror. Adam saw the fear in Nia's eyes as she blinked back and forth in her paralyzed state, begging for his help. Adam went deep inside of himself to muster any leftover energy to free himself from the paralysis. From deep inside of himself he felt the ability to slowly take back his body. He broke free from the frozen state and reached for Nia. But as their hands touched, he was struck with another paralyzing white flash. He helplessly watched Nia's body being dragged off, as her terror-stricken eyes burned a hole through his soul. Adam's heart sank and his eyes gushed with tears and sorrow.

While Adam lied sobbing, a thin figure stepped in front of him, a witch doctor of some sort. He squatted and peered at Adam while smoking his pipe, turning his head from side to side as if he was inspecting the helpless Adam. He pulled out a machete and took aim at Adam's neck. Just then, Adam heard, "Wake up Adam, wake up."

Adam awoke from his dream and jolted up in revolt, as if fighting off the beheading he had expected moments before.

"What the fuck!" he yelled.

While wiping the sweat and tears from his face, he noticed his belongings were whirling and floating about his small room. With the sorrow from the dream turning to anger, Adam began thrashing about his room like a loose bull.

Miles suddenly appeared on the video monitor mounted to the wall in his room.

In a cool, relaxing voice, he said, "Adam, calm down. Everything is okay. If you are not able to calm yourself, we will have to sedate you."

Miles took a moment to see if his words resonated.

"Adam! This part of the base is not designed to handle your energy."

Adam continued to thrash about the small room.

"Adam... Adam, calm down, big fella! We have another floor and a mountain above you. We can't afford for you to be angry in this underground facility."

Adam turned off the video monitor, ignoring Miles and began to mentally settle himself. He plopped back down on his small cot while watching his belongings crash to the ground.

"Arghh, this woman is gonna be the death of me," he mumbled as he used his telepathic abilities to float a toothpick to his mouth.

Talking out loud, with his fingers pressed against his forehead, Adam said, "I haven't quite felt that amount of rage since that day with Winston Chase. I wonder if... nah I'm trippin'... fuck it, it wouldn't hurt to look."

Adam grabbed his tablet and began to study the footage of his run-in with the CEO's goons. He went over the footage again and again, forward and backward. He studied every move he made, every move the henchmen made, until a few drops of blood fell from his nose on his tablet. Before he could remove the blood, Miles interrupted by abruptly knocking on his door.

"Adam... talk to me," in a muffled, frustrated voice from outside the room.

Adam hesitantly dragged his large frame over to let Miles into his room. He entered, assisted by armed guards, and immediately began to focus on the issue at hand.

He picked up a chair and quickly began a tirade of his own, "We have made some amazing progress with your powers in the last six months but have yet to duplicate displays such as this. It seems you display the greatest show of power during these angry emotional tirades. What is all this destruction about? Is there something you are not telling me?"

All Adam had to live for at this point was the woman of his dreams, literally. This dream was obviously connected to the dream he had the morning before he met Winston Chase. It explained the moments leading up to his beloved Nia's gruesome death on the flying silver, oval wheel. The emotional toll of the dream was frustrating enough for Adam, but now all of Adam's dreams with Nia have been further soured by a strange man. Like clockwork, since Adam had been at the underground base, whenever Nia was in his dream, this pipe-smoking witch doctor tagged along. The last luxury Adam had in life had now been taken away from him. He turned angrier and angrier and confused over this phenomenon.

Adam chose to keep his embarrassing love story from Miles.

With his face resting in his palms, Adam took a deep breath and answered Miles' question, "Ever since I've been here, I've been dreaming about this... witch doctor. I don't know, I haven't quite been able to sort through it all."

"A witch doctor," repeated Miles as he motioned the guards to be relieved of duty.

"What does he look like?" asked Miles.

Adam began to describe him, "He is African, has red marks on his face, smokes a pipe, piercings..."

Miles promptly interrupted, "Enough!"

He took in a deep breath while walking over to Adam's in-room camera and cut it off. "Adam, I think it is time you meet someone."

"Who?" Adam questioned.

Miles fidgeted a bit and took another deep breath, "The man you speak of, he is here in this facility."

Lifting his head up, eyes at full alert, Adam blurted out, "What!"

Cautiously, Miles approached the subject with great care not to upset the giant in front of him, "We hired him as a consultant to handle matters...uhm, let's say, not of this realm. He is above top secret. There are only a handful of people who know about him here. You described him to a tee; perhaps he can help unlock this mystery of your powers."

Shaking off the somber mood from his dream, Adam perked up and said, "Well, you got me all cooped up in this place, I could use a change of scenery. You can't expect me to tap into my powers when you keep me in a cage."

"Cage or no cage, per our agreement, I am to be made aware of all neuro-activity and that includes your dreams," lectured Miles.

Adam frowned and cocked his head to the side in disbelief. He snatched the toothpick out of his mouth.

Punctuating his point with it, he snapped back at Miles, "I've been here six months, training and jumping through your hoops every day, and the only thing I can get out of you is where some god damned water fountain is. You got me locked up in this big ass underground secret bunker and I'm supposed to tell you everything? Get the fuck out of here!"

Miles stood up fixing his suit, clearly irked by Adam's comments. He responded with agitation,

"Perhaps you'd prefer to go home! If you don't like the rules here, I'm sure we can arrange for you to leave. It might suit us all better."

Adam was speechless. He downed his head, popped his toothpick back in his mouth, and grabbed his tablet to begin studying the surveillance footage.

Miles continued, "I didn't think so. If you want your leash off, stop throwing tantrums and figure out how the fuck you tossed an SUV across the street. Don't force my hand, Adam. In the meantime, be ready tomorrow morning!"

Adam sighed and tightened his grip on his tablet. He felt like he was on the losing end of Miles' bullying. Growing up in impoverished ghettos across Phoenix molded him into a hood-savvy bully himself. Any tones such as Miles's would often get rewarded with a broken rib or missing teeth. Being between a rock and a hard place, there wasn't much Adam could do about it. Miles had the upper hand and it singed Adam's tail feathers.

Before Miles exited Adam's quarters, he said, "Oh and another thing, turn that damn music down... you're not in Kansas anymore, buddy."

Adam responded with a loud sigh through clenched teeth.

With his hand still on the door knob, Miles turned and warned, "And don't forget to tell me about your little dreams—and I mean everything. You agreed to these terms in the beginning."

He fixed his suit, turned, and finally left.

"Huh... the beginning... whatever, mutha-fucka," murmured the agitated Adam as he lied back down in his bed and rolled his toothpick about his mouth.

He let Miles' last words poke at his ego before he sat up, alarmed, "The beginning... hmmm... I wonder... the beginning... hmmm."

He anxiously grabbed his tablet and began to review the footage with the CEO's goons again. This time he rewound the footage an hour before the incident and put the footage on 10 times the normal speed. He watched every car and person appearing in the scene like a hawk. By some twist of fate, his attention was drawn to the drop of blood that was left on the tablet from his earlier nose bleed. He paused the frame and calmly wiped his blood off with his thumb. Then it hit him like a ton of bricks and his heart skipped a beat. Conveniently hiding under the spec of blood was a woman who looked eerily similar to his Nia. He used the face clarity software installed on the tablet to get a clearer look. It was his Nia!

With butterflies in his stomach, Adam slowly

mouthed, "Ohhhhh ssssssssshit!"

She entered the library 30 minutes before his incident with the CEO's SUV. The shock of a living, breathing Nia sent electrical ripples throughout Adam's body. He lied flat on his bed, mouth agape in awe. He massaged his head with his finger tips in disbelief. He began to contemplate the idea that not only was Nia real but her proximity may somehow have something to do with the strength of his powers.

Chapter 9

Kojo sat in a secure, inconspicuous plumbing van, just three miles away from the point of attack. The van was parked on a busy neighborhood street and filled with high-tech surveillance equipment. There were also computer monitors mounted on one side and high artillery weapons mounted on the other. Staring at his center monitor, he profusely typed on his keyboard. His side monitors displayed current statistics, video footage, and the global position of his team. On the desk behind him were two drones and high-powered assault rifles. He checked the batteries of his drones and loaded a round into his assault rifle. He fired up his cigar and took a deep pull to calm his nerves, letting the sweet taste percolate in his mouth. He took another pull for good measure, then set down his cigar and dived back into his task.

He put on his earpiece and began communication

with his team of five, "Clutch, Echo 1,2,3,4, verify all lines are still secure."

One by one, each team member remotely confirmed line security through their earpieces.

"Okay, I have visual on the engineer. He just sat down and ordered his normal coffee and breakfast," Kojo announced.

After visual confirmation of his target and line security, Kojo began his cyber attack on the traffic engineer for his remote log-on to the Los Angeles traffic control system. With the discipline of a skilled hunter, Kojo had been following the engineer for weeks to get his daily schedule. Every morning before work, the engineer headed to the local coffee shop. During his morning routine, Kojo noticed he used the coffee shop's network in order to remotely log in to check traffic control.

It was that moment that Kojo hatched a brilliant plan to use the traffic engineer as the key tool for the attack. Once Kojo had his username and password, he would effectively be a traffic God on the streets of Los Angeles.

"Clutch, what is your status?" asked Kojo.

Looking at his digital map showing the armored truck's location, Clutch answered, "We are following the target now and approximately five minutes away from the intersection."

"I'm deploying the drones to the coffee shop now. Drones deployed. Once I get his username and password, I'll be jamming all the lights and cameras at the Canyon Blvd. intersection," said Kojo.

"Does everybody copy that?" demanded Clutch.

As if responding to their drill sergeant, all team members chimed in quickly in sequential order, "Affirmative!"

Kojo continued, "Floating the jamming drone. Okay, jamming coffee shop's home network. Network jammed and down. Okay, I'm deploying the mock network drone. New network is up, just waiting for the engineer to bite and logon. Okay, he is logging on."

"How long 'til you get the password?" asked Clutch.

Kojo responded, "Just got it."

Kojo began a furious tirade of typing on his keyboard, "I'm logging into the Los Angeles traffic control now."

With magnificent speed and proficiency, Kojo maneuvered inside the traffic control system with ease, "Bingo, I'm in. Everybody get ready. Alright, the cameras and intersection should be down. Clutch, can you verify?"

"Yes, intersection down both ways and the armored truck is in place," Clutch verified.

The normal morning LA traffic quickly went from a stop-and-go cluster of cars to a miserable parking lot glued together by a soup of rude and highly irritated drivers.

Kojo asked calmly, "Is the pedestrian traffic heavy, as we planned?"

"Affirmative," said Clutch.

Kojo started giving orders, "Okay, I've just dispatched the drone to your location, Clutch. Echo 1, your move. Echo 2, you go in three minutes. Echo 3, you go in five minutes."

Traffic was quickly backing up, all intersections were jammed full of cars and roads were deadlocked for blocks. The snag in the traffic grid granted Kojo and his team the perfect opportunity to strike with a hidden attack.

Blending in with the crowd, Echo 1 rode a skateboard behind the armored truck and inconspicuously put a shaped charge detonator on the back door locks. Three minutes later, Echo 2 walked past the armored truck and discreetly put another shaped charge detonator on the center of the back door. Two minutes later, Echo 3 rode past the armored target and slyly put the final shaped charge detonator on the back door's remaining locks.

All operatives confirmed packages were in place respective of their delivery.

Kojo chimed in, "Echo 4, are the C4 store-front detonators and exit vehicles in place?"

Echo 4 responded, "Affirmative."

"Okay, Clutch, head toward the armored truck—denotation in 10," said Kojo.

Kojo continued, "Drone in route."

He began the countdown, "10, 9, 8, 7, 6, 5, 4, 3, 2, 1." Boom!

The neighboring store front exploded, sending plumes of smoke billowing into the air. Simultaneously, the shape charge explosives on the armored truck detonated, hiding behind the large store-front blast. While most eyes focused on the store-front diversion, Clutch casually walked up to the truck's back door. Wearing an armored truck driver's uniform, he looked through the top window and pointed his weapon inside the seared hole from the donators. While the guards had no time to react, Clutch fired an electric pulse that stunned the men and they fell paralyzed to the ground. Clutch calmly opened the door. He stepped into the truck, ducking his bald head to fit. He used a torch with a black flame to cut through the truck's safe. He grabbed the C-47 vials out of the safe and carefully placed them into a self refrigerated transport container.

"Package in hand," Clutch reported.

Kojo quickly responded, "Okay, the drone is 5 seconds away."

Kojo's drone inconspicuously showed up outside the armored truck, camouflaged by the heavy traffic pollution and plumes of smoke from the blast. While the crowd was still distracted by the store-front explosion, Clutch attached the container to the drone and it covertly flew away. Clutch then calmly walked away and cut down an alley to rendezvous with Echo 4 in the getaway vehicle around the corner.

"Well done, team, we have the package. Okay, Echo 4, I have cleared a route for you," said Kojo.

Kojo easily guided their escape, conveniently turning traffic lights on and off for Echo 4 and Clutch's escape. He made it nearly impossible for them to be followed and pursued.

Chapter 10

"One dead and six hurt in a Los Angeles store front explosion yesterday. Authorities tell us it may have been a diversion for an armored truck robbery, where a rare compound, C-47, was stolen. Authorities are still trying to figure out why anyone would steal the banned substance. It's often illegally made into a serum, used to treat drug addictions. Sources believe the perpetrators are related to the terror group known as the 'Colony', run by suspects known as Kojo and Clutch. The group is known to be responsible for the financial crisis in Nigeria, the bombing of Crow Corp facilities across the globe, and destabilizing U.S. allies. Authorities say..." A knock was heard at Adam's door, interrupting his daily update from the 6:00 a.m. news.

Miles popped into view on Adam's video screen.

"Rise and shine, beautiful. We have work to do," he said.

Adam flew off his bed, grabbed his bag, and left his small room. He headed out, excited to meet the man he hoped would give him some real answers.

"Here, you will need to have this with you at all times. I went through hell and high water to get you this clearance," Miles said as he handed Adam his badge.

"You will need to sign these docs as a precautionary procedure for a level-three base clearance," Miles informed him as he shoved a folder of documents in Adam's chest.

"All this? And there is a level three here?" asked Adam.

Miles smirked at Adam and continued down the hallway, "The person you are about to see is beyond top secret. Our government expects you to keep this meeting a secret upon your life."

Catching up to Miles, Adam questioned, "Really, my life? Come on man, you can't be serious."

"Yes, I'm very serious. And you need to take it seriously too," replied Miles.

Shaking his head, Adam began scanning and

signing the documents. He went through five checkpoints and a series of inquisitions by jumpy security guards before Miles finally led him into a strange dark room. Adam examined the eerie room; it appeared to be some type of living quarters.

"Adam, this is Kano; Kano meet Adam. I'll let you two get acquainted. You're going to be spending a lot of time together," said Miles.

He then briskly left the room.

From the shadows of the room, Kano appeared, gliding toward Adam in tribal clothing. He was identical to the witch doctor in his dreams—a tall, thin man with large invading eyes, and dark, sweaty-looking skin. His face was covered with red paint and large, white bone piercings through his nose and ears. His lips puckered to hold steady the long pipe dangling from the side of his mouth. His living quarters were much bigger than Adam's and decorated with what Adam perceived as occult symbolism. Pentagrams, animal skulls and newspaper articles were scattered about the room with only dimly lit candles for light.

Remembering that the witch doctor put a machete around Adam's neck in his dream made him weary.

Adam got right to business and asked, "For the last six months, you been in my dreams. You put some kind of spell on me?"

Kano, walking around Adam and inspecting him with his smoldering dark eyes said, "I'll ask the questions. How long have you been aware and conscious in your dreams?"

Kano spoke with perfect English diction and a British accent. Adam had expected some sort of African tongue to go with the African garb.

Perplexed, yet anxious to know what he could learn, Adam answered, "Umm... my whole life."

Adam stepped closer to Kano with a furrowed brow, "What's up with that machete bro?"

Still circling, Kano grunted at Adam's nerve to still question him. Ignoring Adam's inquiry, he continued his investigation while watching Adam closely for any emotional reaction.

"This Nia must be real special; who is she?" he asked.

Adam, still a bit embarrassed by his love affair, was careful not to divulge too much information about his Nia.

He looked away, pretending to be more interested in the living quarters than the question, "I don't know, I've been dreaming about her my entire life, but I don't know who she is."

Kano said, "Perhaps she is someone from your past."

Lucky for Adam, Kano wasn't extremely interested in learning much about Nia. With his hands behind his back, he continued circling Adam, pondering his next question.

Standing directly in front of Adam, Kano inspected him as a doctor studies a patient, "I've been made aware that you are somewhat psychic and a telepath, yes?"

Adam nodded lackadaisically.

Kano continued, "How strong is your telepathic ability?"

Adam sighed at the irritation of not getting any of his questions answered but still replied, "It's gotten better with all my training here, but I still have to sit down and really concentrate to get anything worthwhile."

Puffing his pipe, Kano took a moment as if he was conjuring up another question to ask.

He blew the smoke out of his nose and asked, "Anything else?"

He patiently waited, knowing Adam had more to

tell.

Adam shrugged his shoulders and said, "Yeah, umm... I've been seeing these weird colors around some people... kinda like an aura or something. But no one seems to know what it's about. I even see one around you."

"I see, very interesting. And you've always had these abilities, or are they new?" Kano asked.

"The aura thing is new."

"Anything else new or developing?"

Adam sighed, "Well, there are some other things; it's kinda like... I know and understand things but I don't remember ever learning them."

Adam scrambled for a better description, "I can do things, but I don't know where or how I got the ability to do them. Like over the last few months... I discovered I know many different styles of martial arts, but I've never studied them. I just... know them. I know how to fix things too. It's like I have all these skills and I have no idea how I learned them."

That was it—Adam now had Kano's full attention. The combination of Adam's abilities piqued his interest. Kano started nodding and eagerly rubbing his hands together.

A large grin stretched across his face while he said, "Yessss, I knew it, I knew it!"

Pointing and shaking his finger at Adam, he said, "I've been watching you. In all my time here, I've seen nothing like you."

He came closer to Adam and said softly as if he was whispering a secret, "Like you, I also have the ability to interact with the Dreamspace. I have a bit more control than you do, so I'm able to consciously interact with others while in the dream space. This is how I knew about your Nia."

Adam stepped back, contorting his brow, showing his confusion. Kano continued, "I've seen your charts. Your highly evolved DNA has given you incredible powers. What you did takes a high level of spiritual and psychic abilities. You noticed me in your dreams... You have an incredible gift."

Adam shook his head, hunched his shoulders, and asked, "Dreamspace?"

Kano reached out and grabbed Adam's hands, "Tell me son, what am I thinking?"

Adam sighed and closed his eyes. He concentrated and took about two to three minutes to bring in all of the information.

"You think I'm very special; you have heard of my

kind coming and you think I am the one who can change the world. Man, what's going on, playboy," said Adam while letting go of Kano's hands and taking a step backwards.

Such accuracy was all Kano needed to take Adam under his wing.

Kano reassured him with a welcoming smile, "I'm sure you have many questions; I will answer all that I can in due time."

Adam narrowed his eyes and shifted his weight from side to side, showing his discomfort.

He took a defensive stand, "Knock that 'change the world' shit off and tell me what was up with you putting that machete around my neck!"

Kano decided to subdue Adam's restlessness by giving in to his questions.

With a calm tone he said, "The machete was a test to see how well you could defend yourself in the Dreamspace. No harm was to come to you."

Kano motioned for Adam to take a seat. Adam obliged, keeping his eyes dead locked on Kano, as if he was a caged predator. Kano re-lit his pipe and joined Adam in the closest facing chair. He burdened his lungs with a deep blaze of smoke before continuing.

He took a hard stare at Adam while slowly exhaling smoke through his nose.

As the smoke rose into the atmosphere, he said, "There is a place you can go; it is the realm where human souls go when leaving the body. The soul operates freely while the physical body is in a dream-like state. It's called the astral realm."

Adam leaned forward and asked, "Wait, is it kinda like those out-of-body experiences?"

Taking a few more large puffs, Kano answered sharply, "Yes, it is."

Adam grinned and nodded his head while slowly sinking into his chair, "I think I've experienced this, but I thought they were just crazy dreams."

"No, this is different from dreams. In most dreams, you don't see vivid colors, hear, feel, taste or smell. More importantly, you can't master your dreams," Kano responded, cracking a smile and shaking his pipe at Adam.

"I'm confused. Why are you telling me about this and what does this have to do with me?" Adam asked.

"Because, son, you must master this realm—this is where you will hone in on your powers even more. One can create all that they imagine in this realm.

This is the ultimate tool to realize your true power and the first step to seeing the true reality."

"The true reality?"

Happy that Adam was baiting the right questions, Kano continued, "Our eyes, ears, taste, smell, and touch only go so far. At best, they give us only a tiny glimpse of what reality really is. In a sense, you are already in the astral realm; you just can't perceive all of it with your five senses. But upon entering the astral realm, we see and sense everything."

Adam's eyes locked in on Kano. While rubbing his fingers through his five o'clock shadow, he asked, "Can I die in there?"

Waving his finger at Adam dismissively, Kano answered, "There is no such thing as death. A soul never dies. Most people mistakenly believe they only have access to it at death, but that's not true. The astral realm houses the souls who we think are dead."

Adam clasped his hands and said with much vigor, "Well fuck it, I'm in! It sounds like I don't have anything to lose. So, how do I get to this place?"

A slow grin crept across Kano's face. Happy that Adam was on board, he reiterated, "As I said before, this realm is all around you, and has been since your birth. During sleep, the soul is able to leave the body.

Most are unaware of this. With proper training, you can voluntarily enter the realm through sleep, meditation, sex, or even through dance."

Adam was blown back by the deep metaphysical possibilities of this astral realm. Perhaps this would bring him closer to Nia.

"That shit sounds dope. So, how do I get to it," Adam asked again.

Kano grinned with smoke slowly billowing out of his mouth, "I will help you master this realm, and teach you how to enter it at your own will. We must first get your spiritual consciousness high enough. We will start immediately."

Adam perked up over Kano's offer.

Searching his pockets for toothpicks, Adam showcased a rare smile, "Okay now you are speaking my language."

Shifting his toothpick about his mouth and feeling a bit more comfortable about the subject, Adam asked, "So, what do I gotta do?"

Scooting his chair closer to Adam, Kano said, "First we must strengthen your third eye in your mind. After that I will teach you a series of techniques designed to strengthen your mental focus. Once you have complete control over your mental state, you will be able to consciously enter into a meditative trance and from there into the astral realm."

This sounded like absurd pseudoscience mumbo jumbo to Adam... third eye? Astral realm? Still, too much had happened to completely doubt its truth.

***

Over the next month, Kano ran Adam through many mental and mind-strengthening exercises to boost his consciousness in order to prepare him for his training in the astral realm.

A month later, Kano prepared Adam for his first supervised trip into the astral realm. In Kano's quarters, both men made themselves more comfortable on the floor and sat upright. Kano entered first and awaited Adam's entrance. Using the meditative technique Kano prescribed, Adam dove deep into a meditative trance. He slowed his heartbeat, shut down his thoughts, shallowed his breathing, and immersed himself into the moment— no past, no future, just the now. Shortly thereafter, Adam's soul slowly rose out of his body. He was awestruck at the sight of their physical bodies sitting peacefully in their meditative state inside of Kano's quarters. Oddly, he didn't see an aura around their two bodies.

Adam took time to look at his astral self in the mirror and noticed that his body looked like a translucent version of himself. It was luminous, similar to an x-ray or a ghost. It was bright and violet in color. The colors stretched throughout his astral body like millions of jagged bolts of lightning. The bolts glowed and glistened, vibrating with the most beautiful of colors. The same could be said for Kano's astral body, with the exception of a reddish hue.

He awed over the realm's energy and magnificent power. He was essentially a pure, weightless living energy, free of his heavy, fleshy body. Even though he didn't have his physical body, he was amazed he could still feel and touch. He didn't need his eyes; he was able to see with his mind. His visual perception increased from the normal frontal 120 degrees to a whopping 220 degrees of spherical vision.

All colors were more vivid, possessing a visual clarity unmatched and unrivaled by his human eye. He marveled at the shining, glaring, and sparkling beauty the realm offered.

Kano took him above ground, and he saw that everything in the normal world had an astral realm equivalent—the earth, trees, landscape, cities, even people. He was able to float, fly, and pass through walls at will. He didn't need an airplane; he simply focused his attention on a place and he was there instantly. The speed of travel was unfathomable. He marveled at the earth's beauty. He and Kano soared through different countries and regions visiting cathedrals, monuments and beaches, all with a mere thought. Sensations were so real he could feel the cold water dancing about his energy body and the warmth of the sun cradling his face. All the essence of him was essentially the same in the astral realm. He thought clearer, felt the depths of his emotions, and retained all of his memories as normal. Adam felt as though this must be what heaven is like. He thought no human words in existence could properly describe the vastness of the place. Saying it is incredible was an injustice. It was magnificent, just as Kano had described. It made everything Kano said more real and trustworthy. Adam felt forever indebted to him, for granting him this amazing gift. Adam felt the good inside of him blaring out. He felt his connection to all. Simply put, the astral realm changed his life instantly.

They both returned back to their physical bodies.

Adam in full amazement and still sitting in his meditative position slowly mouthed to Kano, "Ohhhh shit, that was super dope!"

While rubbing his hands together and reflecting on the magnitude of what he had just accomplished,

Adam mumbled, "It's on now!"

Kano grinned as he got up and grabbed his pipe.

He lit it and filled his lungs with smoke before saying, "I must caution you on one thing..."

After a few more puffs, "Since you are essentially pure energy in the astral realm, you want to stay above ground. The earth becomes denser the deeper you go underground, and that can disrupt your energy."

"That's it?" said Adam with a another rare grin.

Kano nodded. This voluntary out-of-body experience had completely transformed Adam into a different person; he now understood concepts that made no sense before. He had confirmation that a soul was needed to animate all objects. It was obvious now that energy flows throughout the universe, that energy is the basis of all life and consciousness. It was truly a profound experience that evolved Adam.

With the help of Kano, he knew his gifts would get better, stronger, and more accurate with time.

Perhaps I'd better be a bit more thankful to Miles, Adam thought.

Chapter 11

Over the next few months, Adam toyed with his new astral realm ability by traveling throughout the upper levels of the base. With Kano, he inspected every inch, getting acquainted with the new reality. He saw a silver cord attached from his astral body to his human body. Having increased his psychic and spiritual understanding, he knew this cord was how the soul stayed attached to its physical body while in the astral realm and that all humans possessed one.

During the day Adam continued to further train with scientists to enhance and test his mental abilities.

"Steven, are we just about done in here?" said Adam, sitting in a small room with a half dozen other scientists.

He sat stiffly, tethered to an EEG device, heart

rate monitors, and a host of other body-monitoring machines.

"Just about, but while we're waiting though... I hear you have veridical perception, "Steven said.

"What? What the hell is that?" Adam asked.

Chuckling at Adam's ignorance, Steven answered, "Veridical perception is the ability to project your consciousness outside of your body and observe and retain events in your memory."

Adam sighed and reached for a toothpick.

Before Adam could respond, Steven continued, "Back in 1968, a colleague of mine, Dr. Charles Tart, documented the most infamous veridical perception study in history and published his results in the Journal of the American Society of Psychical Research."

"You talking about the astral realm?" Adam asked with a twinge of irritation.

"Adam, the proper scientific term is veridical perception."

Hissing and rolling his eyes, "Yeah man, I have that ability."

Over the background mic, Adam could hear Steven rambling off Dr. Tart's amazing experiment results to the other scientists, "He successfully documented a young woman using veridical perception. She accurately read a five digit code from another location. All the while, her brain exhibited a flattened EEG with prominent alphoid activity, no REM or skin resistance activity, and normal heart rate. It was truly amazing."

Turning back to Adam, Steven asked, "So, Adam, what is veridical perception really like?"

While seated inside the deprivation room, bored and flicking debris from his nails, Adam sighed, "Veridical perception... No disrespect but trying to explain the astral realm to a scientist is like trying to explain dreaming to a person who has never dreamed."

The scientists all looked at each other, dumbfounded at Adam's profound analogy. Adam sighed again and leaned into the microphone, "Yo, Steven, you gonna at least make it a lil tougher this time? Your shit's been kinda simple lately."

From outside of the room, Steven pushed up his glasses and peered at the video feed of Adam, "Go ahead, tell me what is on the screen?"

Adam chuckled, "Steven... ain't shit on the screen! You know that."

Steven, shaking his head and speaking to another scientist, "This is incredible. There is no change in his brain activity or heart rate; it's like he doesn't even have to think about it."

Shaking his head, Steven said, "Let's give it one more shot. What's on my monitor now?"

Adam took a moment and put a hand to his temple, then a slow grin fought its way to his face; in a joking manner he said, "Something you probably beat off to every night!"

The other scientists burst out in snickers and laughter. "Nah, man, I'm just clownin', it's the periodic table," Adam said while fighting back his own laughter.

Steven sighed, knowing he was the butt of Adam's joke, "You're an asshole. Why are you even here? Doesn't Miles know you are beyond this training?"

Chuckling, Adam shrugged his shoulders, "What can I say, Steven, you know I couldn't let that one go by."

Steven gave Adam a small smile, letting him know there were no hard feelings.

"Alright, you mind freak, I think we're done for the day," Steven announced as he began unhooking

Adam from all of the lab equipment.

Adam was now ready for what he considered his real training.

During the nights Adam met with Kano for extended training in the astral realm. Kano perfected Adam's ability to travel and explore the many vast planes the astral realm had to offer. One night, before entering the astral realm, Kano pulled Adam aside for one of his after-hour lessons.

"Please have a seat," said Kano upon Adam entering his quarters.

Adam obliged, resting his tall frame on Kano's small sofa.

"There is one more piece to your training to make it complete. I need to prepare you for the many malicious human souls you may encounter during your trips to the astral realm."

Adam's eyes narrowed, he scooted forward, "Wha?"

Kano took a seat in front of Adam and puffed his pipe, "You and I are not the only humans that have astral abilities. There are others who have their own agenda in the astral realm, so you will need to learn to defend yourself against them. They can be troublesome if you are not careful. Therefore, you will need to learn certain skills, so I'm going to teach you about astral combat."

"Wait... wait... hold up a minute. Damaged? If I can be damaged, then can't I die?" Adam asked frowning.

"No... No... your physical body can die, but your soul goes on... so no death."

"Awww, man, ain't that about a bitch. So it is dangerous! You should have told me that in the first place!" Adam barked.

"If I did, would you have agreed to go in? There is nothing for you to worry about; you visit this realm every night in your sleep. How many people do you know who die in their dreams? You are more likely to get struck by lightning while riding in an airplane on Christmas, all in the same day you win the lottery. You're fifty times more powerful than any pesky human you may face in the astral realm. Stop worrying," responded Kano.

"Bro! Is there anything else I need to know before we go any further?" asked Adam sternly.

Kano continued, "Can you be damaged? Absolutely. Is it likely to happen? Not in a million years. So, let's move on, shall we?"

Adam sighed, shaking his head and rolling his

eyes at Kano.

"Alright. Soooo how can there be combat if things don't have the same structure as they do in the physical world?"

"For simplicity, we say the things our five senses can't perceive are in the astral realm. So there is still structure, it's just of a higher energy vibration. It's the different levels of vibration that actually make up an object or being. Now, to make it even simpler, your eyes can't see the vibrating wings of a hummingbird, yet they exist and can be disrupted. So just like the physical realm, astral bodies can be damaged by being penetrated, sliced, cut, stabbed even absorbed."

"Damn, that's deep. So how exactly do these attacks happen?" asked Adam.

"Astral combatants have learned that fangs, claws, blades, or any other sharp weapons are strongly interpreted as hostile attack weapons. So when we are clawed, bitten, or struck, we actually expect to manifest damage. Our astral body then absorbs the negative intent and passes it through our silver cord to our physical body, ultimately making the damage real. Likewise, to defend yourself, you must create weapons of defense to do in essence the same thing to your astral opponent."

"Ohhhhh... Crazy, that's on another level, bro. Give me the goods, how do you create weapons?" Adam asked enthusiastically.

"The astral realm allows us greater degrees of freedom for creation. Everything is essentially energy. So by focusing, you can command energy out of the aether into weapons. The key is to choose a weapon that best fits your personally."

"Just like that?" asked Adam.

"Yes, just like that. Just envision the weapon in your hand."

"Dammmm that is super dope!" Adam responded, shifting back into Kano's couch.

Night after night, Kano perfected Adam's ability to create astral weapons in order to defend himself against troublesome human souls.

After wrapping up a training session one evening, Adam hesitantly asked Kano, "I just want to make sure I'm not trippin', but I've been seeing these weird shapes, kinda like blobs of energy wrapped around people's astral bodies here at the base. What the fuck is that?"

Waving his hands in a dismissive manner, Kano quickly put Adam at ease in a reassuring voice, "Oh those, they are nothing more than leaches. They feed off one's residual energy. Nothing to worry about, especially for someone as powerful as you. It's just another one of the creator's infinite creations. If you encounter one, just wish it away."

Swallowing Kano's answer, but still a bit snagged on the subject, Adam scratched his chin and slowly asked, "Sounds simple enough, soooooo uhmm... why did you teach me all these astral weapon techniques if it's just that simple?"

"I told you, for the others like you who have gone rogue. You may need to use your astral abilities to defend against these brutes one day," Kano divulged.

He walked closer to Adam and softly put his hand on his shoulder.

Mustering up a bit of sincerity in his voice, he went on, "We believe these astral abilities are now in the hands of terrorists and they are being used against the state. I don't know what your full mission is, but I suspect you are going to be an elite agent for protection of national security to guard against these kinds of madmen."

Adam sat, perplexed at his situation. He was being forced to do something that he never would have considered. Taking this mission meant he essentially would be a snitch... a difficult jacket for him to wear. Because of his circumstances, there really wasn't much of a choice: either go to prison or do something for the greater good of humanity. The good of humanity wasn't enough to turn Adam; humanity hadn't been good to him and he really couldn't care less. Adam would willfully do time before snitching; after all, he'd have to live with himself. The deciding factor was Nia. Now that he knew she was real, he may have the opportunity to find her.

Adam's mental ability allowed him to master mind-blowing maneuvers that could only be dreamed of inside of comic books. Kano taught Adam the true unimagined potential of the realm; whatever mental items he could conceptualize became real. He gave Adam an idea, and in a blink of an eye it was mastered as soon as the thought appeared in his mind. Kano was right about Adam: his talents were amazing—unmatched and unrivaled by any human to date.

"Let's now get a feel for your combat ability in the astral realm," said Kano.

Adam took the head phones around his neck and nestled them in place. He began searching through his MP3 player.

"What are you doing?" asked Kano.

"Huh?" responded Adam.

Hissing, Kano mouthed louder to Adam, "WHAT ARE YOU DOING WITH THOSE?"

"Oh, music gives me juice, homeboy," Adam said while hitting play to Audio Slave's *Like a Stone.*

A surprising look sprung on Kano's face. He knew Adam was talented, but to no longer need a quiet meditative state to enter into the astral realm was intimidating. Now Adam could easily enter under the motivating sounds of his favorite tunes and Kano didn't teach him how—a slight blow to his ego.

Once in, Kano telepathically said to Adam, "Create your weapon of choice and attack me."

"Let's go, old man," anxiously responded Adam while creating his astral weapon: a double sided spear.

Kano hesitantly grinned, "What made you choose that?"

"Don't know, it's one of those things I told you about. I have no idea how I know about it, it just feels right to me," Adam said while rocking his astral body to the music.

"You hear your music too?" asked Kano.

"Yezzzir," Adam promptly responded.

Another blow to Kano's ego. A bit perplexed, he

nodded and created his own astral weapon: a large astral sword.

"Ready when you are, young pup," he said.

Adam dashed in, aiming his spear at Kano's center. Kano moved and guided Adam's spear away. From there Kano attempted to strike at Adam. Adam instinctively moved away out of range. Kano flew in, swinging at Adam with his sword from the top, then the bottom, then the sides. Adam had an answer for all of Kano's strikes, an unfamiliar experience for Kano. No one had ever stood against his attacks as well as Adam did in the astral realm. Very humbling to Kano's pride once again. Kano felt it was best to stop Adam's training at this point. Teaching Adam any more tricks might make him difficult to contend with, especially if he one day went rogue. It only took Adam six short months to master the astral realm, a feat an experienced projectionist like Kano took a lifetime to accomplish. Their close astral battles clearly challenged Kano's confidence, and Adam's natural abilities didn't help.

"Very good. You have excellent astral reflexes and responses. I believe your training is complete."

"We done already? I feel like I need more sparring sessions to really get a feel for things," said Adam.

Hiding a bruised ego, Kano said, "You now know enough to do your job."

Walking Adam back to his quarters after their last training session, Kano took a moment to give Adam some parting words.

His voice stiffened, "I have reported to Miles that my part with you is complete. Your skills are very remarkable. You will be an excellent addition to our team. It has been my pleasure to have worked with you."

"No doubt, bro. It's been real. Of course I gotta thank the master in the attic for my gifts, but I want to thank you for showing me how to use them. This astral realm shit has rejuvenated my life. I was livin' day to day before, but now I have a real purpose. I gotta give love to you and Miles for that. Good lookin' out, playboy," Adam said sincerely.

An awkward silence lingered before Kano said, "Okay but don't get all bloody mushy on me. Just do your job and that will be thanks enough."

Adam extended his hand to Kano. Kano awkwardly obliged. Adam read a strange melancholy mood from Kano, but didn't get enough time to further the read as Kano pulled away and carried on down the hall. Sad to see him go, Adam watched Kano leave. It had been a full year since he had had his jovial friend, Jolon, in his life. Since then, Kano was the closest thing.

***

The next morning, Adam promptly reported to his first military briefing with Miles. He walked into a conference room with one large video display centered on the wall. A long mahogany table stretched down the center of the room with trays of ice water in the middle. About 20 people sat around the table.

Present were uniformed leaders—Joint Chiefs of Staff from the Army, Navy, Marines, and Air force, most of whom gazed at Adam with a skeptical thunder. Also present were deputy directors from the CIA, NSA, and FBI, along with a few scientists he worked with while at the base.

The room's chatter became muffled at the sight of Adam's presence. All heads swiveled in his direction. Their granite faces bestowed burdening looks to Adam's presence in the briefing. Adam sensed the room was stiff, full of animosity, tension, and stress.

Each person possessed a tablet sitting neatly on their above top-secret files. Adam slowly took a seat, displaying his immediate discomfort. He hadn't been in a room with so many suits since his run-in with Winston Chase a year ago. He breathed a sigh of relief when he realized all of the men had auras, unlike the wicked CEO. The men all slowly constructed narrowed smiles across their faces as Miles introduced Adam to them; Adam nodded at each, not caring to remember any of their names. The lights dimmed and Miles took center stage while presenting Adam with his mission.

Chapter 12

Miles cleared his throat and spoke in a firm manner, being sure to project his voice throughout the room, "Adam, in a nutshell, you are here to combat terrorism. Our first and most deadly target is Kojo and Clutch. You are to use all that you have learned here to find and target these terrorists."

Adam felt a small seed of nervousness take root in the pit of his stomach. He didn't think he was ready to take on such formidable foes just yet.

"We are all aware of the incident in Los Angeles weeks back, where a top-secret compound known as C-47 was taken, resulting in one dead and six injured. Someone hacked into the Los Angeles traffic control system and brought down the traffic lights and cameras in order to heist this chemical. We are not yet sure what they plan to do with the C-47, but we know it's not positive. They wouldn't go through all of that trouble for nothing. That is the good news. The bad news is we believe it is child's play compared to what they are really planning. We believe the C-47 is a cog in the wheel of a much larger plan."

Taking a seat at the end of the table Miles continued, "We believe they are using the astral realm to steal top-secret information and sell it to other governments, corporations, and rogue terrorist groups. This is how they fund their terrorist organization called the Colony. Their destabilization tactics have caused a large increase in U.S. anti-government sentiments around the world. Even worse, we are unsure of what they have stolen, when they will release it, or to whom they will release it. We are now completely transparent, wide open sitting ducks. Essentially, they have become Gods, more powerful than standing governments. They also use this information to crash markets, as they did in Nigeria. NSA surveillance tells us they are planning on bringing down the U.S. market next. The derivative crash in 2008 wouldn't be a blip on the radar compared to the catastrophe they are capable of causing now."

"Do you know what it means if that happens?" asked one of the buzz-cut four star generals from the corner of the room.

Adam shrugged his shoulders and slouched further into his seat, not yet caring to speak out in front of the joint chiefs commanding the U.S. military. Adam took a quick glance at the general's name tag and read 'Brudzinski'.

"Well, I'll tell you, a major fuckin' catastrophe! If they are successful, they can take the world back to the stone age," barked General Brudzinski.

Adam heated up a little at Brudzinski's tone towards him. He took a closer look and saw that he was the Joint Chief's Marine Corpes General.

Miles let the deadening silence stretch a bit before he continued. He waved a device and the large video screen awakened to a picture of Kojo and Clutch.

Nervousness spread to the pit of Adam's gut. Sure he'd handled thugs, hustlers, and gangbangers before, but this was the big leagues.

This is turning out to be some real James Bond shit, he thought.

Watching Adam's temperament closely, Miles continued with his presentation, "Kojo and Clutch are twin brothers born in Nigeria. They were adopted, brought over and raised in the well-to-do parts of San Francisco. They suffered from a condition called twin-to-twin transfusion syndrome or TTTS, which explains the disparity in their size. Because of Kojo's small size, he didn't quite fit into the schools that his adopted parents put him into. Of course, Clutch didn't fare well either, always fighting his brother's battles. Clutch excelled in school academically, but Kojo barely passed. Despite his failing grades in school, it was soon learned that Kojo was some type of genius; he scored a perfect 1600 on the SAT at 12 years old, making him the youngest to ever accomplish such a feat. Now, standing just 4'9", we believe he is most likely the mastermind and lead organizer, with strengths in engineering, weaponry, chemistry, biology, physics, and a wide variety of other sciences. Intel tells us that he can retain 20 times the normal information than that of an average person. Early tests have shown that not only is his IQ off the charts, but his emotional quotient is as well. Having a good balance of emotions allows him to make critical decisions without regret. Due to his brilliance, he has been asked to help lead many anti-government movements in many other parts of the world. But most deadly of all is he seems to have a stirring voice and is very charismatic. Kojo has assembled quite the following off the tone of his inspirational rhetoric."

Miles brought a picture of Clutch on the screen and the mood in the room immediately changed. Clutch possessed the kind of face you wouldn't want to stare at long, especially on a large 100" screen. Adam silenced his ego, put the nervous tingle to rest, and stared forcibly at the screen.

"Clutch is a whole other game. He is a freak of nature; as a high school freshmen, standing over 7 feet and weighing 270 pounds, he ran a 4.4 in the 40 yard dash. He holds the nation's high school bench press record. Back in the Bay Area, Clutch secretly competed in underground tough-men tournaments to help feed him and his brother once they left San Francisco. Fighting against grown men, he never lost. Apparently he isn't just muscle either. His high school teachers were in awe of his intelligence, said he may be one of the more intelligent people in the state."

Clutch's stats brought about discomposure in the joint chiefs, producing a dead silence in the room.

Miles continued, "Just an incredible all-around athletic talent. He and his brother dropped out of school at 16 and lived on the hard streets of Oakland. We haven't been able to track them since. Clutch's main strength is his military might, the kind that would make Sun Zu proud. He is Kojo's right-hand man, handling all of the Colony's military issues, defense, targets, interrogations, and operations. He also has strengths in mechanical engineering and weapon design. Intel tells us that Clutch lacks typical emotional understanding. However, it seems he is made whole by his brother's strengths. In fact, he seems to be perfectly balanced by his brother, and vice versa. We have no idea how he went from football player to a savvy military juggernaut."

Miles replayed surveillance video of the government's last run-in with Kojo and Clutch. Apparently, the agency was tipped off to their whereabouts. Upon arriving on the scene, it became a complete debacle for the government's FBI agents; Kojo and Clutch out-smarted them in every aspect seemingly possible. Rather than accept the embarrassment, it was passed off to the news as a neighboring gang squabble. The FBI deputy director squirmed with embarrassment.

Adam chuckled at the looping footage, "So you telling me with all of your power you can't handle one and a half men?"

Miles jumped in, "For whatever reason, they seem to defy reason with their military tactics. They somehow out wit, out smart, and maintain a technical advantage on us at every turn. Believe it or not, their weapons are superior to ours. We haven't been able to track down who they are buying their weapons from. We haven't seen anything like this before."

Adam hissed, grinned, then chuckled while asking, "You can't handle them and I'm supposed to?"

The room erupted in noisy chatter, protest, and loud sighs.

Miles calmed the outburst with his hands and retorted, "Yes, and I believe you are our best bet."

Dispositions and discomfort shuffled within the room. It was obvious the rest didn't share Miles' sentiment.

While looking around the room with scolding eyes Miles said, "Well it's true that using someone like you in government capacity is, shall we say, uncustomary. We are also facing a different type of enemy that we aren't quite set up for. Simply put, the likes of Kojo and Clutch exist inside a crevice we just can't get too. So we have to use desperate means to protect our country."

The buzz-cut wearing general Brudzinski interrupted Miles, "You find this funny, Mr. Quinn?"

Leaning forward in his chair and peering sternly at Adam, he said with a heightened voice, "There isn't a top-secret building in the world they can't just waltz into undetected. Our nation's security is set up to stop live people, and not some god damned astral body. On one end of the spectrum, they are gods, on the other, they are fuckin' ghosts. Even if we catch them and put them in jail, then what. If we kill them, all of our top-secret information by default will be sent to our worst enemies. You see, Mr. Quinn, this is no laughing matter. I'm sure I'm speaking for everybody here when I say save your fuckin' giggles for a Jim Carey movie."

The seriousness of the general's rant swept the grin off Adam's face. In Adam's mind, that was strike one against the general.

Miles restarted his discussion, "We don't know how they went from stick-up kids to top heads in the Colony. We believe they learned their anti-government sentiment from this man..."

Miles motioned Adam's attention to the screen of a blurry, pixilated picture of a Native America man wearing a cowboy hat.

"All we know is that he goes by Scar. We believe their organization is operating somewhere in the southwest, probably Phoenix. We want you to go back to Phoenix and track this organization. We think they may hide among militia groups, spiritual movements, and fundamentalist religious extremists. You are to use your mental abilities to find information that our traditional means can't. You are to use the astral realm to track and spy into places we are unable to go and cover. Adam, you are not to engage with these individuals, they are extremely dangerous."

Miles made sure to reinforce his statement with a

bit more urgency in his voice, "Adam, do not engage; your job is to track and report only."

Bouncing his glare about the room in confusion, Adam massaged his jaw and asked, "Well, why have me be so weapon-savvy in the astral realm if I'm not to engage?"

Miles quickly clarified, "Because we believe your evolved DNA will give us the upper ground. If a battle takes place in the astral realm, we are confident you are properly prepared and will have the superior position. Still your first option is not to engage. If you can find them in the astral realm, then we can find them in the physical world via their silver cord attached to their bodies. Killing them won't help us expose the nodes of their network and locking them up doesn't contain their astral abilities. As of now, you are our best weapon against them."

Scratching his afro with one hand and frisking his pockets for toothpicks with the other, Adam sought more understanding, "So if I have a run-in with them in the physical world, then what?"

General Brudzinski butted in to answer the question, more irritated than before, "Are you hearing correctly, Mr. Quinn? Report their position, do not engage. You are not properly equipped to deal with this kind of threat physically."

Strike two for the general, Adam thought. Blowing him off, he took a second glance at Kojo and Clutch's mug shots. A feeling of disgust took hold over him. Adam couldn't shake the feeling of what he considered breaking the code. Having to deal with Kojo and ·Clutch was one major irritation, but becoming a spy was another. To Adam, spying was essentially snitching. Even the world ending was easier for him to stomach than him becoming a snitch. The ghost of the street code was still hardwired in his bones.

General Brudzinski continued, "We need you to monitor them in order for us to bring down their network. Most importantly, we need you to stay undetected. If your cover gets blown, then welcome to the terror dome. Do you understand me?"

Adam's eyes narrowed at the general, becoming more and more agitated with his tone.

Noticing Adam and the general's oil-and-water chemistry, Miles intervened, "Adam, start with the markets they shadow, ask questions, shake hands, read minds to get what you need. Use the astral realm to follow leads, listen in on conversations. We need to know their next move, who makes their weapons, their new targets, and governments they are involved with; anything to help prevent this next catastrophe they are planning. You are to report your progress to me every day—every lead, every itch that comes in."

Charismatically, Miles said, "Adam we know your history, the troubles you've endured, the cards that you've been dealt... this is a chance to turn it all around. The lives you save here will make you a god walking among men. The fate of the world now lies in your hands."

Rolling the toothpick between the sides of his mouth, with a sarcastic tone, Adam said, "So all I gotta do is find these cats, report, and I can go free?"

Miles grinned, "Yes, a free man."

Adam fired back, "Yeah right, like y'all gonna let someone like me just fly off to live out his life. I'm just as dangerous as them!"

Fist pounding on the table, General Brudzinski clambered over Adam's statement, "Don't flatter yourself, kiddo! We don't take you to be the same kind of threat. Definitely not enough to lose sleep over. Better not be any funny business either! We control your identity, your money, your life. If you get any bright ideas about joining the other side we'll crush you like a god damned cockroach!"

Adam's voice, filled with anger, firmed up, "Yet you need me to save the world."

The general rose stiffly to his feet and yelled, "Yeah, with our money and intelligence, and last I checked you didn't have either."

Strike three. "Fuck you! I'm not one of your little choir boys. Best believe you gonna learn how to talk to me in a better tone," Adam roared, pounding the table.

Adam sat up in his chair and pointed at the general, "Don't play me! You could have used Kano for this op, but you didn't; you asking me to do your dirty work."

"Dirty work? This is your god-damned country too, and last I checked you're living in it! You better wake up, son!" the general yelled back.

Tired of the ebb and flow between the two, Miles waved the general and Adam down.

Glaring intensely at the general, then shifting to Adam, "I'm sorry, Adam, I'm sure he didn't mean it that way. We are all under a great deal of pressure with this looming attack. Our way of life is weighing in the balance as long as these combatants are free. So can we get back to the mission?"

Half-heartedly, the general nodded while burying his head in a glass of water. Still mulling over the general's last words, Adam slowly rocked back in his chair, and toiled with his lip. He raked his hands through his afro, then slowly floated his toothpick out of his mouth into the General's water. Every eye watched in wonder at Adam's showmanship to the general. Flustered, the general knocked his glass off the table, crashing it against the file cabinet against the wall. Glaring at the general with predator-like intent, Adam let the silence stretch before nodding for Miles to continue.

Attempting to rub the stress off his face, Miles sighed, "You will be given a complete new identity, new expense account, a new name, a new history, a phone, and a car. We have set up a house for you in the Ahwatukee neighborhood. You and I will meet once a week for you to brief me on your weekly findings. This mission is top-secret. You leave at 0600 tomorrow. I remind you again, do not engage— get in, report, get out... that simple. And do not compromise the mission by contacting anybody from your past."

Miles took a deep breath.

He leaned on the table opposite of Adam with both hands and warned, "Adam, if they are successful in Phoenix, thousands could die, and millions could be injured. Good luck."

Those words from Miles set off an instant, internal, panic inside of Adam. If Kojo and Clutch were successful, all chances of him finding Nia may be lost forever. Now that he knew she was a real person, he couldn't just stand around and let her become cannon fodder for some insurgent's agenda. Nia may be the only key to fully understanding his transformation. Worst, the thought of her in any pain or danger stung him deep. For Adam, this was too great a chance to take. He decided that not only would he take this mission, but he would make a point to destroy Kojo and Clutch for the sake of Nia. From the inner depths of his soul he knew it was his business to protect Nia. Whatever fear stowed inside of him was quickly snapped up into brooding anger. A growing obsession was born for the crushing of Kojo and Clutch and the annihilation of the Colony movement.

Chapter 13

The smoky atmosphere spread a hazy gloom about the bar. The low-lit neon light cast dark shadows over their faces, making it easier to identify them by their afros and hair styles. The scene was jumbled with several Black Panthers held up in one corner, the usual dice game in the back and a few pool sharks swimming at the pool tables. Raunchy cleavage with loud, tight-patterned bell bottom pants pranced about the room. The regulars cluttered the dance floor, finger snapping to Chaka Khan's latest song, Sweet Thing. Returning vets bounced to the grooves and stood tall with invincibility after surviving the war intact. The smell of sweat, perfume, booze, and cigarettes littered Adam's nostrils with the familiar scent of being back home.

"Good to have you back, young blood. We wasn't sure you was going to make it over there," said

Adam's friend, Mark, while razzing him.

"Yeah, slick, you should have been like Ali, 'no VietCong ever called me nigga,'" wisecracked Adam's other friend, Cal.

They all burst into laughter. "Did you ever have to use that Kung-fu shit?" Mark asked.

"Yeah, a few times on some jive-ass cats, but mostly for training the other troops," informed Adam while recalling some of the events.

Both friends' eyes grew wide with amazement, "God damn it, we got a real live Bruce Black in here, you understand me," bragged Cal while low-fiving Mark.

"Well the war is over and I'm here now and I ain't goin' back, Jack," said Adam while wrapping his arms around his friends.

"Say, brotha, is that her over there?" asked Mark reluctantly.

Adam swiveled his head over and saw Nia. He felt an immediate ache in the inner chambers of his heart.

"Hey, man, we can get out of here, plenty of other joints we can hang at," Cal said sympathetically.

"Nah, man, I'm good, coo daddy. That was over

three years ago," said Adam, now aware of the ironic coincidence of Chaka Khan's Sweet Thing blaring in the background.

"Let's toast," said Mark, trying to lessen the blow for his buddy.

A conciliatory smile surfaced on Adam's face as he raised his glass, "To moving forward. Cheers."

After tapping glasses, Adam plopped back down on his bar stool. He stared deep into the depths of his rum and Coke, regretting the draft now more than ever. The inconvenient timing of his draft card wedged a gap too big to fill between him and Nia. The blunt pain of seeing her ripped through his insides more than he thought possible. The fresh, reawakened, agitated love deafened Adam to the sounds in the bar. His eyes locked in on her with his mind frozen in recall from moments pasts. Her wavy hair, long enticing neck line, and her curvy, smooth skin reminded him that not only was she still in his heart, but she was also still etched deep in his bones. Nia's magnetic beauty was intoxicating enough to pull looks from anybody in the bar.

Adam sulked with the thought that she wasn't in his life. He eyed Nia as she got up to head to the ladies room. He slowly popped a toothpick in his mouth and his eyes slid across their sockets, tracking Nia. The painful lure of just looking at Nia became profoundly unbearable. He had to talk to her. Adam perfected his afro, sprung off his stool, and leaped into action—hell bent for Nia.

"Hey, where you going, cool daddy?" asked Cal.

Locked in and mesmerized by Nia, Adam didn't hear the question. He fought through the crowd, being careful not to take his eyes off of her. The closer he came to her, the more energy and excitement he felt. Within arm's reach, he extended a hand to her shoulder.

She felt his presence and turned to greet him. Adam stopped, dropped his hand, and was locked into her beautiful gaze, lost in her brown, almond-shaped eyes. Her gaze volleyed back and forth about his face while a knowing smile crept to hers. The seductive pull of her smooth, slick, caramel-brown skin lured Adam like always. Her wavy dark hair flowed down over her succulent breasts. Her lips were full and moist; oh how drawn he was to them. Over the music, he could hear her breathing and felt her heart beat. It had been well over three years, yet he still had the taste of her in his mouth. The regret of being drafted further beat on him, robbing him of his chance to rekindle his love. Time slowed down for Adam at this moment. How thankful he was to once again take in her beauty. The energy between them was strong enough to make them both uncomfortable.

They stayed locked in a tangled daze until a voice broke the moment, "Hey, baby, is there a problem? Is this cat bothering you?" interrupted a man while flashing his wedding ring to Adam.

Adam was jarred awake by air plane turbulence on the flight to Phoenix. Another haunting dream, and another cold reminder of no Nia in his life. It was worse than a nightmare, she was with someone else. Adam sighed with the heartache and rested his head against the airplane window. In silence, he gazed at the sun. The tingling feeling of the rays temporarily distracted him from Nia. The light's photons performed a choreographed dance on Adams face, bringing him a new charge of vigor. Hidden away in the underground base, Adam hadn't felt the sun on his skin in over a year. He recalled how the sun sparked a heightened sense of clarity, strength, and understanding in his thoughts. He remembered how it recharged him that day outside of his apartment, making his bruises go away faster. He also recalled how it made his skills sharper and stronger that same day. He could feel it recharging him now, a well-needed jewel to an emotional nightmare of a dream. Coming back to the dream brought heaviness on his heart. These reoccurring dreams were becoming more of a nuisance.

He thought, *I gotta figure this shit out.*

He went over his circumstances.

Mumbling out loud, just under the airplane hum, he said, "The sun gives me strength and Nia gives me power."

Staring at the seat in front of him, his eyes swiveled back and forth as he tried to make sense of the information.

I know I'm not crazy. I know I have these abilities, and I know she was there that day I grew stronger, he thought.

The passenger next to him uncomfortably looked over as Adam conversed with himself.

He continued talking to himself under his breath, "What combination of things could make all this happen?"

"Are you okay, sir," asked the older lady passenger next to him.

Immersed in his thoughts, Adam ignored her question. She scoffed and rolled her eyes at Adam's impolite behavior. He narrowed down the possibilities by taking out his tablet and Googling any words or phrases he could think of that might help him solve the riddle. He franticly typed, "powerful love energy" into the search engine. He began reading through random articles about love energy and powerful love spells. None of them seemed to fit. Eventually he ran across an intriguing concept called twin flames. Pulling up the definition, he read from an online encyclopedia:

In the beginning of time we were created as a perfect soul that was split into two soul halves—one half female, the other half male—that would then be cast upon Earth to be forever looking for one-another.

Hmmmm...one half male, the other half female... to make one perfect soul, Adam pondered while scratching his unshaven jaw line.

He pondered the validity of Nia not merely being just a woman he had been dreaming about, but possibly his twin flame. It would explain his bewitchment for her. His evolved DNA had taught him not to question strange paradoxes. After all, he was a telepath, could move objects with his mind, travel in the astral realm, and see auras, not to mention that his abilities were enhanced by the sun's rays.

"Oh wowwww," mouthed Adam after he was hit with the epiphany of a lifetime.

Out loud again, while nodding his head, Adam said, "It makes perfect sense. Nia being across the street at the library was why I was stronger that day Winston Chase's men tried to kill me. And that would also explain why my powers weren't as strong at the base. She wasn't around me."

That's it… I need the sun and Nia, he thought.

Adam was even more intrigued so he kept searching the internet. He found blogs and videos on how the sun's rays have been evolving human DNA for millennia. A year ago, he would have considered these people crazy, but after all that had happened, he thought this was incredible stuff. It was all a stretch, yet it seemed to rest easy on his soul. This understanding didn't answer all of his questions, but it was a start. It helped the irritation from his dream fade away.

Being content with this new understanding, he happily turned and acknowledged the lady next to him, "My bad Ma'am. I was just lost in thought, but I'm fine. Things just got better."

She smiled, "Good, I was worried about you for a while."

Adam gave her a half grin and sank back into his chair. He continued to wonder, if Nia was his twin flame, did this mean they have had past lives together? What else could explain him knowing so much about her? He remembered her voice was always soft, warm, sexy and alluring. Her smile was strong enough to run icy tingles throughout his nerves. It always caused him to get lost in her. She often had different hair, or a different skin color, but her eyes were always the same; one glimpse and he'd know it was her. Her big brown eyes always told him when she was smiling from within. He remembered the unique way her eyes would talk to him like no other person could. They seemed to always let him in to connect with her soul. Her skin oozed a familiar scent akin to a natural spring breeze that Adam loved to fill his lungs with.

This twin flame idea really could explain all too clearly why the love of this woman had doomed him throughout his life. He thought this could be an unfair curse of unmated twin flames. In his heart he knew there was only one way to know for sure: he had to find Nia, especially before her potential harm. Adam couldn't imagine what kind of life he'd have knowing Nia was dead. He couldn't fathom not finding her, knowing she was his other half, knowing she completed him like no other could. Adam knew he may never live a life to his full potential without her. And worse, if he didn't find her, he could be haunted by his dreams of her for the rest of his life. Another moment of rage settled again over Adam at the thought of Kojo and Clutch harming Nia or preventing him from getting the answers he needed. It was enough stored rage and anger to plunder Clutch's head to an unrecognizable pulp. Nia, being his twin flame was a game changer. This made finding Kojo and Clutch all the more motivating.

A few minutes after landing in Phoenix's Sky Harbor Airport, an arranged car took Adam to his corporate house near the edge of town. It was in the southern suburb of Phoenix called Ahwatukee, named after its Native American settlers. The area was populated with newly built homes, well manicured yards, desert mountain views and neighbors speaking to neighbors. The agency put Adam up into a neatly furnished 2Bd/2Bath corporate rental under his new alias, De'sean Colter.

A standard issue 2015 Ford Taurus was parked in the garage. The house was furnished with the bare essentials; the main bedroom had a queen sized bed, a nightstand and TV. The other bedroom was set up as an office. Adam hardly took time to settle into his house before he got busy running down every lead he could. He started with internet chat rooms, anti-government news feeds, and conspiracy blogs.

Miles sent him daily leads of interest from illegally monitored sources: library activity, website traffic, emails, phone calls, key word searches, video downloads, social media activity, and text conversations among others. Adam combed through each lead with the driven intensity of the migrating African wildebeest, continually burning the midnight oil. He also scoured key locations in the astral realm nightly, looking for clues that could lead to the whereabouts of Kojo and Clutch.

His new obsession caused him to ruffle feathers at bars, mosques, churches and synagogues, ruining any chance of establishing allies in the hunt for his new nemeses. He visited the library every day, where he saw the surveillance footage of Nia. He thought if only one day she'd return to the scene, he would finally get his chance to meet her. Every day she wasn't there caused him to grow more angry and desperate in his search.

A month into the Phoenix operation there was little to no progress made, despite his insistent tenacity to go after the mission. Miles was still thoroughly impressed by Adam's drive.

One late night at his house, Adam received a call from Miles, "Sup, Miles?"

He got right down to business.

"Adam, other than speculative internet chatter, Phoenix has gone dark. There is nothing here. It is time to move on."

Not wanting to miss the possibility of seeing Nia at the library, Adam hesitated, "I'm working on a strong lead that I believe is our best bet. It's a target..."

Miles interrupted, "Look Adam, we appreciate your insistency and we're actually thoroughly impressed by your drive. But we believe we had a Clutch sighting back in his home town of Oakland. We need to move fast, before the lead goes cold."

Adam chimed in, "But if I miss..."

"No buts, Adam, you have your orders! Plus, this lead is minutes old, get a flight out as soon as you can," Miles insisted.

Adam sighed, "I'll take the first flight out tomorrow morning."

He slammed the phone down and slouched into his bed. Knowing time was winding down, Adam felt an increasing flow of desperation seeping in from the mission's pressure. Going after a hot lead that would bring him closer to Kojo and Clutch was good for the mission but bad for his heart. He hated to leave without finding Nia. There was no telling where this mission might take him. In actuality, he may never get back to Phoenix. Pacing about in his bedroom he descended deeper into a downward Nia spiral. The tailspin resurfaced Adam's old habit with the bottle. Lucky for him Miles surprised him with a rum and Coke house warming gift. The pressure and the daunting task of finding Nia weighed heavy on him. He pulled out his tablet and began to replay the footage of Nia. He continued drinking and obsessing while staring at her pixilated face. Apathy about his twin flame hypothesis started to set in. Plunging deeper into a funk, he surmised that if he couldn't have Nia to lift his spirits, perhaps Jolon could. Despite strict orders from Miles not to contact anyone, he decided to call the only friend he'd ever known.

Chapter 14

"Man, fuck it! I got one last night to kick it—I'ma holla at my dude," Adam said with a boost in confidence from the alcohol.

Reaching for his phone, he dialed Jolon's number from memory, hoping the number was still the same. The phone rang twice before a voice answered, "Hello."

Adam smiled, recognizing Jolon's voice, "Jolon, wus up, bro."

"What's up, but who is this?" Jolon asked hesitantly.

Holding back his snickers, Adam said, "My name don't matter, but what does matter is you got my girl pregnant and we need to talk about it, homeboy."

"I...uh...huh," stumbled Jolon.

Breaking out into laughter, Adam teased, "Hahaha... look at you! You was scared as fuck about to piss on yourself. It's Adam bro!"

"Awwwwwww, mannnnnn," Jolon whined.

Interrupting and practically bursting into tears, Adam continued, "I told you to keep that lil pecker in ya pants."

Jolon broke in with cheers and jeers over the phone, "Aww, man, you got me good on that one, bro. Look at you, tall dark and lonely finally cracked a joke."

"Yeah man... at any given time there prolly is at least six girls possibly pregnant by your old ass," clowned Adam.

"That's right, bitch, I'm the original sperm bank. Don't be jealous. Man, I thought you was done, I heard some crazy stuff about you, bro."

"Nah, man, I'm good, can't trust all what you hear," said Adam while holding back his grin.

"Man, where you at? Let's get together... I'm headed out to my spot on the reservation," said Jolon.

Knowing he was pushing mission protocol, Adam paused and hesitantly said, "I can't, I have an early flight...."

Jolon interrupted, not taking no for an answer, "Ahh man... don't give me that bull shit. Man, I haven't seen you in a year. We gotta catch up, plus Sonya's sister Rachel is gonna be there, and you knowwwww how crazy she is about you, bro!"

Adam knew he needed a break. He hadn't had RnR in well over a year. The steady grind of the mission was starting to take its toll. After all, it was Jolon.

Man I can't pass up an opportunity to hang with my dude, he thought.

He caved under the welcomed Jolon pressure and assisting alcohol, "Yeah, okay. I can't stay though. I'll drop in for a sec."

"Tha's what I'm talking about my brotha, bring that big bullet head of yours on down. And don't be actin' all scary with Rachel either. It's time to put those good looks to work," Jolon chuckled.

Adam hung up the phone, took a deep breath, and began to get himself ready. He took a shower and put on some comfy jeans and a t-shirt and headed to the reservation. Although tipsy, a big framed man like Adam could easily pound down a few more beers before it affected his driving.

From Ahwatukee, the bar on the reservation was about a forty five minute drive. The drive was along the southern Baseline corridor of Phoenix, a scenic view that trailed on the edge of Phoenix's South Mountain. Even at night the mountain rose out of the earth like a large wall gating off the city. Adam found brief moments of peace glancing at the behemoth mound of rock. He rolled the window down and let the warm desert air knock about his afro. Finally at the bar, he was excited to see his buddy Jolon.

The bar was about a mile deep into the Indian reservation, west of Phoenix, nestled around corn fields hidden from the rest of the city. The grungy bar could easily bounce between a dive or sports bar. It was populated mostly with natives from the reservation and sprinkled with a few loyal locals.

Adam walked into a friendly, festive, dimly lit atmosphere of pool, darts, and Bob Marley blasting on the juke box. His tall, handsome, muscular frame immediately garnered attention from the lady patrons. Dodging their eye contact, he surveyed the bar for Jolon. Seconds later, he found him already being the life of the party. He watched Jolon for a few minutes and stole a few laughs off his animated behavior. He took a few more flirtatious comments from the ladies before confidently cruising over to meet him.

Jolon spotted Adam and broadcast a wide grin as

he approached him, "Heyyyy, man. What's uuuup?"

Laughing and punching at Adam, Jolon said, "What's been up, bro?" Adam fought to hold back his grin but gave Jolon a hug.

"See, now I know you're getting too lonely. We don't hug, bro... We don't hug," teased Jolon.

"Good to see you, let's get this party started!" yelled Jolon while clapping his hands and shimmying his pudgy body to the tunes of Bob Marley.

Adam grinned at Jolon's rounded body gyrating. In a way, he envied Jolon. He knew how to have a good time, a skill that eluded Adam his entire life. Perhaps that was why he and Jolon worked.

During a break from Marley's chorus, Jolon yelled while pointing with a scolding finger, "Let me introduce you to your princess for the night, and don't give me that stick in the mud business either."

Before Jolon could make the introduction, Rachel swooped in toward Adam.

"Awww shit," Jolon crudely mumbled in the background.

"While you two lovebirds chat, I'm going to drain the dragon. In the meantime, girl, you go easy on him... he's prolly a virgin," Jolon laughed.

While Rachel's back was turned, Jolon gyrated sexual innuendos for Adam before heading to the bathroom.

Adam slipped out a chuckle from Jolon's background instructions. He obliged Rachel's eager flirtatious pass and let her lead him to the bar. She motioned the bartender for drinks and turned toward Adam with excitement.

"You look really good! How have you been?" Rachel asked while rubbing Adam's hands.

Adam looked down at her hands before answering.

"Let's just say I've been laying low," said Adam, sarcastically referring to living deep inside an underground base.

"Nothing wrong with taking it a lil easy, baby," said the bubbly smiling Rachel while scooting closer to Adam.

"So, Jolon told me you had a run-in with some guys who were trying to kill you. Is that true?" Rachel asked, now hooking her arm around Adam's.

Paying her flirtatious advance and question little mind, Adam shrugged his shoulders and said, "Big mix up, let's just say they had the wrong guy."

Rachel heated up the side of Adam's face with her flirtatious gaze.

"Oh my God, you have always been so sexy and mysterious," Rachel said while coiling her fingers around Adam's hands.

Then in a flash her eyes bounced up in fear.

"No no... it's not what you think," begged Rachel.

Adam followed her nervous eyes, only to be rudely brushed aside into the bar by a stranger.

"Bitch, you want to come to my spot and embarrass me like this?" yelled the stranger to Rachel.

"Who is this clown," he said, motioning to Adam.

He grabbed a wad of her hair, snatched her close to him, and continued barking insults at her.

"Chill out, homie, her and I are just friends," said Adam, softly putting his hands on the man's shoulders so as to try to calm him.

Still irate, the man said with a ragged rage in his voice, "Mind your fucking business, chump."

Cracking his head to the side, Adam said with a calm but bitter tone, "I will as soon as you get your hands off the lady like that."

The angry man slowly let his fist of her hair go, shoving Rachel out of his way. He turned to Adam with inflamed hate in his eyes.

"Like I told you, mind your fuckin' business," said the man while coming within inches of Adam's face.

"And I'm tellin' you... partna, keep ya fuckin' hands off the lady," scolded Adam.

The man's face tightened. Adam knew what that look meant. He'd seen it a thousand times before. Truth be told, these kinds of moments were the ones in which Adam was most comfortable. He had already sized the man up. He was left-handed, plagued by anger issues, easily frustrated, and a bully.

As expected, the man fired a wide left hook. Instinctually, Adam blocked the left hook with his right arm, then reached and grabbed the man's neck, perfectly pitting his thumb on the ball of his larynx. With brute strength, Adam lifted the man slightly off the ground. The gagging man's eyes widened with fear, which was confirmed by Adam's telepathic ability; a clear understanding of a heartbroken boyfriend driven into rage by the pipe-bursting pressure of love. Adam thought there was no need to be rough on the guy since he could obviously relate and understand his predicament. Adam was temporarily distracted by the thought of how clear, fast and easily he was able to read the boyfriend. He usually had to concentrate to get that much information. He wondered if this had something to do with Nia increasing his abilities, like the day with the CEO's goons. Is she close? he wondered. The thought was interrupted by a blindsided crushing blow to Adam's left jaw. He immediately dropped the boyfriend and crashed up against the bar.

"It's always the punch you don't see," said Adam as he refocused his vision and realigned his jaw. Lifting himself off the bar, he eyed and faced his most recent attacker. From the corner of his eye, he noticed the boyfriend now had a knife and another brute flanking on the left, looking to join in on their assault. Adam probed the gash in his mouth with his tongue, gathering incentive for the beating he was going to deliver. In an instant, he could feel hundreds of deadly combat techniques surging through his veins. He felt he had an answer to every potential punch, kick, head butt, or weapon attack the brutes could possibly throw at him. He didn't know for sure where these techniques came from, but he was sure he was going to use them.

Is this another gift of my evolving DNA? he wondered.

It was something he would have to get to later; the boyfriend was rushing him with a knife. With crushing speed and power, Adam kicked the knife out of the rushing boyfriend's hand, then delivered a knife-like chop to his already weakened throat. The boyfriend dropped like a bag of potatoes. He clutched his throat, gagging, rolling over the floor, and gasping for air. The next assailant grabbed a chair and tossed it at Adam while charging at him. Adam thought fast and grabbed a bar stool to toss at the flying chair in an effort to deaden its approach. The chairs crashed midway between the two men, splintering into multiple parts. The momentum of the stool toss set the rushing assailant up for Adam's perfectly timed round-house kick to the side of his face. The body of the attacker flew like a flimsy rag doll and crashed into a group of onlookers. Most of the crowd scattered away from the ruckus, but a few curious barflies scampered to be entertained by the action. Still in full defensive mode, Adam prepared for a possible third attacker. From the corner of his eye he saw a pool stick swinging his way. He covered his face and took the brunt of the blow on his iron-like forearms, breaking the stick. Slowly pulling his hands from his face, Adam dialed in on the attacker. Tonguing the inside of his gashed cheek again, Adam relished in his growing anger.

"I'm gonna enjoy this!" said Adam to his jumpy attacker.

The man lashed in at Adam, trying to stab him with the broken pool stick. Adam quickly sidestepped, paring the stick away to avoid being impaled. The move simultaneously brought Adam close enough to toss the man several feet away. The man crashed to the floor on his shoulder. He lied screaming on the floor, grabbing his snapped collar bone. While Adam admired his handy work, two hands grabbed his head from behind like a basketball and lifted him effortlessly off the ground. Before he could read the temperament of this new attacker he was thrown by his head across the room and against the wall. Adam hit the wall with a thudding force, causing the bar's jukebox to fall silent. He lurched out of the basketball-sized hole in the drywall and slid down the wall, taking plaques and pictures with him. He landed on the jukebox and fell to the floor, now really angry. With blurred vision Adam quickly got to his feet to finish the melee once and for all. Shuffling to his feet, he focused in on his attacker as his vision came to. It was Clutch, glued into an icy gaze at Adam. His face was balled up in a contorted way that matched the viciousness of the toss. The bar fell silent, and only the footsteps of scampering insects could be heard. In strode the pint-sized Kojo, smoking his cigar and casually walking along the top of the bar. He stopped next to his massive brother and peered down at Adam arrogantly. Blood trickling out of his mouth, Adam felt a rippling shock throughout his body. He glared at them with the harbored hate only a captive prisoner of war could understand. The muscle under his eye violently twitched, as the deep seeded rage blossomed out the pit of his gut.

Don't engage, don't engage, replayed the general's voice over and over in his head.

Adam tried to honor the mission, but the contorted anger seeping into his bones blinded him. Before he could analyze anything further, Clutch gritted his teeth, contorted his brow, and sprung toward Adam, letting out a horrid groan. Being a low level snitch was a hard enough blow for Adam to stomach, but being a coward was simply bad odds. After all, he still had to live with himself. The line had been drawn. Adam wasn't going to leave and report; he was going to engage. Adam's face tightened while fixing his fro.

Fuck that! This cat wants it, then I'm gonna bring it... time to chop this big tree down, Adam thought, firing off the ground and exploding toward Clutch.

Chapter 15

Tapping and two stepping to Bob Marley's "Could This Be Love," Jolon washed his hands at the bathroom sink. He heard the music abruptly stop.

"Dammmm! Why they cut the music off, that was my jam!" he whined.

"Oh well," he said a few seconds later while fixing his hair in the mirror.

"I guess it's gonna be up to me to get this party back crackin'," he said while grabbing a paper towel.

Blowing his nose, he heard a loud thud.

"What was that?" he questioned.

He paused a couple of seconds to try to identify the sound. When no other sounds were heard he shifted his focus back to the female bar flies. Feeling good about the night, he blew his nose and washed his hands again before he left the bathroom. Bouncing down the hallway he was jilted with screams.

"What the fuck," he muttered.

He ran around the corner and came face to face with a spirit-shattering event. The bar was a mess, with broken tables and chairs everywhere. The lights were on and most of the crowd had dwindled. The few patrons who remained gathered around in a circle with two combatants in the center.

Jolon was frozen in his tracks when he spotted Clutch towering over the crowd. His abnormally massive frame extended beyond the average height like a single redwood tree growing in the desert. Jolon was floored with shock when he saw his buddy Adam getting off the ground.

"You gotta be fuckin' kiddin' me," Jolon said nervously.

He bolted to Adam's aid. Adam wouldn't have started the fight, but he damn sure would try to finish it. Against Clutch, it was a bad combination. He grabbed a pool stick to even the odd and was met by a few younger bar mates. They stepped in front of him and snatched the pool stick, "Don't even try it, old man. Let them hash this one out!"

Adam and Clutch charged at each other with the violent intensity of two male rams in battle. As Adam approached Clutch, he noticed an unfamiliar look of comfort in his eyes. Seeing fear and panic was normal during his brawls, but seeing comfort was disturbing. Nonetheless, Adam pushed the confidence-breaking thought aside by taking the offense first. He fired a powerful overhand right toward Clutch's jaw. Clutch, the master brawler, read the attempt with perfect accuracy and fired off a front snap kick to Adam's chest. The blow sent Adam tumbling back. Adam recovered from the blow with incredible athleticism, almost as if he was a gymnast. In the blink of an eye, Adam grabbed and tossed two chairs at Clutch. Clutch blocked the chair by covering his face. Now Adam was upon him and hurling a barrage of lightning quick blows on Clutch's large frame; right hook, left hook, body blow, upper cut. Clutch, covering from the heat of Adam's heavy-handed blows, stepped back in an instant and blasted Adam with a thunderous round of house kicks to his jaw. The timely kick landed flush on Adam's face with a smacking force, enough to send him tumbling into the crowd. Clutch probed his jaw for any problems that Adam may have caused it. He then beelined toward Adam's fallen body, flipping and flinging tables and chairs out of his way with ease. Adam jumped to his feet, hardly showing any signs of slowing down. Adam wiped the trickling blood from his mouth and braced for the mountain of a man approaching him. Still bugged by the comforting look in Clutch's eyes, Adam decided to switch up his strategy. Bouncing on the balls of his feet, he peppered Clutch with a series of timely jabs, none of which Clutch seemed to be able to time. Adam snapped Clutch's head back with surprising ease. After one of his lightning quick sneaky jabs, Adam launched a clubbing right hand to Clutch's chin. Clutch pulled slightly back from the punch before it landed. With incredible accuracy, he reached and hyper extended Adam's punching right arm, taking it out of the fight. Adam winced from the sharp pain. Clutch, being a master strategist, was testing Adam. The successfully landed jabs were nothing more than bait for Clutch to time Adam's punches. After the hyperextension, Adam tried throwing a short inside left hook. Clutch slammed Adam's left hook with a deliberate elbow to the center of his bicep. Groaning from the blow, and billowing over in pain, Adam knew Clutch had deadened his left arm for the night. Clutch didn't stop there. He kicked the back of Adam's left foot, bringing him down to one knee. Immediately Adam used the power in his coiled legs to launch a head butt into Clutch's chin. The blow shuffled the unsuspecting Clutch back. While Clutch stumbled back, Adam launched one of his sickle kicks. Clutch partially blocked Adam's kick with one arm. With his free arm he grabbed the weary Adam and tossed him into the bar wall again. Adam's large frame smashed the wall, leaving wood, bar stools and glass everywhere. Adam's ability to recall martial art techniques was not enough to outwork or out think the brawling Clutch. The situation was drastically worsening. It was obvious he was out of his league. The sinking odds didn't matter to Adam. If he was to find Nia, he was going to have to go through Clutch first.

After being flung into the wall, Adam rolled to one knee; carefully keeping an eye on Clutch.

I'll blind him, Adam thought while filling his hands with debris.

He exploded off the ground, tossing a fistful of rubbish at Clutch's eyes. His withered arms put little velocity on the flying fragments. Reflexively, Clutch shielded his eyes and cruised toward Adam with ease. Adam's charge was met with another front snap kick to his solar plexus. The freezing kick halted Adam's attack as he gasped at the air leaving his body. After the kick, Clutch seemed to have six hands; with speed and power he banged around on Adam's body like a sparring session with a practice dummy.

Adam always made a point to look deep in his enemies' eyes during combat to get a better understanding of their toughness. A glance at Clutch's face revealed comfort, calmness, confidence and resolve; this was highly disturbing to him.

What kind of man fights with comfort on his face? Adam pondered.

While Adam's face expressed the beating of his life, Clutch's face looked as if it was just another day at the office. More oddly, Adam noticed Clutch's pupils were dilated. They were large, similar to the eyes of hostile cats, another phenomenon majorly disturbing to him. With his pupils appearing as large black circles, Clutch continued the beat down. He took Adam down with a low sweep, putting him on his back. Hitting the ground with a thud, Adam coughed and clamored for air. Adam eyed the towering giant upon him. About the only thing good about the situation was that Clutch had a surprisingly calming aura. Clutch reached down and grabbed Adam off the ground. He lifted Adam's dangling, rag doll-like body with one hand. With the other hand, he drew back with a clenched fist to hammer Adam one last time. Adam began to plummet emotionally, not because of the beating, but because he fretted he would no longer be able to save Nia. Adam's soul would never let him settle for such a thought. The realization drove a telekinetic rage. As that thought was marinating, his veins began to pulsate and throb. The few standing tables and chairs around Clutch started to vibrate violently. Clutch's brow gathered, his mouth gaped, and his eyes volleyed back and forth at the vibrating furniture. The crowd slowly backed away, bracing for the unknown. One chair flew at Clutch. Then one more. Then two more. Crashing violently against his head, face and body, each chair made Clutch stumble backward. Clutch dropped Adam to shield himself from the onslaught. Then Adam telekinetically threw a series of bar stools, then a few tables. Clutch crashed into the bar and toppled from the last set of stools. The crowd gasped at what their eyes were witnessing: two super behemoths enthralled in battle. Even Kojo was extremely more interested in the brawl, witnessing for the first time his brother being bested. Adam slowly rose to his feet with clenched fists and teeth. He turned to face Kojo. He glared at Kojo as a lion eyes its kill on the plains of Africa. Adam moved forward with small trickles of blood dripping from his nose. Kojo, still smoking his cigar, looked at Adam with a newly heightened interest. His eyes never showed fear, despite the raging Adam coming his way.

Adam cleared the few crooks in his neck and slid a trusted toothpick in his mouth. After a few nibbles, he popped his knuckles and said to Kojo, "I'm gonna serve your little ass with my bare hands."

Kojo calmly took the cigar out of his mouth. He grinned while exhaling smoke, "Your hands aren't big enough for me."

He waved his hands and the last few bystanders popped Adam with their Tasers. It took three jolts to bring Adam down and disrupt his telekinetic powers. Adam convulsed and hit the ground like falling timber.

Jolon ran over to help, "Get the fuck off him, bro!"

Covering Adam, Jolon waved off the fight with the street version of surrender, "Okay, the fight is over, let him be."

He was easily pushed off by the now pissed off Clutch. He hammered Jolon with a right cross, knocking him unconscious. Then he looked at Adam, frowning his brow in disgust. He pulled his clenched fist back and hammered Adam, knocking him out cold.

***

When Adam came to, he was tied to a chair. He looked over and saw Jolon restrained next to him, cheek swollen and still knocked out from Clutch's thudding blow. Adam lifted his wobbly, weary head to observe his location. He was in a small brick room with no windows and a single interrogation-like light dangling above him. His newly awakened body reminded him that his jaw ached, ribs were sore, arms hurt, and a few teeth felt loose. In front of him sat Clutch with a stone face, staring at him with a hard yet indifferent gaze. His large liquid eyes zoned in on every inch of Adam. He straddled a chair, showcasing Adam's blood on his knuckles. Resting on his lap was some sort of battle ax, doubling as a shotgun. He was wearing a teal green military tactical vest, with a few protein bars oddly peaking from the pockets where clips would normally go. A few other barely indistinguishable faces were leaning against the walls with their fingers wrapped tightly around their stun Tasers.

"Who are you?" Clutch barked when Adam's eyes met his.

Hearing Clutch's voice bounce around the small room for the first time was another reminder of the intimidating nature of his large physique.

Spitting blood at Clutch and still simmering with anger, Adam screamed, "Fuck you, take these ropes off and find out!"

Clutch calmly got up and clenched Jolon's throat with his massive hand. Jolon awoke with a surge, gagging and coughing for air. Blood and saliva spewed out of his mouth like a newly erupting volcano as he wiggled for air.

"De'sean Colter," yelled Adam, caving from the

visual strain of Jolon's torture.

Clutch's eyes tightened as he applied an even deeper squeeze to Jolon's throat, "Then why does he call you Adam?"

Adam's face cracked at the sight of Clutch's python-like grip around Jolon's windpipe. Adam knew it took less than twenty pounds to collapse someone's throat. From the looks of it, Clutch's grip was well beyond ten. He needed to buy more time. If he failed here, Nia may not be safe. But how could he cost the faultless Jolon his life? After all, it was Adam's own heinous act that sabotaged the mission and put Jolon in danger. He shouldn't have engaged. It was abundantly clear that he wasn't properly prepared to deal with Kojo and Clutch, but his ego and anger got the better of him. One thing was for sure, Kojo and Clutch would kill Jolon. The thought was too toxic to stomach—he had to save Jolon.

"Okay... okay, I'll talk, just leave him be. He has nothing to do with this," Adam hissed intently.

Clutch eased his grip around Jolon's throat; the windpipe still bore a dented imprint from Clutch's clamp. Jolon gagged, coughed, and fell back out of consciousness. Clutch eased back into his seat, calmly placing his battle ax back in his lap. He grabbed one of his protein bars, ripped the wrapping, and placed the entire bar in his mouth.

With his mouth full, Clutch ordered, "You got the floor. Speak!"

"You's a real tough son of a bitch, torturing a man bound to a chair, unconscious and half your size," said Adam with a ragged voice and a crinkled brow.

The taunt bounced off Clutch like bare feet off a hot Arizona sidewalk. Clutch took a seat in front of Adam and pulled out a stun gun, "I remind you, telekinetic abilities are disrupted by electricity. So don't get any funny ideas. If you do, I'll finish him and start with you. So let's get started, shall we. Who the fuck are you?"

Clutch's steamy dark eyes broadcast an unmistakable heat that meant serious business. Adam decided to go with a partial lie that hugged the truth close enough. He figured it might give him enough time to salvage the mission and protect Nia. After all, there was no way they could possible know about the true nature of his mission.

"My real name is Adam, I work for a government program that trains telepaths and telekinetics around the country. We used to work together, so we were just catching up when some jealous bitch lost his cool about his ex and couldn't hold back his anger."

From the back shadows of the room, Kojo came forward puffing his cigar. His eyes narrowed at Adam.

He took a deep pull from the cigar and slowly walked over to him. He rested his hand on Adam's forehead and put his cigar out on Clutch's massive shoulder.

"Telepaths, huh? So what am I thinking?" asked Kojo.

Adam tried to ignore Kojo's cigar stunt but was awed at its inability to break Clutch's skin. It took Adam a few seconds to break free from the haunting durability of Clutch before he could focus in on Kojo's thoughts. Adam thought this was a perfect opportunity and planned to make this count. Adam tried to pull any and all information out of Kojo's head. With the right focus, he could enter the astral realm, message Kano of Kojo and Clutch's position, and hopefully end this nightmare.

Adam focused. A few seconds into the read, Adam's eyes widened with bewilderment.

"What! What tha fuck! Oh my God, what!" yelled Adam from the brief tour inside Kojo's mind.

Kojo grinned, pleased with Adam's reaction to what was in his head.

"There is someone you need to meet," Kojo said, hiding his smile in his voice.

Clutch sighed, then barked to Kojo, "You gonna trust this pretty boy fuck?"

Kojo turned sharply to his brother, in a calm manner, "How many telekinetics can put you down? He might be what we are looking for. You know this isn't an intentional coincidence... right?" Clutch grunted and hissed to his brother's point, rolling his eyes in disgust.

"I don't understand. What's going on," Adam questioned while bouncing his head between the two brothers.

Adam sighed, "Sooo you haven't done any of those things?"

"Bingo," said Kojo, pointing to Adam.

"How could you not, but the news, Nigeria, Cali..." Adam muttered randomly.

Kojo motioned to Clutch to let Adam read him as well. Clutch grunted and hesitantly rested his large hand on Adam's neck. Adam focused in. After his reading, he dropped his head and shook it back and forth in disbelief. He had climbed throughout Kojo and Clutch's conscious and subconscious mind, finding nil trace or connection between any alleged or planned crimes that Miles warned him about. Worse yet, he found the exact opposite. They had been trying to boost, uplift, and liberate all of mankind. He read compassionate, insightful, humbled, conscious, spiritually sound individuals. The shock of the information knotted his stomach and completely turned his world upside down.

"Well, you aren't the first who's been brainwashed to come after us, but certainly the strongest," said Kojo.

"But I've read them, and they wasn't lying either," scoffed Adam.

"You mean your handlers?" Kojo chuckled.

Adam scoffed, "Handlers? Nah, playboy, I mean top heads of states, scientists, agents. Good people."

"Who to believe when both sides are telling the truth?" Kojo cackled.

"That is quite the conundrum, isn't it, Adam?" Kojo said pacing about the small room with his hands behind his back.

"They technically wasn't lying though... just deceived of the truth," said Kojo with a smug grin.

Adam's face tightened, "What truth? What's the fuckin' truth?"

Chapter 16

In walked an older man with a cowboy hat and boots. He didn't have an aura, making Adam extremely uneasy. Adam tried to familiarize himself with the man's face. He had strange slanted eyes, high Native American cheekbones, and a tall, thin frame. His skin had a light olive tint, with hard creases in his face. A large facial scar stretched across his left eye down to his chin. He sat in front of Adam and looked very punctiliously in his eyes.

"This will hurt," the man said to Adam.

His voice was deep but had a slight digital echo behind it like an android. It was unlike anything Adam had ever heard. The man nodded to Clutch and pulled out an odd shaped silver and grey gadget that fit snug in the palm of his hand. Clutch further restrained Adam's head with his massive arms.

"Wha... what the fuck are you doing?" Adam asked while he started to wiggle profusely.

The man shined the device at Adam's eyes. A slow growl rumbled up Adam's throat before he erupted in screams of pain. A sliver of flesh under his right eye began to separate, next the muscle, then the nerves separated. With his blood flow staying intact, the separation continued down to the bone under Adam's eye sockets. The man reached into the separated tissue and pulled at a silver device attached firmly to Adam's skull. The device was small, oval, flat, and possessed tentacles that reached around into Adam's brain stem. Prying the device away from Adam's flesh tormented him with pain. The agony brought on convulsive spasms. The device's tentacles sheered, grounded, and rubbed against Adam's tissue as it was being pulled out. The pulling, stretching and separating of Adam's flesh took him well beyond his nauseating pain limits. Once the man detached the oval device, Adam's pain began to subside, but not before he vomited nearly everything inside his stomach. The lights on the gadget in the man's hand changed color. Instantly, Adam's flesh and skin started to mend itself in reverse fashion, leaving no sign of damage.

The man showed Adam the device before laying it on the table, "This is a CrowMedia chip. They have been tracking your thoughts, ideas, dreams, visions, and whereabouts."

Recovering from the trauma of the agonizing incision, slobbering and barely holding his head steady, Adam stared, bewildered with his mouth agape at the insect like device. He pondered the familiarity of CrowMedia. The growing questions in his head pushed the pain out of his body. The thought of when, why, and who put the tracker in him further ignited the growing rage within.

The man swiveled over to Kojo and Clutch, "This isn't good. Once they realize the tracker is no longer reporting information, they will send a team to its last known position. We have until morning before they have agents outside our doors. From then, it will only take them a couple of hours to connect the rest of the Colonies together. We must initiate a shutdown protocol. Notify all of the other Colonies, and burn and destroy everything except DNA sequencing equipment in labs 34-37 by morning."

On the man's orders, the rest of the nameless faces left the room, jockeying to execute his orders.

He turned to Adam, his eyes widened as he slowly spoke in a low groveling voice, "You coming here has put everything we've worked for in jeopardy. Lives of good people will now be lost."

His voice lightened, "Yet, ironically, Kojo seems to

think you are our only hope."

Adam's eyes widened when he realized the man before him was Scar. He could see the resemblance from the badly pixilated picture Miles showed him at the base briefing.

A dead calm stretched across Adam's face for a few seconds before Clutch interrupted with his baritone voice, "How can we really trust him?"

"How can he trust us? He came here for drinks, not to scout. It doesn't matter anyway, they will kill him by morning regardless. We are his only hope, and he is ours," Kojo retorted, defending his decision to trust Adam.

The possible attempt on Adam's life brought a rumble of anger across his face, "Who will kill me? Anybody gonna tell me what the fuck is going on?"

"Sorry about your associate, we took him upstairs and he is safe getting treatment. You both are safe, we mean you no harm. I'm sure you now understand why we had to take such dramatic measures," Scar said while pointing to the tracking device.

He motioned to Clutch to release Adam. Adam massaged his unbound hands and wrists, unsure if he should thank Clutch or belt him. He explored his face with his fingers, feeling for any deformity left by the tracker.

"You may call me Scar, and I have a bit of bad news for you," he said.

Scar waited until he had Adam's full, undivided attention. Adam slowly shifted his full focus to Scar.

"There is no easy way to say this, but you are a serf. A slave. You were born, designed and manipulated to serve a purpose not of your own," said Scar.

Before Adam could give Scar's story legs, he flinched his shoulders, and his face tightened before saying, "Mannnnn the whole slavery, banker, 911 conspiracy theory thing is old news. Please tell me we not going down this road?"

Kojo chimed in, arms folded and leaning against the wall, "That level of slavery is heaven compared to what we are talking about here."

With his let's-get-on-with-it face, Adam shrugged again, flailing his hands in the air, "Okay, soooooo what kind of slavery are we talking about here? Let's cut to the chase, shall we, fellas?"

Kojo settled in against the back wall and braced himself for the coming story. Clutch chomped into another protein bar. With his arms folded, he leaned against the wall with one leg cocked against it.

Scar slowly rested back in his chair and took a deep breath before continuing, "About 40,000 years ago, a universal war was being waged throughout the galaxies. One of the combatants in this war took refuge on earth and created a base here. A smaller war broke out between the humans of the earth and the invading combatants. Of course, the humans lost."

Adam looked around the room, jokingly hissing and chuckling at the beginning of Scar's story.

Puffing his cigar, Kojo said, "Before you are so dismissive, my friend, do you know what often happens to the group who loses the war?"

"I don't know, maybe... killed!" Adam sneered with sarcasm.

"The resistors are killed, the rest are turned into slaves. You can see examples of this all over the planet and all throughout history. And what these aliens did to us humans is no different. So it is not out of the question that you are a slave today because of the war your human ancestors lost thousands of years ago. Keep that in mind," Kojo said with a serious gleam in his eyes.

Adam's sarcastic grin receded.

Scar continued, "After the humans lost the war, a new strategy was hatched by the invading aliens. On this foreign planet, the aliens needed a power source to help fight the larger galactic war. So as a strategy, they enslaved the humans and modified them to be their food and energy source. They have designed an elaborate means of farming and caging humans by manipulating their understanding of reality so that they won't recognize their slavery. Earth has been a power plant and a food farm for the aliens for thousands of years. Myself, Kojo, and Clutch, and everybody else in the Colony, are fighting this shadow war to free the humans."

Adam rubbed his face, raked his hands through his hair, and sighed, searching for words. Kojo and Clutch stared emotionless and watched Adam fight with cognitive dissonance.

"Are you fuckin' kidding me? Who is they? And what do you mean modified," asked Adam in an irritated voice.

Scar continued from the back of his seat, "They are called the Ky. They are an alien race from a distant galaxy. They anonymously reside and rule from deep inside the earth."

Adam squinted, looking for more information.

Scar obliged Adam's confused gaze, looked upon him with a halting stare and said, "What I'm about to tell you is going to sound impossible, but you have to remember that their technology is thousands of years beyond earth's."

Giving Adam a second to open up his mind, he continued, "The human body is a vessel for the soul. The body's DNA had the ability to store and retrieve a soul's purpose. Upon the soul entering the body, it typically had access to this information, helping it remember why it came here. The plan was for the soul to incarnate here, fulfill its purpose and move on to its next experience. When the humans lost the war, the Ky began modifying their DNA to disrupt this natural process, ultimately blocking souls from knowing their true purpose. In most cases, the soul becomes trapped. By forgetting and not fulfilling its purpose, the soul reincarnates over and over again in an endless cycle, trying to complete its purpose. In these endless cycles, you are harvested to become food and energy. Every child born is born with modified DNA—or Kode-X, as it's called by Ky scientists. Ever since then, humans have been trapped and preyed on for thousands of their life cycles on earth."

Kojo chimed in, "This is why most of the ancient wisdom cultures and traditions were more spiritually advanced than we are today. They acquired wisdom with their spiritual gifts before the Ky's modifications, whereas today our culture has adopted materialism. They need machines today to verify what the ancients knew internally thousands of years ago."

Adam grinned and laughed at the ridiculousness of their tall tale. The smile was quickly blown off of his face like a spring breeze when he witnessed Clutch, Kojo, and Scar's stoic faces.

Fretting to go down this dispiriting path, Adam took a deep breath and rubbed the hairs down on the nape of his neck before he continued, "Okay, you know this sounds ridiculous, but I'll humor you, explain this whole 'humans being trapped' business."

Scar nodded and continued to lay into Adam, "You are trapped by being deceived of your true potential. The human reality here on earth is typically one of the lowest forms of existence a soul can experience. Humans have a far greater potential than they are told. Buried within each human body's DNA are dynamic abilities, like being telepathic, telekinetic, pyrokinetic, hydrokinetic, psychic, precognitive, clairvoyant, multidimensional, and boundless other abilities. Many of these abilities were once active in the human DNA. You even once had the ability to create your own starship and travel the universe. It's called the merkaba. The Ky turned off all the gifts that conflicted with their agenda. Those genetic sequences now lie dormant and are conveniently referred to as junk DNA."

Adam briefly tuned out Scar to recall Miles' words

that day in his apartment: "The human body's DNA is evolving, mutating if you will, and birthing super talents such as yourself."

Then he remembered one of his dreams in which his Zulu master taught him about the merkaba, and how the Zulu elders used it to travel to earth from another world.

They also used the merkaba to bring down the strange flying wheels. "What an odd connection," he thought.

"Could there be a connection between my DNA and my dreams?" he pondered. Adam knew now that there may be an ounce of truth in Scar's story.

"Alright, you got my attention. I'm listening," said Adam while wrestling a toothpick out of his pocket and into his mouth.

Scar continued, "You have the capacity to free yourself from any pains, mental or physical. You have the ability to manifest any thought you desire. There is no need for space craft, the human body is capable of traveling to infinite worlds and dimensions using the merkaba. Humans can have a blissful, god-like existence compared to what they know now. You were made for much more than the stressful, repetitive, monotonous, soul-draining jobs that torment your life today. The Ky make sure you know nothing of this, and they ensure it is publicly frowned upon even if the thought is suggested."

Adam's face fell blank from the heavy likely odds of Scar's story. The reality he once knew now vacated into the aether.

He squinted, cleared out his eyes, and creeped back into the conversation, "Does the astral realm have anything to do with all of this?"

A slick smile slid across Kojo's face from the presumed direction Adam's question would take the conversation.

More stoically than before, Scar answered, "Yes, the astral realm is just the beginning. With your five senses you are essentially blind. For example, your eyes can only detect a small sliver of light, and your ears can only hear a small range of sound. But when the soul sheds the flesh for the astral realm, it can detect much more. It becomes free to see the spiritual reality, the reality that has been hidden from you. The Ky keep humans blind to this to further suppress and deceive them of their spiritual gifts."

This hit closer to home for Adam. His lowly mood was beginning to show on his face. He had experienced the divine power of the astral realm and often wondered why it wasn't common knowledge. The spiritual experience in the astral realm had ignited the spiritual revolution in him. Scar was right, knowledge of the astral realm most likely would spark an unimagined spiritual renaissance within mankind.

Adam gnawed harder on his toothpick, leaned in, rested his elbows on his knees, and asked directly, "So what does this have to do with me?"

Scar's stern glare didn't waver from Adam's face.

He leaned in to match Adam's renewed interest before continuing, "In order to maintain their BioGrid and weaken the humans, the Ky have instituted a series of crusades to prevent your DNA from naturally evolving. You are besieged with malicious campaigns from vaccinations, poisonous foods, spiritual deceptions, lies, war, and a plethora of divide-and-conquer strategies. However, you are what the Ky are fighting so hard to prevent. Despite all of their efforts, your DNA has evolved... naturally. Your DNA activation has connected your soul with your body's original blueprints."

Scar paused and watched Adam closely, hoping the thought imbedded itself deep in Adam's subconscious. Adam hovered a vacant gaze about the room before he conjured a slow nod of understanding.

With his face blanketed with apathy Scar carried on, "Once awakened, your type are impossible to enslave, impossible to stop. Seven billion people like you, and the Ky will lose their food and energy source, a dramatic setback in the universal war. Your impressive telekinetic, telepathic, and psychic abilities make us believe you are the first to get this far in the evolutionary cycle since the Ky's modification."

Adam flopped back against his chair while staring numbly at Scar, then Kojo, and finally Clutch. The story was getting more real and hitting its mark. The pit of Adam's stomach churned. Deep inside, he could feel his soul nudging him to the truth in Scar's story. He'd known his entire life that the system discouraged his gifts. He pondered if that was the effect of the Ky's top-down policies. He saw how the system made it unpopular and unrewarding to have such talents. Yet Scar's story didn't give a credible explanation as to why the astral realm and his gifts had all been kept out of the mainstream understanding. He eagerly listened for more.

Scar continued with his slow, precise, robotic voice, "Not only have the Ky modified your DNA, but they have infected your mind with a virus as well. The human mind is so infected with this virus that it's difficult to rely on it for true understanding. An infectious, crippling idea is created and then it is unknowingly spread throughout the population through television, music, movies, family, books, schools, and person-to-person interactions. Ideas are made real and public opinion swayed through mass media campaigns. These ideas are continually crammed in the minds of humans until they become accepted and owned. Those who don't accept these ideas are ostracized, but those who do are rewarded. These ideas continue to stir the population away from the truth. Since humans are weak at consulting their own souls for understanding, these ideas catch hold and continue spreading like wildfire, manipulating the human population. In fact, you can hardly come to a true understanding with an infected mind, you have to consult your soul."

Speaking in a muffled tone from the slit beside his cigar, Kojo said, "In other words, it's hard to measure with a bent ruler."

Adam's eyes tightened while his head tilted, still in obvious confusion.

Scar read Adam's befuddled body language and decided to take a more subtle approach.

He scooted his chair forward and with praying hands resting on his face, he asked in a soft voice, "Which one of your five senses is telling you how you feel right now?"

Before Adam could answer, Scar blurted, "Is it your sight... or your hearing... what about taste... how about your touch... or do you smell it?"

He watched as Adam scrambled to answer before he continued.

"It isn't any of them, is it Adam? Yet something inside of you senses how you feel. What is sensing how you feel?"

Adam blankly stared at Scar, still scrambling to answer.

"Something besides your five senses is able to tell you how you feel. Why haven't you been told about that sense?" Scar asked.

Adam struggled, searching for an answer while gnawing on his toothpick.

Scar continued, "That something that is sensing how you feel is your soul. It's hard for humans to relate because you have it backwards. Because of the Ky's modification, you have been trained to put the mind and body before the soul. But that's not the real way of the universe; the soul comes first... it should feel the mind and body. The human body is a vehicle that souls pass in and out of. The soul is far more powerful than the physical body and its five senses. Connecting with your soul will liberate you. Of course, this philosophy contradicts the Ky's ideology, so you are kept blinded to this spiritual truth."

Scar continued, "The human mind only lives on

average 70-80 years, but the soul is infinite. All the information in your mind comes from the Ky one way or another—through influence of their vast media and financial empires. So being taught to use your mind instead of your soul disconnects you from the universal order, making it easier for the Ky to purposefully misguide your perceptions. In other words, humans are infected with a mental virus; that virus is what further traps you within their BioGrid. To determine what is true, it is best to consult the soul; it is of a much higher intelligence."

Pressing the tips of his fingers against his eyes, Adam exhaled a long sigh and was speechless for some time. The accuracy of Scar's subtle approach stung him to his core.

He blinked profusely and asked with a face locked in shock, "So you telling me our whole civilization is a lie, a fucking sham, and that our entire way of life has been guided and hijacked by aliens in order for us to be their slaves and food?"

Scar shifted back deep into his seat and returned to his rested stoic face, "Simply put, yes. Man has fought a spiritual war with the Ky for thousands of years. If mankind can become more conscious and spiritually enlightened, they can repair their own damaged DNA. This can only be accomplished by living in balance with the earth, and living by the creed that all is one and one is all. When these abilities are mastered, the DNA begins to reprogram itself back to its original form. Fully active DNA will allow humans to circumvent their slavery. When humans realize this, mankind will rise and no longer be cogs in the Ky's BioGrid. The more enlightened humans become, the clearer their purpose will be. Many were killed for spreading this message of enlightenment. In fact, all liberating messages are stripped of its transformative properties before being endorsed by the Ky's counsel; the messages are then released back to the people."

Scar paused to check on his new pupil, as he knew this was overwhelming.

After a few seconds, he continued, "They have been guiding humans away from any liberating phenomenon or principles for centuries, only giving them enough to become effective slaves."

Adam swallowed and blinked his eyes as the reality he once knew was ripped into mental shards in his mind.

Shifting his toothpick side to side in his mouth and still not ready to let the world he once knew go, Adam asked, "But some people are happy and live good lives and they don't feel like slaves. So you are basically saying that they have trained our minds to not see the enslavement?"

"Bingo, the last thing a fish will notice is the water," Kojo stated from the back of the room.

"I freed a thousand slaves, I could have freed a thousand more if only they knew they were slaves," Clutch barked in his bone-shattering voice, referencing Harriet Tubman.

"I feel you on some of your points... but these dudes couldn't make a solar panel or some fucking wind turbine to get their energy from? You say they are thousands of years ahead of us. Why go through all this trouble?"

"They don't eat solar panels and wind turbines," Scar said.

Wincing and pulling at his afro with both hands, Adam asked, "Okay, but how in the hell are they feeding off me, I'm not giving these dudes shit?"

Arms folded and still leaning up against the wall, Clutch said, "Brace yourself" in anticipation of the coming answer.

Scar peered at Adam for a few moments in silence as if he was searching for words before he began, "This is perhaps the most difficult part for the human to understand. It requires a level of understanding that the Ky made impossible for humans to grasp. It is best to process this from your soul rather than your mind."

Adam's face was ripe with anticipation as he dialed in on Scar, "Man, enough with this hand holding shit, just give it to me raw... how do they feed?"

Obliging Adam's eagerness, Scar nodded and began, "They feed off humans primarily in two ways; first they feed off of your emotional energy. The human body essentially takes food, extracts the energy out of it and transfers it to the soul. The Ky, however, can feed directly off of the energy a soul emits. As an eel is equipped to pass electricity through water or how a shark can detect blood miles away, the biological makeup of the Ky allows them to harness energy directly emitted by a soul. So humans are pushed and swayed to think and feel certain ways in order for their souls to exhibit certain energies. The energy of choice is anything that produces emotional suffering. The more suffering created, the more powerful the beings grow. This perhaps will help explain the perpetual negative state of your planet. They keep war and turmoil in a never-ending cycle from behind the scenes. This is all done with total disregard for anything resembling ethics, respect for life, concern for the ecosystem, or compassion for human health and consciousness. All in all, this keeps the human DNA from ever having a fair chance at evolving and makes a breeding ground for negative emotions for them to feed off you."

Adam snapped his fingers and blurted out, "Yeah, I worked at a news station and the majority of it was always negative. I even read that negative, warring, pain, and evil spirit on Winston Chase. I thought he was some type of demon; it was so bad."

Scar's eyes widened and he perked up, questioning Adam in an excited tone, "You've met Winston? Winston Chase, CEO of Crow Corp?

"Yes, about a year ago," Adam responded.

"He is in charge of earth's BioGrid and a descendant of the military coup that killed off my family!"Scar said.

"Not only have I met him, but he tried to kill me," Adam responded, nodding profusely.

Reaching in his pocket for his phone, Adam cued up the surveillance video of the run-in with the CEO's grunts. Kojo and Clutch all gathered behind Scar to view the footage. Kojo looked up in amazement, grinning and nodding at his spot on instinct about Adam.

Adam continued, "I was given the option to go to jail for murder or help the government track down terrorists. At that time, it was a no brainer. They said if I helped I could go free, and that is how I ended up here."

"The ol' find'em and we'll set you free bit, huh! I can't believe this clown is going to wreck everything we got going. By you coming here you have exposed the whole Colony, putting countless lives in danger," Clutch squawked, teeming with animosity.

Still fuming with his own hostility toward Clutch, Adam yelled, "How was I supposed to know? I came here to hang out with my boy. Maybe you shouldn't have put your mutha fuckin' hands on me in the first place and we wouldn't be here!"

Moving a bit closer to Adam, and with a resounding roar, Clutch yelled, "Look here, chump, you mean to tell me with all those so-called skills you couldn't figure out they was playing you. Hell, they opened up ya dome to put a tracker in it, you couldn't sense that?"

"Let's put one in yo big-ass head and see if you sense it," Adam shot back.

Scar interrupted while waving down Adam and Clutch, "Gentlemen, please."

Both men eased after painting each other with dirty looks.

Scar continued in his mechanical, edgy voice, "Winston Chase knew you were far more powerful and felt he could, as you humans say, kill two birds with one stone by duping you this way, but it doesn't matter. Perhaps fate is playing a cruel trick on us all. By you simply walking into this bar, you have either single-handedly destroyed the Colony or helped it. That is going to be for all of us to decide."

Ego still ablaze from Clutch's comments, Adam refocused his attention back to Scar, "So how do you know all of this?"

"Because I am Ky," Scar divulged.

Chapter 17

Adam's breath locked up, his heartbeat soared and a golf ball-sized swallow bowled down his throat at the confirmation of a live alien in front of him. Adam looked nervously around the room. Leaning against the wall with their arms folded, Kojo and Clutch peered at Adam.

Scar slowly took his hat off and placed it on the table, "It's time you see for yourself."

Adam braced himself and prepared for the unknown. Scar steadied himself and slowly began to morph into his alien form. His face was light grey, having large slanted eyes with no eyelashes or visible hair. Unlike the human eye, Scar's were devoid of irises and were wet and shiny black in color. Scar's head was long and oval, with part of his cranium protruding backward, similar to the statues of Nefertiti of Egypt. A ridge was present for his nose, but no nostrils, just two small barely visible holes. His skin had a rough scaly texture with a light greenish transparent tint. His lips were thin with a slit for a mouth and the same color as his outer skin. Adam could see his skin loosening and tightening as if it was breathing and taking in energy across the aether. He was at least Adam's height, with thin, weak-looking limbs.

Scar's dark eyes gave off a focused and determined gaze, devoid of emotion. All in all, Adam could feel the peaceful energy flowing from Scar's skin.

Truly amazing, thought Adam.

He could still see a tint of human features residing on Scar's face.

Adam pondered, *This must be why I wasn't able to see an aura around the CEO; their alien souls emit a different energy than my eyes can see.*

He slowly reached toward Adam and telepathically told Adam to take his hand. Glued in amazement to Scar's alien face, Adam hesitantly reached out and grabbed his hands. He immediately felt a clammy difference from most humans. Now that his skills were more focused and accurate, he read deep into Scar's mind to ensure he wasn't getting manipulated again. He matched and confirmed every word of Scar's story with his telepathic skills.

"I don't share the Ky sentiment. Thousands of years ago, the ruling Ky family was overthrown in order to make way for the conquering of earth. The overthrowing rebels murdered and sent the rest of that family into exile. That family was my ancestors. For generations, my family and I have been fighting to reclaim our throne and bring down the Ky BioGrid," Scar relayed telepathically to Adam.

Adam turned his head to gaze upon the wall as if he was surveying grassy green pastures out of an invisible window. Frowning and shaking his head in disgust, he acknowledged with his soul that it was all making sense.

Still pinned to the immensity of the moment, Adam dove deeper, "This reincarnation, you mean to tell me I've been here before?"

As he asked his own question, an idea exploded in his head. Adam had thousands of past memories that he hadn't personally experienced but remembered as if he had, especially with Nia.

"Wait... Is the Kode-X modification supposed to block memory of our past lives too?" Adam asked.

Shifting back into his more acceptable human

face, Scar replied, "Absolutely, humans waking up to their past lives will alert them to their true potential. Those ideas are too risky to permeate throughout the world, so that was deleted out of your DNA."

Adam sighed and rested his face into his palm. It all made sense now; he had been here on earth before. His dreams were not just dreams or strange fantasies, but reincarnations of his past lives, including the strange flying oval wheels over his Zulu village, Vietnam, and memories with Nia. It all happened. The reincarnations were becoming more and more real. Specifically, the one where he was captured, chained, and marched to his death on the flying oval wheels. The recalled trauma was so great that it seared a response in his body's DNA, bruising his wrist, ankles, and feet, and parching his tongue. His evolved DNA had connected him to all of his stored memories and allowed him to recall them since he was a young boy. He had recalled hundreds of past friends, parents, events, even deaths from his previous lives.

All over the world, the Ky's large silver oval wheels were showing up, testing and destroying the original humans' DNA. He had witnessed the beginning of it and actually been a part of the original war with the Ky. They were preparing to seed the world with a new man; one to be forever enslaved to them. Now it made sense why the CEO so eagerly wanted to test his psychic abilities. He wanted to see how strong Adam's evolving DNA had become. Being able to mentally see the CEO for who he really was proved to be a clear sign of Adam's evolved DNA, making it enough to warrant his death and/or his manipulation by Miles. It further explained why Nia was so etched in his soul. She was his twin flame, and he had found her in many of his past lives. Adam recalled the full definition of a twin flame:

In the beginning of time we were created as a perfect soul, that was split into two halves—one half female, the other half male—that would then be cast in the universe to be forever looking for one another. They would reincarnate over lifetimes with this longing for each other, and once they were ready, they would unite and be in love and then leave this physical plane as one whole individual soul.

The confirmation of Nia being his twin flame was a game changer. He lifted his head and with renewed spark rejoiced, "I remember my past lives!"

Kojo and Clutch looked at each other with a tinge of excitement. Whatever doubts may have existed before were now being slowly molded into hope.

Bewildered, taking the toothpick out of his mouth, Adam asked, "But how could they be so stupid to risk us talking and you telling me all this?

Scar assured Adam, "Once the tracker was in your head, you were already dead. It would have been only a matter of time before they found and killed you. You were only necessary to get them closer to us. Of course, they preferred that we not talk but if we did, it wasn't a deal killer."

"Or so they thought," Adam fired back, pounding his fist on the table.

He could feel the anger creeping up his spine. He'd had enough threats on his life.

Adam's purpose began to loom heavy on his shoulders, "So what are we supposed to do?"

With a rare nib of emotion, Scar said, "We must awaken the people to this reality. I have been trying for years to sequence the human DNA to restore the strands closer to their pre-modified state. But I don't have an original strand to work from. You, on the other hand, are a natural wonder. Your DNA is a gift from God. With your DNA, I can create a counter agent that can start to repair the human DNA back to its aboriginal state."

"Ohhhh, so that's why you guys took the C-47 compound, to make some kind of serum to return human DNA back into its original state," Adam reckoned.

Nodding at the brilliance of Scar's plan, Adam asked, "So how are you going to vaccinate seven billion people?"

Scar leaned forward and shook his head and finger at Adam, "We don't need to vaccinate seven billion, just the willing souls around the world within our own ranks, inside the Colony. This group will further unplug from the BioGrid, influencing others and birthing uninhibited free-thinking children."

Coming off of the back wall again, Kojo said, "In other words, once the world sees humans with your gifts, it will be enough to spark the revolution. Everybody will want to be telepathic, telekinetic, pyrokinetic, hydrokinetic, psychic, precognitive, clairvoyant, or experience multi-dimensions. At that point the cat will be out of the bag."

Adam's eyes brightened as he began to grasp the intent and design of the plan.

Scar continued, "The Ky know the earth's sun always evolves DNA through an evolutionary process. So they have accounted for gradual and spotty evolutionary changes in humans. But this counter agent will be beyond their methods of containment. By the time they suspect anything, it will be too late. Thousands will be blossoming free from the BioGrid with a new understanding of reality. This will slowly start to disrupt the Ky's power. We can have a completely new earth in five years."

Adam threw Scar's statement about the sun around in his mind. He felt the sun recharging him before. He felt firsthand the sun sparking evolutionary changes in him. The truth of the sun giving him strength confirmed that Nia would give him more power.

Kojo interrupted Adam's thoughts, leading off Scar's words, "And simultaneously we continue to teach the people what their true potential is. Until the counter agent takes full effect, you are proof of this potential. The evolved ability in you will start to awaken those who haven't received the counter agent. DNA is programmed by the soul's will and intent. So getting the people to believe will help their DNA evolve. This is the most powerful opportunity we've had to get the message out to the masses. Before, we were nothing more than a bunch of backroom conspiracy kooks or terrorists with no proof and no ability to convince the masses at large. But you bring undeniable proof of the truth. This is perfect timing."

Shaking his head in disgust, and throbbing with anger, Adam whined, "Well shit, bro... Is there even a God?"

Kojo and Clutch both looked to Scar to tackle the question.

Scar perked up, "Yes, but not like..."

Boom! Just then, the tracking device pulled out of Adam's head exploded, leaving a basketball-sized hole in the table and choking the room with a cloud of thick, white smoke. Instinctively, Clutch jumped into action, shielding Scar, Kojo, and Adam from any other possible damage.

Waving the smoke down, Clutch caught a visual of the charred remains of Scar's face. The wood and metal from the table, along with the tracker material, wedged through his flesh like hot shrapnel. His head was agape, missing the nose and left eye. Out oozed a tan, alien-like sludge from the singed seams of Scar's still-stoic face. In Clutch's hands dangled Scar's lifeless body.

He let out a long growl, holding back his immediate rage.

Still crouching over Scar's body, Clutch roared, "Fuck... they are putting detonators in the trackers now. They're on to us sooner than we thought!"

Kojo and Clutch gathered around Scar in a moment of silence, honoring him for the work he'd done for humanity. Clutch bore down on Adam with an icy stare, all the while flexing his throbbing jaw muscle from grinding his teeth. Adam's eyes bucked in shock at the seared table, envisioning what his head would have looked like had it not been pulled out. When he saw Scar's mangled face, bolts of anger surged throughout his body's nerve endings.

Clutch interrupted Adam's trance by barking orders, "Shit, we have to pack up and prepare the rest of the Colony. They will be here soon—looking for a body!"

Plagued with little emotion, Kojo resolved, "We are going to most likely lose the Colony, labs, even some lives. Nothing can be done about it now. We knew it would come to this one day. We may lose the Colony, but as long as we have Adam we are strong. I believe I can synthesize the counter agent, but we need to get Adam to safety or all is lost."

A door opened into the basement, and a voice yelled, "Flyers!"

Indiscriminate gun fire could be heard in the back ground. By reflex, Clutch franticly reached into a secret panel hidden in the wall and grabbed some weapons, tossing some to Kojo and Adam, and bolting upstairs with his battle ax.

Before exiting the basement door, he turned to Kojo and said, "You know what to do if they breach this door!"

Wide-eyed, Adam asked, "What does he mean?"

Kojo whispered to Adam with a finger over his lips, "Shhh, keep quiet. They have sent a bunch of A.I. drones to investigate. They can pick up the smallest chatter and bio signatures."

Both men waited in silence as the gun battle got louder and presumably more heated upstairs.

Chapter 18

While lying silent and still on the floor, Adam heard Clutch's voice roaring orders upstairs. The gun fire blast spilled flashes of visible light through the cracks of the dimly lit basement door. Adam got up to run upstairs to help Clutch in battle. Kojo grabbed his leg.

"How can we stay here and let him fight by himself," Adam whispered.

"Think about it, they think you are dead. If you show your face, we lose what little surprise we have left. Trust me, Clutch can handle this!" Kojo uttered under his breath.

Adam sighed, looked at the door, looked back to Kojo, then back to the door again. Finally, he kneeled next to Kojo, "I hope you are right."

Clutch kicked in the basement door with a crash. His eyes were dark, focused, and dilated. He ran downstairs with Jolon scampering behind him.

"We have been overrun by agents, they have us surrounded! We have to go!" Clutch yelled.

Adam and Jolon reunited and reassured each other that they were both okay. Kojo and Clutch frantically ran to the secret panel in the wall and began to load up supplies. They stuffed their pockets and backpacks with guns, ammo, water, first aid, batteries, lights, and food.

"Give me your phone," Clutch demanded.

Adam looked puzzled, "Why?"

"Because they will also be able to track you through your phone, Einstein!" yelled Clutch.

Adam quickly took out his memory card, desperate to preserve his music and the all too important video footage of Nia. Clutch snatched Adam's phone and tossed it on Scar's lifeless body. He drew his weapon and fired a steady, light blue flash into Scar's body, completely disintegrating the body and phone. Adam and Jolon observed Clutch with an unsettled nervousness.

"Why the fuck you do that?" Adam yelled.

"If they found Scar's alien body, they would know we likely have alien technology. We can't afford to lose that element of surprise. His body had to go," Kojo responded, as calmly as ever.

Clutch carried on firing another weapon into the basement wall. A large oval section of the wall began to liquefy and wither in a transparent pattern like a portal. Kojo jumped on a chair, then a table, and vaulted up Clutch's back and seated himself into a readymade pouch.

"Let's go, and stay close or the portal will close on you," Clutch ordered to Adam and Jolon.

Without hesitation, Clutch and Kojo breached into the wavy, liquefied wall. Adam and Jolon anxiously looked at each other before darting cautiously through the portal behind them. Astonished, Adam noticed they were running underground. The weapon Clutch was firing rearranged the molecular structure of the underground bedrock, allowing them to pass through solid earth and escape undetected by the agents.

After running for about a mile, Clutch screamed, "Shit, the MolGun batteries are running low; we will have to surface."

Clutch began to take them to the surface by slightly pointing the MolGun up and following its path. They breeched the surface in the thick of a full grown corn field. The sweet aroma of the plants and the crisp desert air filled their nostrils with relief over the underground bedrock. The calm cool of the night gave a temporarily tranquil feeling to the men. It was a typical calm Arizona night, with chirping from crickets and the occasional coyote howl. The corn rows were barely lit by the moon. Deep in the corn fields, all the directions looked identical. At 7'4", Clutch was the only one tall enough to discern any difference in orientation. In the far distance, flashing lights and faint sounds of agents' chatter could be heard.

Barely breathing, Clutch tore into one of his protein bars.

Scarfing the bar down, he said impatiently, "You have five minutes to catch your breath, then we continue."

Jolon fell over from exhaustion. His fifty-year-old frame had been pushed beyond its capable limits. Lying on his back, he lazily turned his head and vomited involuntarily. Kojo climbed down from the pouch latched to Clutch's back, pulled out his tablet, and began to reassess the mission's objectives.

Adam sank into deep thought. His whole life he had felt unwanted, unworthy, unable, and now he was being told he was the key to free the human race. Adam was feeling inundated with emotions.

He thought to himself, *Wow, saving the world*!

But even with all of this excitement, finding Nia was still his main agenda. At this point, he had flipped an SUV with his mind, learned of his spiritual enslavement, remembered his past lives, met an alien, yet none of it felt more meaningful than his love for Nia. Adam was snapped out of his daydream by Kojo.

"It's just as I thought. They have raided all of our other locations—bank accounts and labs," said Kojo.

The glum look spreading across his face made obvious the pending doom they were likely facing.

"I'm afraid the retaliation by the Ky's agents will be swift and powerful," Kojo warned.

He showed them live news coverage from around the world, further exposing and demonizing the Colony as an extremely dangerous terrorist organization:

Breaking news: we have just learned that the FBI has won a major victory against the terrorist organization who calls themselves "the Colony." Authorities say the group is responsible for crashing markets in several countries and they have confirmed that the U.S. was their next target. An FBI spokesperson says they have seized the group's bank accounts, affiliates, paper trails, and locations. Take a look at this video showing boxes of assets that were confiscated in London, Africa, South America, and the U.S.

They all sat speechless, pondering the doom to come.

Clutch broke the silence, concerned about the future, "Shit, do we still have enough equipment to synthesize the counter agent?"

"At this point, I'd say no, we don't have access to Scar's labs and his technology. Plus, now it is going to be immensely more difficult to travel to our other safe houses throughout the states without detection," Kojo said grimly.

"That's easy—we could use the astral realm to check the bases. We could cover them all in one night," Adam said.

"No, they will eventually unravel all of our bases, and they will probably park some of their demons around the buildings to wait for us. That will be too dangerous," said Kojo.

"Demons? There ain't no demons. My astral trainer, Kano, said the astral realm isn't dangerous like that," Adam corrected Kojo.

"Kano?" Clutch butted in, contorting his brow.

"Yeah, do you know him?" Adam asked while taking a seat on the ground.

With anger stabbed on his face Clutch answered, "Yeah, we know that clown. He used to be one of us until he switched sides. He sold us out. That bitch gladly set us all back just so he could have a few riches to himself."

Shocked, Adam asked, "What? What the hell happened?"

"To make a long story short, he got tired of fighting the good fight. He woke up one day and looked at his life and didn't like it. Turns out he'd rather be a rich slave than a free man. In exchange, he struck a deal with the Ky to help crush all evolutionarily progressive humans," Kojo explained.

"Fuck that muthafucka. I wouldn't piss on him if he was on fire," said Clutch.

Adam was speechless. He dropped his head in between his knees while sitting on the ground.

With disappointment heavy in his voice, he said, "I thought he was helping me. I actually considered the dude my friend. I sensed something strange about him after our last sparring session but..."

Coughing and catching his breath, Jolon said, "Nah bro, I'm your friend. I got ya back!"

"Good lookin' Jolon," Adam said.

He then turned to Kojo, "Tell me what I need to know about the astral realm."

Kojo nodded, "Here is the truth about it. It can be extremely dangerous. It houses the souls who we think are dead. In fact, most ghouls, ghosts, demons, and other paranormal activity are nothing more than souls or spirits in the astral realm. Many of the malevolent souls are controlled by the Ky."

Adam's eyes widened as his comprehension grew.

"I presume Kano didn't tell you about this?" said Kojo.

"No, he didn't. He told me it was basically like purgatory and there would maybe be a troublesome person or two. Worst case, some energy leeches," Adam answered.

Shaking his head in disgust, Kojo said, "They purposely lied to you. The astral realm is definitely much more than purgatory. It contains heaven and hell; that's why demons are present. Heaven is in the higher reaches and hell in the lower reaches."

"You gotta be shit'n me," Adam responded, shaking his head.

Then it hit him like tonnage against his chest, Kano and Miles purposely stirred him away from knowing the full dangers in the astral realm. He never would have been able to fend off these Ky controlled demons if they were called to attack him. Since they purposely never prepared him for them, they would have a better ability to attack and destroy him. This must have been Miles's ace card in case Adam went rogue. A sobering thought waned over Adam—he was nothing more than a pawn, a play piece, pointless fodder. Worse yet, he was essentially limited and ill prepared for the astral realm.

He remembered some of Scar's last words, "The CEO knew you were incredibly powerful and felt, as you humans say, he could kill two birds with one stone by duping you this way."

The CEO's wicked and malicious manipulation of him stirred a burning deep inside his soul's core.

Kojo continued, "Well, Adam, let me give you a two minute crash course on the dangers of the astral realm. If your soul is weak, you'll become an easy target for the demons to attack. There are infinite low-level demons, souls, spirits, and spooks all waiting for any opportunity to grab the next available body and get back into the material world; they will do and say whatever it takes to manipulate your mind in order to possess your body. If you are strong enough to get past that, then you have to worry about the higher level Ky-controlled demons; we call them the Shadows. And they are on another level. Avoid them at all cost. They are extremely powerful, wicked, hateful, mischievous, combative and worst of all hungry for your soul. Many who weren't properly prepared entered the astral realm and were attacked, torn, and ripped from their material bodies all to discover they were no longer able to return back to their homes. The ones who did return home lost their grip on reality in the material world, hearing voices, having compulsive thoughts, feeling insane, having emotional breakdowns, or worse—they would lose control of their bodies. If you don't know what you're doing, it's best to stay out; it's one big bad neighborhood!"

Kojo paused to let the thought penetrate deep into Adam's head.

"These demons can get into your mind and control you, sometimes convincing you to kill... inception, deception," Kojo added.

"Ahhh, so that's what possession is all about," Adam stated, having an epiphanous moment.

"Yes. The Ky hacked human DNA to leave a back door open for repossession. Keeping humans in a state of fear weakens their DNA and keeps them vulnerable for repossession. This allows the Ky to take over any unsuspecting mind whenever necessary with these demons. In fact, some multiple personality disorders are a form of possession. Even certain levels of sleepwalking can be defined as such. Since humans can't perceive the astral realm with their eyes, they are blind to the demons' attacks. The only way to see the demons is to shed the flesh and enter into the astral realm. Unfortunately, most humans don't know how to do this. So this gives the Ky the ability to take over and control anyone's mind at will—uncontested," Kojo clarified.

He paused and took a deep breath, "For example, have you ever had a thought that didn't seem it belonged, or wasn't yours?

Adam answered, "Yeah, all the time."

"That could be them tempting you, whispering at you. People confuse these thoughts with their own and live them through. This is how heads of states are compromised and how governments are eventually corrupted."

"Oh shit. When I was in the astral realm, I did see those demons wrapped around the scientists' astral bodies. But Kano told me they were nothing more than harmless, low-level leaches and that there was nothing to worry about," Adam noted.

Rather than his normally smug look, Kojo glanced

at Adam sympathetically, feeling sorry for his gullible and naive understanding.

"Leaches are very dangerous. They harness energy and thoughts from unsuspecting victims. Having no astral abilities, most people carry them around their entire life and know nothing about them. It's a simple way they get the best scientists to go along with their agenda," Kojo clarified.

With anguish, Adam said, "Kano taught me some light-weight astral combat techniques... But shit! It sounds like I'm gonna need a lot more than that. How about guns, can I create those?"

"Yes, you certainly can, but the demons have to recognize the gun can actually cause them damage. If not, it will be useless. This is why most astral combat is done with blades, swords, claws, or some other sharp object—a universal understanding of hostility. The astral realm is so huge they barely even know about our guns, and the ones who do don't fear them. So our physical guns hold little to no value."

Looking at Kojo with concern, Adam humbly asked, "So, how can you really protect yourself if the astral realm is that fuckin' dangerous?

"First, be aware of your soul. Some mistake their mind and soul to be the same thing. But that's not true, they are separate. In fact, most people's minds are not even consciously aware of their soul. That's why you have to train your mind to be conscious. That way the mind becomes aware of the soul's presence, in and out of the astral realm. If you can connect the mind to the soul, you can connect with your higher senses and be aware of the demons. That is the first step to fending them off," said Kojo.

Adam interrupted, "Yes, I remember Scar saying the Ky modified us so that we wouldn't easily connect with our souls."

Kojo continued, "Next is to become enlightened and have no fear. Fear weakens you. Although evil is present, good is also present; just like in the material world. They can only prey on the unsuspecting or the weak. So you must have master control over your emotions, your anger, and your ego. Lastly, never—I mean never—let yourself lose consciousness while in the astral realm. Losing consciousness will separate you from your physical body; in other words, death of this current life. You start your reincarnation process all over, and we don't know when or where that will happen."

Kojo let his words sink in and become fully digested by Adam before continuing, "You must become compassionate, conscious, insightful, selfless, rid yourself of prejudices, and know that all is the One, and the One is in all, and most of all, connect with the principle of love. We call this the god frequency, it makes you immensely powerful. Vibrating with the emotion of love makes you a god compared to these demons."

Another piece of the puzzle fell into Adam's lap. Not only was it the proximity of Nia that made him stronger, it was also the love he felt for her. She was the source that could power him beyond all odds. Nia completed him—his other half and the key to unlocking his powers. This made finding Nia all the more important to him.

Still keeping Nia to himself, Adam fell into a stoic gaze at the night sky before falling back into the conversation.

Still snagged on the dangers of the astral realm, Adam asked, "So why risk it, why even go?"

"Dude, was you even listening to Scar!" Clutch scolded.

Waving Clutch down, Kojo said, "Clutch, I got this, let me handle it."

With an angry scowl, Clutch honored his older brother's request. He rolled his eyes away and returned to cautiously surveying the corn field.

"I'll give you two more minutes," he said.

Kojo turned back to Adam. Understanding his new pupil's naivety, he explained, "The astral realm is a gift from our creator; it helps us find our purpose. It helps us to recall past lives, confirming that there is no death, and it gives us the ability to meet so-called deceased loved ones. Even more, the astral realm enables us to converse with angels. It also helps increase our psychic abilities, knowledge, and wisdom."

Adam's eyes grew with amazement.

Kojo grinned, "Oh I'm not done yet... it gets better."

"Just for fun, you can fly and travel beyond your material body's limit. You can even witness other realities—I'm talking increased mental and physical healing. But the biggest strength of the astral realm is that it can be instrumental at waking humanity to their full potential," Kojo said, showing something resembling joy for the first time.

Adam shook his head while staring off in the distance, as if he was running the conversation past his soul for confirmation. He nodded, realizing the superb duping that had been done by Miles and Kano via Winston Chase's diabolical plan. He connected with the rage he felt for the CEO that day in his office. Adam spiraled deeper into thought. He saw how lifetime after lifetime the Ky had taken Nia away from him, even killing their first child on the flying wheels. He felt that in all likelihood the Ky were behind all wars, manipulating mankind into misery, including the Vietnam War, which ultimately put an unrecoverable wedge between him and Nia. In fact, the Ky were guilty for torturing and murdering billions of human souls, taking them beyond the worst imaginable hell. They had physically and mentally tormented humans throughout earth's history, causing hunger, famine, suffering, racism, ignorance, and hatred.

They had pitted humans against each other for centuries. They purposefully turned the beautiful gift of life into a miserable armpit of an existence. It was obvious to Adam that the Ky saw humans as farmed cattle, nothing more than genetically modified organisms, rats in a cage, or cockroaches to be squashed. Worse yet, they trapped the souls to do it all again—lifetime after lifetime. Like steady inflation, they brought about a constant increase in misery every year without any consideration, compassion, or care for humans, a well-oiled machine of misery. They are invaders, foreigners who care very little for the planet. Adam felt at this very moment they were probably surveying other planets across the galaxy to do the same thing. Taking bigger breaths and popping his knuckles, Adam fantasized about having that day back with Winston Chase; hindsight was 20/20.

His boiling anger gave rise to the beginning

stages of an anxiety attack.

Ahh... if I ever... if I ever have the opportunity... I swear... Adam thought.

Adam's mind flashed to the people all over the world, children's faces who had no idea of what they were born into. It broke him. Tears began to well up and stream down his face. He broke into a quiet, slow, steady sob. Jolon patted him on the back. Clutch looked away, discomforted by the show of emotion.

Kojo welcomed the much needed cry. He knew Adam would need to grab from it in order to fight the coming battle.

"For this reason, you must be changed from your old self to be a more focused and balanced person as to not be controlled by evil. If you don't, you will become prey in the astral realm. Typically, it takes years for someone to be ready and safely travel in the astral realm," he said.

"Quiet!" hissed Clutch, motioning with his hands to curtail the chatter. Once again, his pupils dilated. A long stretch of silence ensued as his eyes probed through the barely visible corn fields. His eye lids slowly narrowed while his head swiveled in all directions to inspect the fields. Clutch's slow gaze locked frontward like an attacking lion. He slowly unlatched the battle ax attached to his back, with his eyes locked in alertness.

"Ky-otes!" he whispered.

"We can't go back underground, the MolGun is dead so don't move," Clutch quietly whispered while drawing his weapon.

The rest of the gang followed his eyes. The men all froze with terror at the sight of four glowing sets of eyes creeping through the corn field. The beasts were large, double the size of a typical Arizona coyote. They possessed a bulky, muscular frame, with large saber teeth jutting out of their jaw line. Their eyes were set deep in their heads to protect them from the action of their hunts. Their shoulders were large and bulky, leading to large paws. Their tails were long with exposed spikes along the end. Shocked by the enormity, Jolon stepped back and snapped a twig, producing a loud cracking sound. The Ky-otes' heads swung up with speed and looked their way. Locked in on their targets, the four Ky-otes combusted toward the men, shattering the nighttime calm with barks and howls. Kojo jumped into action, grabbing his weapon, climbing up Clutch to once again nestle himself in the pouch on Clutch's back.

"Hold here, pull this back, wait for the blue light, then fire," said Clutch, throwing a weapon to Adam.

"Now will be a good time for your gifts," he added.

"What the fuck are those!" screamed Adam.

Snatching Jolon close, Clutch said, "They are desert coyotes, mixed with animal DNA from the Ky's planet, highly intelligent."

"Holy shit, man, those aren't coyotes those are grizzlies," Jolon shrieked.

The Ky-otes rushed to attack, darting and swaying in and out to avoid taking fire by the men. Thirty yards out, the beasts split up and surrounded the men. Hiding themselves amongst the corn stalks, they slowly crawled and inched closer to their prey.

All fell silent, except the busy breathing between the men before Clutch yelled, "Everybody back to back, wait until you see their eyes before firing."

More silence ensued. All back to back, the men huddled against each other and nervously waited for the wave of terror. The first Ky-ote attacked the slower Jolon. Clutch pivoted, "boom," and pumped a liquid blue slug into the first Ky-ote's skull. The Ky-ote fell from the blast and slid just inches from Jolon's feet.

"They want to wound Jolon to slow us down," Clutch yelled.

In a brilliant flash of strategy, Clutch lifted the massive animal, "I can't keep covering you—Jolon, get under it, you will be safer."

Jolon scooted as much of himself under the dead beast as possible.

"Bang Bang," Kojo hit another attacking Ky-ote while Clutch was distracted with Jolon.

The beast hit the ground, belching an unbearable scream. Still screaming and squirming, Clutch put the beast out of his misery with a slash to the head with his battle ax. Another silence ensued.

"They won't attack anymore. They are going to try to hold us here until their master can radio in," Clutch said.

"Clutch, how much time do we have?" Kojo asked.

"Ten minutes, but only if we take them out before the agents at the bar know they have picked up our scent," Clutch said.

"We can't stay here. We have to get off the reservation and get to a safe house in the city. We have one that I'm sure is not compromised," Kojo said.

"We have to make a run for it!" Clutch shouted to

the others.

He reached down and snatched Jolon up like a rag doll, putting him across his shoulder.

Clutch turned to Adam and motioned with his finger, "Stay by my side; Kojo will watch our six. Let's go!"

Adam nodded. They dashed through the fields, all the while hearing the Ky-otes zigzagging outside their eye's view. One of the Ky-otes made a move, attacking Clutch from his side before he could fire his weapon. The force of the 400 pound beast knocked Clutch backward, pinning all the weight on Kojo and Jolon. The Ky-otes vicious bite was inches away from Clutch's jugular. He guarded off the bite by shoving his battle ax weapon in the beast's mouth. Adam was set to fire on the beast but was blindsided by the other attacking Ky-ote, knocking his weapon to the ground. The marauding beast mounted itself on top of Adam, attempting to gnaw into his neck. In the back of Adam's mind, he knew the combined weight of the Ky-ote and Clutch on top of Kojo would crush him. Not only was he fighting for his life but Kojo's as well. He must fight the ravenous beast off first. Still lying on his back, he grabbed the beast around the head, pitting his elbows in his own abdomen to prevent the beast from biting him. He dug his thumbs in the beast's eyes, scraping and scratching. He felt the beast's eyes pop—fluid seeped out like cracked eggs. The beast yelped and waddled enough for Adam to grab its windpipe with crushing pressure. The suffocating beast gagged and flailed its limbs. Adam locked one of his arms around the beast's head and steadied it to further clamp down on its throat. After about two minutes the beast flopped down on Adam's chest. He rolled the heavy beast to the side and ran to save Clutch, Kojo, and Jolon. He grabbed his weapon and turned to help, only to find Clutch already on his feet, standing eye to eye with the beast. One of his hands was around the beast's throat, the other on his weapon that was crammed in the Ky-ote's mouth. The inhuman strength Clutch exhibited with his bare hands, all while the beast pawed and snapped at him, was beyond impressive. Adam thought perhaps he wasn't the only one with advanced DNA. With a look of satisfaction, Clutch fired, taking off the beast's head. Bits of exploding flesh burst, spraying the corn stalks. Clutch dusted himself off, cleaned his weapon, and looked at Adam—as if offended he had offered help. Kojo, whose head was back buried in his tablet, said with a smug smile, "I know what we need to do!"

Chapter 19

"We have a car on the reservation just around the way. Once we get to the safe house I'll explain the plan, but for now we have to get out of here before they realize their Ky-otes are dead," Kojo said urgently while packing away his tablet.

Clutch reached into his backpack and pulled out three square, pocket-sized devices. He kept one for himself and tossed the other two to Kojo and Adam. Kojo and Clutch quickly nestled the devices to their belts. With a push of a button, the device disguised Clutch into an older Native American man, similar to Scar's Native American disguise. Kojo transformed next, cloaking into a male Caucasian, about mid-forties. Kojo then hinged Adam's device to his belt. He calibrated the device to Adam's biometrics, also changing him into a middle-aged white man.

"Just be yourself, the device will do the rest," Kojo instructed. Adam and Jolon gawked in amazement at the flawless transformations, barely comprehending Kojo's instructions.

The device even slightly modified their voices.

"These are BioMods; they alter people's audio and visual perception of you. This is how we travel undetected. Video cameras are okay, but stay away from photographs," Clutch said while handing out identification cards to fit their new identities.

"What happens with photos?" Adam asked.

"We haven't been able to get the biometrics to stick with photos. If photographed, your cover will be blown," Kojo said.

Meticulously covering all of his bases, Clutch advised Jolon with his forceful scowl, "Since you left your car back at the bar, eventually they will be looking for you so for now use this ID 'till we get to the safe house."

The getaway car was a very inconspicuous grey 2000 Buick Rainier SUV. It had lightly tinted windows to ease the desert sun, a few scrapes, and was quite dusty from the previous week's dust storms. The crew piled into the SUV and began the mile-long drive to the reservation's border. Their eyes all hitched on a police barricade a few yards outside the Indian reservation. The police, swirling red and blue lights, scattered about the road and night sky. Four police officers were investigating all traffic leaving the reservation, with their cruisers staggered in the road.

Pulling onto the main highway, Clutch sternly instructed, "Remember, relax and just be yourselves. No sudden movements. They are not looking for these new faces... no reason to get jumpy."

The mile-long drive out of the reservation built a rising anxiousness, thick enough to touch. Composed in his Native American face, Clutch set his weapon to stun before hiding it under his large thigh. Their low-key Buick slowly pulled to the road block. There were four officers, three Caucasians and one African American. The youngest officer directed the spotlight from his cruiser on the SUV. He began his approach to the SUV while the other officers continued to stand watch. He was a Caucasian male in his mid-thirties with neatly combed dark hair. His face carried a tense, stressed, urgent look. He cautiously crept to the SUV, hands resting near his firearm and eyes locked forward. On approach, he grabbed his flashlight and rudely flashed the light in the men's faces while peering cautiously in the SUV.

"Good evening, officer... Hutchinson," said Clutch, reading the officers tag.

Ignoring Clutch's greeting, the officer discourteously replied, "I'm going to need to see everyone's identification."

"Sure, no problem," Clutch responded while reaching to collect everyone's ID.

A tense, unbearable stretch of silence dwelled as Clutch handed the officer the IDs. While taking the identification, Officer Hutchinson glared at Jolon's swollen cheek from Clutch hammering him back at the bar. Beads of sweat poured from Jolon's face from the added attention. The officer's eyes narrowed from Jolon and slowly rolled to inspect the ID's, scrutinizing each face.

"Where are you gentlemen coming from so late in the night?" the officer asked.

"Apparently, making the casino very happy," Clutch chuckled.

"We gave 'em a good chunk of our money tonight," Clutch added with a rare smirk.

"He lost the most, his wife is gonna kill him," chuckled Clutch, pointing toward Jolon to cover for his nervousness.

Jolon's face squeezed out a clammy smile to play the part.

The officer gave Clutch a suspicious glance, "License and registration please!"

"Sure, but is there a problem officer," he said while handing the officer the paperwork.

"Sit tight," demanded the officer while he walked back to his cruiser. The other officers watched the car intently, thickening the already distressed mood. Inside of his cruiser, the officer began to punch in data on his computer. Five minutes later, he emerged and discussed his findings with the other officers, showing them the IDs and pointing at the SUV.

"Fuck man, they know something," Jolon cried.

"Shhhh... relax," Clutch said in a whisper.

Hutchinson nodded in the huddle with the other officers. He beelined straight to the SUV, "I'm going to need you gentlemen to step out of the vehicle, please."

Adam's hammering heart picked up its pace, thumping harder and harder. Clutch sighed and began to unbuckle his seat belt to exit the vehicle. Kojo did the same. Adam and Jolon looked at each other with a nervous bemusement. Clutch began to slowly roll out of the truck, inconspicuously grabbing his weapon. Just then, indiscriminate chatter crackled across the officers' radios.

"Copy that," said Officer Hutchinson while handing back the men's identification.

"It's your lucky day, you are free to go," said the officer.

He trotted back to his cruiser with the other officers. They hit their sirens and began speeding towards the bar, screeching down the highway. The men all sighed with relief, savoring the moment of peace before heading on their way.

"Shit, that was close," Adam remarked.

A sly grin grew across Clutch's face, "Good ol' BioGrams— works every time."

"Bio what?" Adam asked.

Studying the rearview mirror before driving off, Clutch continued, "Works the same way as the BioMods technology. Basically projects a biological hologram in the mind. I dropped a few of our last chips by the bar in case they were close on our tail. They are designed to make someone think they have sighted us. The officers basically call the citing in, and it draws them off our ass."

"One of Scar's greatest weapons in keeping the Colony hidden throughout the world," Kojo explained.

"Fuck, bro, no wonder why ya'll have been so

hard to find," Adam said in amazement.

After a few minutes of silence, Adam asked, "Okay, I gotta know, how did you guys meet Scar?"

"Well, I guess you can say he is our father!" said Kojo while peering back at Adam.

"Wha?" Adam exclaimed, flinging forward from the back seat.

"You're Ky, too?"

"No, not like that. Scar was a high-level Ky scientist. He had secretly been trying to restore human DNA for some time. He actually synthesized our DNA back in Nigeria. That's why we have more abilities than most humans. He smuggled us out of Nigeria through the Lost Boys Adoption program and later contacted us in Oakland. He was eventually found out on March 13, 1997, the day of Phoenix Lights incident. Do you remember that?"

"Yea, I do!" Jolon said with a raised brow.

Shoulders sulking, Adam flopped back against the back seat, "Nah, I was pretty much homeless in that part of my life. What was it about?"

Kojo continued, "A large UFO was identified over Phoenix. Thousands saw it. Scar was on that ship. When the Ky found out about his insurgency, a battle ensued on the ship. In an effort to get away, Scar distracted his security officers by disabling the ship's cloaking mechanism, allowing the ship to become visible above Phoenix. They believed they killed Scar, but he escaped undetected into the Phoenix desert. He fled to the Indian reservation since it had no government jurisdiction. From there, the Colony was established and eventually spread to other reservations throughout the states. The Native Americans became the lifeblood of the movement. They have been providing us funding and cover ever since. The Colony became headquartered here in Phoenix, and the rest is history."

"Ohhh... So, Scar is the reason you have all these high-tech weapons. And the Ky have no idea that he was actually one of their own?" Adam asked with growing understanding.

"Correct, we can easily beat the highest government agencies, surveillance, and weaponry. We are years ahead of them; that is why we have been able to hide so well," Kojo explained.

"Wait, Kano... If he is a trader, I'm sure he has told the Ky about Scar, and him helping the Colony," Adam said astutely.

"No, Kano didn't know about Scar's true identity. Scar never trusted Kano completely. Clutch and I are the only people who knew Scar was a terrestrial. Of course, if the Ky did know about Scar helping us, we would have been destroyed long ago," Kojo said.

"Ahhhhh... I see. Do you call him Scar from the injuries he received that day on the ship?" Adam asked.

"Yes, but it is mostly because his real name is far too difficult for humans to pronounce," Kojo replied.

The rest of the car ride was silent. They arrived to the safe house just after 3 a.m. It was a typical south Phoenix home: bars on the windows, a chain-link fence, desert landscaping in the front yard, and dirt in the back.

Clutch entered first, closely inspecting the house with his battle ax weapon in hand. Kojo entered second, assisting with Clutch's security sweep. Adam and Jolon quietly crept in last. The house had a simple layout: kitchen, family room in the front, and bedrooms in the back. There was minimal furniture throughout the house, only a couch and a scarred coffee table in the family room, along with a 27 inch TV set on a small, square coffee table. An old, dated, white refrigerator hummed in the kitchen. A little more than a foot away sat an aged, wooden table and chairs. The walls and baseboards were painted Swiss coffee white, with bright white, twelve inch tile throughout. The house reeked of cigarette smoke, like a well worn rental. Small twin beds were neatly arranged in each bedroom corner.

Clutch continued his security detail, ducking his bald head down the hallway while he secured each room.

Adam and Jolon jolted to a halt at the sight of a large Ky-ote head on the front room wall.

"What the fuck," Jolon whispered.

Adam studied the beast, pricking his fingers on its large fangs.

"Revolutionaries by day, taxidermist by night," Jolon joked.

"The Colony is much more than myself, Clutch, and Scar. We literally have thousands of resistors across the world. One of our native brothers gave us this head as a gift."

"Wouldn't a watch have been better... jeez?" Jolon joked.

"Our native brothers and sisters have had many interactions with the Ky and their genetic abominations on their lands for years. Originally, they didn't know what this beast was, until Scar. To commemorate the Colony's union with the Native nations, it was given as a gift to Clutch," Kojo said.

"Cut off your BioMods, we have to conserve

batteries until we can properly rig a way to recharge them," Clutch directed while coming up the hall way.

Adam and Jolon nodded in agreement and set themselves on the living room couch. Clutch pulled out a smaller device and swept the house for any bugs, recorders, or cameras to his satisfaction. Once he was done, a calm rested on his shoulders.

He turned to Kojo, "Okay, big bro, what's the plan?"

Kojo nodded while shielding the flame lighting his cigar. He took a few pulls from his cigar before taking stage on the coffee table.

"His name is Mark Green and he is revolutionizing human genetics. All cells are pretty much equipped with a way to check its DNA sequence for mistakes before and after cell division. Mark found a way to isolate this process. He found the quality control process of the human DNA. This quality control process has identified the gene sequences that have been turned on and off, or simply junk DNA. With this quality control process Mark could eventually decode what the junk DNA sequences actually do. That means he will discover what humans are actually capable of."

Kojo paused, shaking his fingers, "And of course you know the Ky is not having that. They already understand this genetic science, but the arrogant bastards never thought we humans would. But every once in awhile one of us does something incredible like this..."

"Is everybody with me so far," Kojo said, eyeing everyone in the room.

All heads nodded in agreement, giving Kojo the sign to continue. "With that being said, our intel about Mark says he is a bit anti-government and as far as we know isn't controlled by the Ky. The bastards at Crow Corp have been attempting to buy his research, but he hasn't sold. He is a wealthy philanthropist, right up our alley. He might just be the person we need to continue financing the agenda, which will allow us to re-establish cover to produce the counter agent. He is speaking today downtown at the Hyatt Regency Hotel. With Adam and his powers, we can prove the Ky's agenda is real. He will have no choice but to believe us and climb on board," Kojo said.

"That's fuckin' perfect," Adam grinned while rubbing his hands together.

"No, that's fuckin' risky," Clutch shouted.

"You want us to just walk up and ask this dude for money? Even if your plan works, who are we gonna vaccinate... the Colony is no more!" Clutch argued.

"Clutch, no matter what, we have to try to produce the counter agent. We have no money, no labs, no cover, and Mark Green is only in town today. What other choices do we have?" Kojo reasoned.

"Lay low for a while, do some research, see who else is out there. Worst case, we catch him at a later date," Clutch retorted as his voice echoed throughout the empty house.

"You know the Ky are putting the next phase of their plan in motion. You know as well as I do, if Mark doesn't sell off his patents they'll kill him. We have to try now or it will be too late," Kojo said to Clutch.

"We don't have much battery left in the BioMods, nor Scar here to help charge them. If the battery goes, so does our cover. Plus, you know how it goes—for years the media has marked us as terrorists. What makes you think Mark is going to see us as any different. Do you really think Adam will be enough to change his thinking?" Clutch asked.

Adam and Jolon's heads volleyed back and forth between the two brothers debate.

"Wait, wait, hold up, what is the next phase of their plan?" Adam interrupted.

Kojo backed off his focus on Clutch and turned to Adam. "They want to recycle the souls faster and eliminate any chances of human DNA evolving. So they plan to shorten the human life span to between 40 and 50 years. They plan on doing this by flooding the world with false information about health, foods, medicines, treatments, diseases, and sickness. And they are going to back it all with faked pseudoscience and then have it endorsed by the world's top news pundits, entertainers, and spokespersons, making it seem authentic to the masses. Phase two of the plan is to essentially render humans sterile. Humans will have to use the Ky's technology in order to reproduce, giving them complete control over our population. I'm talking complete control of ethnic races, genders, number of children and how long they live."

"Oh God, Oh God... I can't believe this is happening," Jolon cried while resting his head in his lap.

Kojo continued, "This would slowly but surely create another group of modified humans incapable of sensing their enslavement. This group of humans will be more easily controlled, mentally and physically, as per the Ky agenda, and would ensure no chance of human evolution—ever! Everyone will be trapped in misery, reincarnating as slaves over and over— forever!"

Adam growled, "Clutch, we don't have a choice! If they win, they'll reset our evolutionary clocks back thousands of years. Do you want to reincarnate for another thousand years before you wake up? I sure as hell don't!"

"He is right, Clutch. It is now or never," Kojo agreed.

Clutch hissed, and shook his head in disbelief, "This is madness, there's too much heat out there right now. It's smarter to live to fight another day."

Leaning back and resting against the couch, Adam telekinetically floated his proverbial toothpick into his mouth, "How can he not believe me? Plus, we have the BioMods as further proof. If we can convince him of the struggle, surely he'd be down for the Colony. He's already anti-government."

"So what! That doesn't mean Mark is willing to fight and put his neck on the line. Truth be told, some people are fine with being slaves. To be honest, he could be another mutha fucka like Kano, just lookin' for the limelight," Clutch argued.

Kojo took a big pull on his cigar. He jumped down from the coffee table and walked closer to Clutch, "Look, lil bro, I know you've lost faith in mankind, but I haven't. I have to do this. We have to do this."

"What about him?" Clutch asked, motioning to Jolon. "Can we really trust him? We don't know shit about him."

"It's too late to ask that now. He knows everything. We have no choice but to trust him at this point," Kojo replied.

"Well, I trust him," Adam assured them.

Slowly raising his head, Jolon said, "Bro, you said it yourself, Native Americans are the lifeblood to the Colony. I'm 100% Cherokee, I want in."

"How do we know Mark Green isn't with the Ky already? We could be walking into a trap," Clutch said.

"That is where I come in," Adam responded. "I can read everything about him, so we'd know ahead of time. All I need to do is shake his hand and I'll know."

Clutch looked in silence at Kojo and shook his head while letting out a large sigh.

He looked down at his shoes while his large chest surged in and out from his breath.

After rolling Adam's idea around in his head, he said, "I don't like it and I still don't think it is a good idea. I'll do it, but only if we do it my way. We go toward the end of the seminar to save battery on the BioMods, and Jolon has to stay here. Jolon, you left your car at the bar, they're likely looking for your face by now. We have no more BioMods for you."

Everyone nodded, knowing this was all the budging they would get out of Clutch.

Looking at his watch, Clutch said, "Okay, it's 0400 now. I'm going to need everyone sharp, so we rest now and we leave at 1300."

He paused and looked at Kojo, "You better hope this isn't an ambush."

Before Kojo could answer, Clutch turned and headed down the hallway.

Thirty minutes later, Adam struggled to sleep. Clutch destroyed his phone with his music back at the bar. Without it, it would be impossible to silence his thoughts. As he lied on the living room couch, his mind wandered. He tossed and turned with each idea. With the exception of Nia, he hoped deep down this was all a dream. His mind pulled at all convenient possibilities in an attempt to dispel the current reality. No getting around it, this was all very real. He attempted to strike up a conversation with Jolon, but he was out like a baby, nursing his swollen cheek with a bag of frozen veggies. He then heard Kojo was still up typing away on his computer. From the intensity of Kojo's key strokes, he thought it wouldn't be a good idea to interrupt him, and Clutch was definitely a no-go. He cringed at the thought of shooting the shit with him, considering their oil-and-water relationship.

An hour later, he finally drifted into a light sleep, dreaming as usual. But this time his dream was different—Nia wasn't there.

From the outer depths of space, Adam saw earth peacefully and quietly rotating in the darkness. He could see that electricity was thousands of years away from being discovered. The night side of the earth was cloaked in complete darkness. As he descended closer to the earth, he saw the clouds slowly slipping past the earth's quiescent surface. Occasional lightning strikes and thunderous rumbles were the only signs of activity he witnessed. The lands were pure, rich, and practically untouched by man. He continued spiraling downward toward the earth and noticed his form looked similar to his astral body. The closer he came to the earth, the more it coalesced and molded itself into a human shape. His energy body began to glow and throb before heading to southern Africa. In a flash, he saw himself slipping inside a fetus, comfortably being prepared inside its mother's cozy womb. As he nestled himself into his new home, his first physical movements were felt by his loving mother. He could sense her rubbing her stomach and acknowledging his arrival.

Suddenly, Adam was jarred awake by revving

blenders, clanking spoons, and cabinets slamming in the kitchen by Clutch.

Lying on his back, Adam glared hard at the popcorn ceiling. He let go a long sigh at Clutch for disturbing a rare and peaceful dream.

He pondered, What could it mean? Did it mean anything? Was it just a dream or was it another past life memory?

"Fucking thorn in my side," Adam mumbled for Clutch ruining the possibility of learning what the dream could have meant.

He sighed again while massaging his eye sockets. He'd have to let it go for now and prepare for the momentous day ahead. Looking at the time, he realized he put in three hours of sleep. Adam shuffled down the hall toward Jolon's bedroom. Before he got there, he saw Kojo was still up in his bedroom, still working on his laptop. Kojo's room was retrofitted into an office with a desk, a few plastic chairs, and blank white walls.

Adam gently knocked on Kojo's door before entering, "You're still up?"

"I rarely sleep," Kojo said, motioning for Adam to come in.

"You're up kinda early." said Kojo.

"Yeah, well, I didn't have a choice. Your baby bro is making smoothies and shit in the kitchen!" Adam cracked while scrunching his large frame into one of the small chairs in the room.

Kojo glumly stared back at Adam, "Not a smoothie, a protein shake."

"Yeaaaah, I've noticed. Dude carries protein bars around like Tic Tacs. What's up with that?"

"It is out of necessity. Being a product of the Ky's genetic modification, Clutch was designed to be a super human. Due to his extreme muscle mass and strength, Clutch burns through enormous amounts of calories. He has to supplement his protein to stay in his normal operating ranges. Though an insufficient amount of protein never takes away from his strength, it does affect the sharpness of his senses, which makes for a very unpleasant person to be around when he's running low."

"Ohooooooo, so that's why he could lift that 500 pound ky-ote," Adam said.

"Yes, Clutch is a near physical masterpiece with some emotional flaws. So, you don't want to push him. He doesn't feel fear, remorse, or regret like a normal person. His mind is the clearest during combat. Depending on the situation, Clutch's rage can peak in a split second. When he hits his peak level of agitation, his brain releases a chemical into his body that triggers a modified type of adrenaline, which fuels his combative rage against his opponent. When you see his eyes dilate, stand clear... You don't want no part of him like that."

"Damn, I did see that in his eyes during our fight!" Adam recalled.

"Yeah, it's a side effect of his genetic modification," said Kojo.

Just then, Clutch barged in on the conversation. He came in the room carrying a breakfast shake. He set the glass down in front of Kojo.

"Here you go big bro, load up," he said while his deep voice echoed around the slightly empty room.

He gave Adam a half nod before ducking his head to leave the room.

Gulping down Clutch's concoction, Kojo said, "Because of my modification, my mind burns incredible amounts of energy, so I need to eat more than a normal human even though I'm smaller."

"So, are you saying you were made in a lab?"

"No, we were born of a normal vaginal birth. We had a mother and father. In Africa, the Ky pretty much do what they want. No one cares what happens in

Africa, so it's a perfect breeding ground for the Ky's sinister experiments. They've been modifying a long line of our ancestors. In their super human program, I was to be the sacrificial twin for Clutch. They designed our gestation with Twin to Twin Transfusion Syndrome in the genes so that Clutch would continue to feed off me while we were both in our mother's womb. Usually, the smaller fetus dies, but I survived. Scar's orders were to keep Clutch and toss me into the incinerator. Being that he was the head geneticist at the time, I guess he somehow felt a connection with me as well as a responsibility. Scar took us both in. Clutch and I were never handed over to the Ky for cloning purposes. He smuggled us out of Africa into the States."

Kojo paused to drink more of Clutch's breakfast shake before continuing, "The majority of my modification came after my birth. Scar would often abduct me for the purposes of restoring my DNA and restoring much of my brain function lost in the womb. My strengths are having a fully functional pineal gland and twenty times the normal human brain capacity."

"Damn, bro, so you are telling me your whole purpose was to be food for your twin brother? Fuck, that's terrible... I don't even know what to say," Adam said, realizing his life was a party compared to Kojo and Clutch.

"From youth, we were guided by Scar. Once Clutch and I were of age to fully understand the Ky's plan, we vowed to be a thorn in their side. The Colony didn't form until that night after the Phoenix Lights and with the aid of the Native American nation. Although Scar was technologically leaps and bounds ahead of us, he didn't understand human emotions very well. Because of my intricate understanding of humans, I usually take the lead role in the Colony's affairs. For that reason, Scar was just as much of an assistant to me as I was to him."

Suddenly Adam understood Kojo and Clutch's animosity and drive to destroy the Ky, even down to Scar avenging his family's empire. It was highly personal—something Adam could fully understand, being that his personal driving factor was Nia. Adam sighed and took a moment to reflect. Here it was that the majority of the population was oblivious to aliens, yet there had been star battles going on for thousands of years right underneath their noses'.

Chapter 20

Walking out of the safe house, Adam felt the sun's rays lightly cascade over his body. He felt once again its immediate rejuvenating power, similar to the day outside of his apartment door after waking up from his first reincarnation nightmare. He had felt the sun many times before since he'd been back in Phoenix, and every time it felt amazing. Adam quickly noticed his skills were more increased, more focused and his thoughts were clearer. He felt physically stronger, more telekinetic, and more telepathic. Adam even recalled more details from his past lives, like fighting techniques, weapons used and battle strategies. Over the last couple of hours, his growing consciousness and sun exposure had evolved his abilities. He felt ready for whatever would come.

Piling back into the inconspicuous SUV, Adam, Kojo, and Clutch headed for the Hyatt in downtown

Phoenix. Sitting in the back seat, Adam stared out of the window in a listless daze, daydreaming about Nia. He thought of their time together back at their Zulu village before their tragic run-in with the Ky. He contemplated many of their other tragic circumstances together that the Ky were behind, including their last life together leading up to the Vietnam War and how it drove a deep, unrecoverable divide between them.

Adam remembered things like her favorite colors, her favorite poems, her favorite flowers, and her favorite smells. He could even replay her laugh in his head. He reminisced about intimate details during their different lifetimes together, like riding the rapids of Blyde River Canyon and walking the Legzira beaches of Morocco. Last but not least, he fantasized about her touch and how he loved touching her. He was haunted by all the lifetimes of finding Nia, and not ultimately ending up with her.

Adam realized at this moment that the goal was to become tuned to his highest potential in order to be right for his twin flame. In each of his lives, he was madly in love with Nia, but he hadn't reached his point of enlightenment to keep her. Perhaps fate had played a cruel joke on Adam and Nia, allowing them to find each other too soon. Today, Adam was completely in tune with Nia; he would at stop nothing short of death to be with her. If he ever had the opportunity again, he'd make it his business to love her forever—the right way. Adam knew that loving her was essentially loving himself; they were two halves of the same soul.

Adam's thoughts of Nia were interrupted when they arrived at their destination. They parked in a nearby underground car garage. With their BioMods on, they walked inconspicuously into the Phoenix hotel. The Hyatt Regency was a typical four star convention hotel nestled in the bustling downtown Phoenix. The inside of the hotel was cluttered with business suits briskly moving about. The hotel was decorated with earth-tone colors and soothing dark flooring. The tinted light and alternative jazz created a cool, calm lounge atmosphere. They walked into the large convention room, seating about 500. The lecture was already in progress. Speaking behind a wooden podium was Mark Green.

His smooth baritone voice captured every person's undivided attention. Clutch's eyes intimately probed every crevice of the room. He made detailed mental notes of all exits, security guards, cameras and even fire extinguishers. Adam and Kojo's eyes locked on Mark Green while taking a seat in the back of the auditorium.

Adam immediately nudged Kojo, "He has an aura, Mark's human. So far, so good."

Ten minutes into the lecture, Adam began to sense a presence.

Leaning over and whispering into Kojo's ear, Adam said, "Something doesn't feel right. Do you notice that at times Mark is speaking smooth and other times he's stuttering and stumbling over his words?"

Nodding his head with firm lips and an intense gaze, Kojo said, "Yeah, I noticed."

He continued, "I'm going to investigate and see what's going on in the astral realm. I'll need you and Clutch to watch over me, wake me if you see anything suspicious."

Clutch and Adam both nodded in agreement. Kojo put his shades on and comfortably shifted into a quiet, meditative state to begin his journey in the astral realm. Over the next few minutes, Clutch continued to scan the room with his security-minded eye. Adam's attention volleyed between Mark and Kojo.

Suddenly, Kojo started to lightly flinch and twitch in his meditative state. Minutes later, his flinches became more violent. Adam looked across to Clutch, sitting on the other side of Kojo.

"Does this normally happen," he whispered to Clutch.

Clutch shrugged in confusion, showing concern on his granite face.

Both men turned to watch Kojo more closely. Nervously, Adam and Clutch observed as Kojo's face began to contort. Kojo's condition continued to worsen.

When he began to gag and spasm, Clutch whispered, "We have to wake him."

"Good idea," Adam agreed.

They both lightly shook Kojo, to no avail. Kojo erupted in a torrent of seizure-like convulsions. Clawing welts started to appear across his BioMod body, face, arms and wrist. Clutch tried to coil Kojo's odd behavior by holding and restraining him, hoping to keep the audience from noticing.

Pressing the heels of his hands into his eye sockets, Adam said, "That's it, I'm going in!"

While Adam prepared to enter the astral realm, Clutch argued, "You are not ready, you might make it worse! Then I'd have the both of you to worry about!"

"I'm going in, he's in danger!" Adam hissed back.

Clutch, not having astral abilities himself, had no choice but to trust Adam.

"Fuck!" Clutch angrily whispered while glaring

back at Adam with his I-knew-this-was-a-bad-idea face.

Adam ignored Clutch's burning eye beams.

"I'm going in deep, It may be tough to wake me. You might have to use your Taser if you really need me out," he said.

Adam turned back to Kojo.

"Hold on, Kojo, I'm coming," he said as he prepared himself.

He put on his shades, leaned back in his seat, and slowed his heart beat. Adam sank into a meditative state and began his rescue mission into the astral realm.

As Adam's soul rose out of his body, he beheld an epic scene of paranormal proportion. On stage with Mark were clans of small grotesque demons swirling and engulfing him. Upon Adam's closer inspection, he saw a few leeches feeding off of Mark's energy, similar to the leeches at the base. He also saw demons whispering swaying thoughts into Mark's mind. His psychic gifts made it apparent to Adam that these demons were controlled by the Ky, and their job was to weaken and bend Mark to their agenda. Adam understood that in all likelihood these demons had been whispering wicked ideas into Mark's head for some time. Adam now knew Clutch was right, this was a bad idea. Like all in the audience, Mark had no awareness of their presence. They had no idea that a grim battle was taking place right under their noses. A few feet away from Mark, Adam spotted Kojo's astral body. Kojo was being ransacked, overwhelmed, and ravaged by a gang of marauding astral demons. The demons were small, about the size of a two-year-old child with semi-transparent skin. They possessed large heads and mouths with large teeth and fangs. Their heads had no visible eyes or ears. Their arms were thin with three long fingers and large claws attached.

Kano completely kept Adam in the dark about other demons such as these in the astral realm. Besides the occasional leech, Adam's previous visits were all positive, without any suffering or attacks.

Right away, Adam felt a flood of overwhelming emotions. Normally, he physically displayed his feelings through facial expressions, sweating, and hand movements. But in the astral realm, the rules were different. One's emotional state is shown through the colors of the astral body, like a spectrum, a mixture of colors in a rainbow. Experiencing upper, loving emotions causes astral vibrations to soar, emitting colors like violets and blues. Before now, those were the only emotions Adam had experienced in the astral realm. In this moment, the sight of vicious demons filled Adam's soul with fear and anxiety. These lower emotions dropped his vibrations, causing his astral body to emit the lower colors of energy: red and orange.

Adam's glowing, bright red astral body began to get the attention of the demons. He replayed Kojo's strict instructions when dealing with the astral realm, "Show no fear, it weakens you."

He looked at the audience, sitting oblivious to the astral clash. Sadly, some of the audience members were unknowingly preyed on by the beasts and leeches. His fellow human brothers and sisters were helpless fodder. He had to rise to the occasion.

Focusing in on Kojo's astral body, he could see it emitting a lowly red hue.

That ain't good, he thought.

His instincts told him Kojo didn't have long before he was permanently damaged. Adam began to get a grip on himself, putting his fear aside. He must save Kojo from being gorged on by the demons or the mission would fail. He powered up his confidence by thinking of Kojo, Mark, the audience, the world, and lastly Nia. His increasing confidence raised his vibration, shifting his astral body to display a powerful blue hue. The rise in emotion quickly got the attention of the marauding demons. A few of them broke off from gorging on Kojo and rushed Adam's way.

Adam's peeking confidence gave him the strength to face the incoming demons. Like his sparring session with Kano, he materialized with his mind his most comfortable weapon, a double sided Zulu Lklwa stabbing spear. Adam's evolved DNA allowed him to be connected with his past life as a Zulu warrior. Now he was ever more keenly aware of how to maneuver it. The spear was sixty inches long with a twelve inch, two sided blade at one end. With his weapon in hand, Adam darted to face the demons.

Chapter 21

Completely oblivious to the occult battle Adam was facing in the astral realm, Mark's audience continued listening to his speech. Adam focused his entire energy on the intense battle that lied before him. Like a star athlete, all his attention and focus was on the moment. Adam was completely aware that if he was not successful in conquering the demons attacking Kojo, this entire mission would fail. Even worse, he knew he may never unite with his twin flame, Nia. A nervous ripple cascaded through his soul.

With his weapon in hand, Adam swooped toward Kojo. Careful to not damage Kojo's astral body, he stabbed, swiped, and sliced at them, inching closer and closer to Kojo's rescue. His Zulu skill overwhelmed the small demons, sending them screaming and retreating back into the aether. The demons were no match for his well trained abilities. Knowing this, they began to retreat from their attack on Kojo.

Adam felt victory at the ends of his spear, reflecting in his rising astral colors. His confidence soared from the demons abandoning their attack on Kojo. However, unknown to Adam, a few of the demons regrouped, spotting his silver cord. This exposure gave the demons the location of Adam's physical body, leaving it vulnerable to attack. In retaliation, the Ky-controlled demons started to possess the minds of the security guards positioned near Adam's physical body. One by one, like a domino effect, the demons began to systematically possess the minds of every security guard in the convention hall. The possession rendered the guards as pawns, programmed to blindly execute the Ky's sinister plans. The demon-entities planted the seeds of annihilation and set the plan of elimination in motion; Adam and his group must be destroyed at all cost. In a trance-like state and with a mission to kill, the guards began to approach Adam's physical body as it sat meditating.

Clutch watched as the guards slowly started to pool around his crew. The gathering guards were of grave concern to Clutch, still unaware of their possessed state.

"This can't be good," mumbled Clutch as he gripped his weapon inside of his pocket.

Hoping to stay incognito, he decided against it. Any blast from his weapon would surely blow their cover. He slowly loosened his grip on his gun. Instead, he stood his large frame up to barricade the guards from Kojo and Adam.

Hiding behind his BioMod identity, Clutch curiously whispered to the security guard, "Is there a problem sir?"

Ignoring Clutch's question, the first blank-faced security guard raised his stun gun to attack Adam. Clutch's eyes grew with alertness. With a strong downward parry, he knocked the guard's stun gun out of his hand. Handling security guards was no problem for Clutch. However, handling them in a quiet, crowded room, while being the most wanted criminals in the world was a different story.

As difficult as the task may be, Clutch knew he must stop the guards from disrupting Adam's meditative state at all costs. Adam was his only hope of saving his older brother. A few more stone-faced security guards appeared, stun guns and batons in hand. Clutch now suspected they were possibly possessed. For many, the conundrum would be knowing for sure who was or wasn't possessed. For Clutch, it didn't matter. If it came down to it he would never hesitate to use deadly force to protect the Colony and its members. He was willing to accept the burden that came with taking a life. He was built for it. It was one of the reasons he had his name. He was always ready for battle, even if it was with innocent, possessed security guards. The colony must thrive at all cost.

After batting down the first security guard's stun gun, Clutch stomped and crushed it. Looking up, Clutch eyed even more approaching guards. The situation was quickly escalating and getting out of hand. The guards moved in, raising their stun guns. Clutch quickly reacted. He continued batting down and parrying the guards' guns. Still, the security guards continued their attack like mindless zombies. Their attempts to reach Adam were futile. Clutch was able to fend off each guard one by one; blocking, shoving, and pushing some to the ground. Despite his attempt to keep the fight quiet, the audience began to notice the commotion in the auditorium. A few of the audience members' heads began to swivel back, curiously observing the commotion. Realizing the single attack was no match for Clutch's might, the possessed guards attempted another avenue of attack. In unison, the security guards all decided to rush Clutch at once. They attempted to shove him out of the way while another guard attempted to shock Adam with a stun gun. A man strong enough to lift a

500 pound Ky-ote with one hand had no problem with raging possessed guards. Holding off the rushing guards with one arm, he calculated a timely blow with his other arm. With one massive looping punch, he cracked the guard trying to attack Adam. The guard crumbled to the ground and was out cold. After dropping the guard, he turned his attention to the other attackers. He went all out—hook, jab, right cross, left cross, and uppercut to the other possessed guards. Bone-crunching sounds bellowed throughout the neighboring rows. One by one, they dropped, each hitting the ground with a thud. One guard actually shot Clutch with a Taser, but 50,000 volts weren't nearly enough to bring him down. He unpinned the prongs and continued his defense.

The snapping sounds of the stun gun and Tasers alerted more audience members to the melee. Many turned around and witnessed bodies sprawled out. The rough commotion began to panic the crowd. They gasped and cupped their hands over their mouths at the sight. It didn't matter that the guards' physical bodies were stopped; the persistent astral demons were still present. They changed up their strategy. While Clutch was distracted with the other guards, the demons started possessing people in the crowd. The audience members being stressed, shocked, scared, or panicked were easier targets for the demons. The demons began attacking again in their new physical forms. Some members came with purses, some with mace, others with knives.

Mark halted his lecture. "Uh, can we get more security please... looks like we have a disturbance in the back row that is getting out of hand," he said while peering into the back row with his hands shielding the light.

A swoosh was heard as the entire crowd shuffled and turned to the ruckus.

Being disguised by the BioMod, the other members in the crowd were completely unaware that the epic battle in the back was comprised of the world's three most wanted fugitives. Clutch continued brawling with the possessed. As Clutch knocked out one possessed soul, another came forward. He'd have to fight the entire auditorium before it was over.

"Whomp, whomp," warned Clutch's BioMod; the power source was running dangerously low. All the motion from the melee had severely drained the battery. Staying any longer could reveal their true identities at any moment. As the BioMod's alarm continued to sound, he knew the mission had utterly failed. There was no way now to make contact with Mark. He had warned them that this was a bad idea. The more the 'I told you so,' theme grew in his head, the harder his punches got. He had to get out of there.

In the midst of the commotion, he decided to get Adam and Kojo to safety. Once he saw a slight break in the action, he turned to Kojo and Adam. Careful to not disturb Adam's meditative state, Clutch gently grabbed the both of them. He put them over his shoulder and briskly walked out to the parking garage. A few possessed audience members and reawakened security guards stumbled behind him. Just as he was placing Adam and Kojo in the SUV he heard the parking lot doors fly open. The possessed henchmen pointed in his direction. Clutch looked up and eyed an audience member and security guard in pursuit. He sighed and continued securing Adam and Kojo in the SUV. First he latched Adam in the front seat. He then quickly moved to the back seat and secured Kojo. Sliding across the hood, he sprung to start the SUV. Clutch's large frame crinkled the hood, sending an echo throughout the garage. By this time, the guard and audience member approached on both sides of the vehicle. The audience member opened the SUV door on the passenger side and pointed his gun toward Adam in the front seat. No longer stun guns or Tasers, the man from the audience was wielding a semi-automatic Glock. With his weapon already set to stun, Clutch quickly fired upon the audience member on the passenger side. "Bang bang," went Clutch's weapon, dropping the audience member to the ground. Clutch then quickly swiveled and fired on the guard who was approaching him,

"Bang bang," Clutch's weapon knocked the guard unconscious, but not before he was able to fire a few rounds into the SUV. He nervously checked on his team. Relieved that Adam and Kojo were okay, he now understood that as long as Adam and Kojo were in the astral realm, possessed humans would continue to come. He knew that Adam and Kojo's silver cords were connected to their physical bodies in the astral realm. All the demons had to do was follow their cords and possess any nearby human. They could theoretically continue this process indefinitely, as long as Adam and Kojo were in the astral realm. They no longer had cover, leaving them with no way to hide. This was the worst imaginable outcome: Clutch's nightmare.

After firing on the guards, Clutch jumped in the SUV and sped out of the garage, smashing through the parking arm gate. "Bang bang," Clutch heard. He looked at his rear view and saw pursuing guards firing. He heard bullets zooming past his ears and hitting the back of his SUV. "Crash," a bullet flew through the back window, leaving a spiraling webbed crack.

As Clutch fought with every essence of his being to protect Adam and Kojo, Adam was still in a deep focused meditation. While bullets were being flung past his physical body, he continued his own battle in the astral realm. Now that Kojo's astral body was clear of demons, Adam inspected his astral state. He could see Kojo was very weak. Adam knew he must somehow raise Kojo's energy vibration. If he didn't, Kojo's astral body could become separated from his physical body, leaving him to aimlessly wonder the astral realm or reincarnate.

"Kojo... Kojo," Adam called telepathically.

While waiting for a response, Adam began to feel a tightness in his astral body. He noticed he had a reddish line wrapped around his body, starting with his neck down. He could feel its suffocating grip around his neck. His sides ached from its crushing pressure. At second glance, Adam could see the line was more of a whip, and it belonged to a goliath of a demon beast. Adam's astral body surged with a high bandwidth of fear, hesitation, shock, and awe at the sight of the beast. The demon was at least four times his height. It was humanoid in form with bulky shoulders, arms, and legs. The demon had no fingers, but large talons for claws. It had two large, sharp horns extending back out of its head, and slanted red eyes. Its face was a grotesque mixture between goat and lion. This must be one of the shadow demons Kojo warned him about. Further wrapping Adam in its weapon, the demon slowly pulled him closer. The weapon was starting to possess and control Adam's soul. His astral color plummeted, emitting the lower reds, a clear sign he was being drained of his essence. With too much of this, Adam knew he could be sent back to the aether.

The beast pulled him closer. Now face to face with the devilish shadow beast, Adam felt its menacing evil. Its eyes seared Adam with malevolent hate.

It telepathically taunted Adam, "We will feast on your soul!"

A high-octane rage spread itself throughout Adam's astral body. Verbal assaults were always the catalysts that caused Adam to explode against threatening forces. Perhaps a ramification of being homeless for a big part of his life, he always found a way to deal with threats. Surviving with nothing to live for molded Adam into a machine that could throw caution to the wind.

Recalling Kojo's words to have no fear, Adam thought, *Fuck this*!

He fueled himself by the demon's threat and burst out of the beast's restraint.

"We will have to see about that!" Adam responded with rage. He swiveled free and eyed the shadow goliath. He took a second or two to formulate his strike. Rematerializing his Zulu spear, Adam flew directly at the heart of the shadow beast. With lightning speed, he swiped, struck, and stabbed at the shadow demon, knocking it back. However, the beast responded with a mighty strike of its own. Adam quickly created his version of a Zulu shield in time to deflect the demon's strike. He turned the battle to his advantage by throwing a series of spears at the demon's center. The beast moaned as the spears penetrated. It attempted to latch a hold on Adam again. It drew back with its muscular arm—whip attached—and lashed at Adam. Adam then countered the demon's attack by slicing at the demon's forward-striking whip. He followed up with more strikes to the beast's center. The beast howled again and began to retreat. Adam rushed closer to the beast with more strikes.

"Those little demons are tougher than you!" Adam telepathically taunted while he continued stabbing, slicing, and jabbing at the beast.

Adam's momentary victory was not void of consequence. While he was engaged in battle with the first shadow demon, he didn't notice a second was approaching. Just as he was about to strike his last blow to send the first beast into the aether, the second beast latched its whip around Adam's neck. He felt tightness in his astral throat. It was the same painful choking sensation he felt earlier. Now that the beast had a firm grasp around Adam's neck, it easily pulled and yanked his astral body backward. He began to feel his head ache from the suffocating effects of the whip. No breath was necessary in the astral realm, but Adam knew the stifling affects were being passed on to his physical body. While the new beast choked Adam, the other beast recovered. It then whipped its weapon around the lower portion of Adam's body.

"Who'ssss tough nowwwwww," hissed the beast.

Now both shadow demons pulled and tugged at Adam in an effort to possess, control, and feast on his soul.

He could telepathically hear the beasts clamoring for his soul, "Yesss, thissss one has the energy of a godddd."

Apparently, a soul like Adam's fetched quite a big bounty in the astral realm. Meanwhile, the smaller beasts were back gorging on Kojo. A few of them glided over and began feasting on Adam's astral body. Adam twisted and turned, attempting to fight his way free from the demons' binding whips.

Fuck... I got myself in some shit now! Adam thought as he felt himself drifting away.

The battle was getting the best of him. As he was fading, he heard that familiar voice, Nia's voice, "Wake up Adam... Wake up!"

While Adam struggled to keep his soul in the astral realm, Clutch was speeding away from the parking garage, avoiding gun fire. He glanced back at Kojo and Adam, and noticed the welts on their faces and their bodies convulsing. His heart was pounding; he was starting to feel that he was now out of his league. Since Adam and Kojo's astral bodies revealed the location of their physical bodies, he had no chance of hiding. In a sense, their bodies were like GPS units, subjecting Clutch to a form of constant surveillance, something he wasn't used to. Worse yet, because their location was known, the demons could possess any human close to their vicinity. If anybody else had brought this much attention to him or the Colony, they'd be dead by now. But his brother was his only weakness. If the Colony failed, it most likely would be due to Clutch's sympathetic heart toward his brother. "Boom boom boom," the back window was shattered from a spray of bullets. The possessed security guards were in a car behind them. They fired again, "Boom boom boom". Clutch was now in a high-speed chase. He turned his weapon up to full force. Knowing everybody was counting on him, Clutch began to return fire. He knew the likelihood of success was slim to none at this point. His only hope was to avoid capture as long as possible in order to give Adam enough time to rescue Kojo. With his large frame scrunched in the seat, he weaved in and out of traffic, avoiding gun fire.

Meanwhile, simultaneously in the astral world, the sound of Nia's voice calmed Adam. He thought of Nia. He'd give anything to be with her now. In this dismal moment of his soul being pulled apart, Adam began to give up. He decided that if this was it, he wanted to spend his last moments thinking of Nia.

God—if I could just see her, he thought. The realization of the fantasy brought him to the obvious— none of it would be possible if he didn't deal with these demons. The very thought of being with Nia began to energize him, reminding him of his purpose. He slowly started to raise his astral vibration. He went from red, to blue, to violet. Thriving at the higher spectrum, powered by his love for Nia, he began to fully awaken. Kojo was right, vibrating with love gives you the power of a god. Fully conscious and aware, he summoned enough energy to spin free, unwinding his horizontally stretched body.

After freeing himself, he grabbed both whips and wrapped them around his arms. With intense thought and focus he began to imagine himself draining the shadow demon's energy. As he thought it, the beast's energy began to draw into his body, weakening both shadow goliaths, a small trick he learned from Kano. The beasts tried to fight back, to no avail. Adam, with thoughts of his twin flame, was too powerful. He continued to absorb their energies, getting stronger and stronger. The demons twisted and squirmed during Adam's energy drain. Eventually they were no more, being dispersed back into the aether. Adam quickly flew back over to tend to Kojo. Vibrating with the higher frequencies of love, Adam had no problem dispatching the smaller demons who were foraging on Kojo's astral body. Strikes by his double-sided spear quickly sent them back into the aether. Adam poured some of the residual energy he took from the shadow demons into Kojo. Kojo's astral body was emitting the lower red frequencies, but showing signs of recovering. Satisfied with the state of Kojo's recovering astral body, Adam rushed over to finish saving Mark's mind from being corrupted.

As Adam fought the demons off Mark's astral body, he still had no idea of what troubles Clutch was facing in the physical world. Clutch was in a high-speed car chase, being hotly pursued by the possessed security guards. To make matters worse, his BioMod was still warning of its low battery.

One guard drove while the other hung out the window, shooting at Clutch's SUV. Ducking from the gun shots, Clutch was barely able to see as he weaved in and out of traffic. Clutch toiled with the idea of either waking Adam to be a side gunner or continue letting him help Kojo. He felt the disposition of a rock and a hard place while reaching for mental straws to solve his circumstances. The whole of the Colony had come down to this.

Clutch took a hard left and drifted around a building into one-way traffic. Motorist wildly swerved and honked while Clutch wheeled the SUV in and out of the oncoming traffic. He checked his rearview mirror; the guards were still in high pursuit. Shifting his eyes back to the road, he was caught off guard by a residential moving truck coming his way. He franticly weaved trying to avoid the truck. He turned rapidly, getting t-boned by another car. The pursuing security guards pulled close enough to fire a few rounds into Clutch's driver side door. He ducked down to avoid the gun fire. The shots missed him, ricocheting and hitting Kojo in the side. Clutch sped off in the opposite direction of his shooters, burning rubber and fishtailing away. He hauled off down the street before being rammed by another group of possessed guards, sending the SUV rolling over.

Adam was still oblivious to the plight Clutch faced in the physical world. In the astral realm, Adam had no problem dispatching the smaller demons with his Zulu spear. He finished off the smaller demons and turned his attention to the last demon, who was whispering persuading thoughts into Mark's mind. This was the demon that had been assigned to him, to sway his thoughts, and turn them to the Ky's agenda. Not knowing these thoughts were from a demon, Mark would live by them and follow them to be his own. Once they set in, there would be no convincing Mark otherwise. This was exactly what the Ky wanted. This demon was non-humanoid. It was shaped like a billowing dark cloud, engulfing Mark's astral body. The demon's head was located on the top of the cloud. Its eyes were red, with a slight upward slant. It was keenly aware of Adam's presence, but offered no attack or resistance to him. Its wicked eyes just glared down on him in silence. Adam studied the oddly shaped demon. This was the moment. Destroying this demon would bring him a step closer to Nia. He raised his spear and dashed to annihilate the demon. Suddenly, he felt himself being yanked back into his body.

Adam awoke to a scene of flying glass, metal crashing, and a tumbling SUV. While the vehicle was rolling, Adam's seat belt snapped, tossing him. The SUV eventually came to a stop, resting on its back while nosey onlookers stared, cupping their hands over their mouths in shock. When Adam came to full awareness, he heard his BioMod warning him of a low battery. He had no idea how much time his BioMod had left. Any minute he may be exposed for who he really was. He pulled himself off the ground, moving to his hands and knees. He looked at his hands and could see the singed flesh from his clash in the astral realm. His wounds from the astral battle and car crash began to throb. He felt his neck and ribs burning. He felt the smoldering road rash bruises from being tossed out of the vehicle. Adam eyed the SUV and saw Kojo's body dangling inside, still latched to his seat belt with blood trickling down his face. He also spotted Clutch lying unconscious inside the SUV. To make matters worse, he also heard Clutch's BioMod warning of low battery.

Gathering himself, Adam crawled back into the SUV to first attend to Kojo. Upon closer inspection, he saw Kojo was badly bleeding and grimly hurt from the crash. Using his telepathic powers, he reached to touch Clutch to get a fill of what had just transpired. Adam was able to pull from Clutch's subconscious mind the events leading up to the crash.

He saw the melee in the auditorium, the high speed car chase, Kojo being shot, and the crash.

"Shit!" Adam yelled.

The information also told him they were still in imminent danger. Adam's heartbeat picked up. One minute he was fighting for his life in the astral realm and now he would have to fight for his life in the physical world. He swiveled his head around, looking for any approaching guards or civilians. He saw two security guards getting out of their car, coming his way. He scrambled for the glove box; he knew Clutch had a 9mm hand gun inside. He snatched the gun and checked its rounds. As he desperately crawled out of the mangled car, the two security guards began firing at him. He crouched and fired back while taking cover. The first guard laid down cover fire, and the other inched closer to the SUV. Now the closest guard began to lay down his cover fire and the first guard began his approach. All the while, they laid a constant barrage of bullets in Adam's direction. In a flash, Adam looked under the car, dropped to the ground and fired, hitting both security guards. "Bang bang bang bang," perfect shots to the chest put them both down. He didn't actually want to kill the guards. He also knew there was no time to negotiate.

Just when he thought he was free to begin Kojo and Clutch's rescue, he took on more fire. Apparently the original chasing security guards who shot Kojo were back. "Bang bang bang," the guard was firing and approaching Adam fast. He continued to scrunch down and avoid the gunfire. He heard the bullets flying past his head and piercing the SUV. Lucky for Adam, the guard ran out of ammo. Adam popped his head from cover, fired two rounds and put him down. Now Adam was out of ammo and another guard was approaching and firing. Adam took cover. Gun forward and running toward Adam, the guard laid down a slew of bullets to pin Adam in his location. Clutch began to come to. Still groggy, he bolted into action by unbuckling himself out of his seat. He flopped to the ground with a thud. Clutch patted his body, desperately looking and feeling for his weapon.

He spotted his gun outside his SUV about seven feet away. He began crawling on his elbows to his firearm.

Adam saw the guard was still firing and Clutch was exposed. He had to think fast or Clutch was dead. Out of bullets, Adam franticly looked about the scene for an object he could telekinetically throw. Without Nia, he knew he could throw no more than his own weight. He looked up the street, down the street, inside the car, but there was nothing light enough for him to throw. With no rocks or gravel in his vicinity, as a long shot he tried to telekinetically toss the guard. He concentrated. Too late, the security guard was upon Clutch, gun raised and finger on the trigger.

While shaking his head and wide eyed, Adam slowly mouthed, "Noooo... not like this!"

Suddenly, the security guard's face started to contort, twitch, and convulse. His body oddly twisted and bent as if something was fighting from within. Then he calmed, grinned, and crouched next to Clutch while slowly bringing his gun down from aim.

In a strained voice he said, "You don't have much time. You will have to break the slab in the kitchen. There you will find what you need. I have equipment to charge your BioMods. That will buy you more time. Once you do that, I have a secret lab inside the Grand Canyon. There you will find other Ky willing to help. The equipment underneath the kitchen slab will give you the location, and tell them Scar sent you."

Clutch cleared his vision and stuttered, "Scccaar...?"

"Yes, I will contact you later," said the security guard whose body was newly possessed by Scar.

"Take the security guard's car... hurry," he said while pointing to the guard's still-running silver Taurus.

Instantly, the security guard began to contort again before falling to the ground.

He came to a foggy daze, "Wha...what... happened... Where am I?"

Scar's physical body was dead in the human world, but his soul was alive and well in the astral realm. He'd been watching over his group after the incident at the bar. Scar was able to attack the possessing demons who were controlling the security guard's mind. Taking advantage of the backdoor built into humans, he took control of the security guard's body and mind long enough to deliver an all-important message to Clutch.

Adam scrambled from his cover position to Clutch.

"You good, bro?" he asked, catching his breath.

Clutch grunted and flew past Adam to Kojo's side of the car.

Adam took another glance at Kojo and panicked, "Oh shit Clutch, Ko...."

"Shut the fuck up, no names!" Clutch quickly hissed as he motioned to the gathering crowd.

Adam gave a half nod and whispered, "Was that who I think it was?"

"We have to go...now! We are still in danger," Clutch yelled, ignoring Adam's question while unbuckling Kojo.

Clutch delicately took Kojo out of the SUV. Carrying Kojo past the increasingly nosey crowd, he bolted to the security guard's car. Adam quickly followed. Clutch gently buckled Kojo in behind the driver's seat. He probed the crowd to see if any more possessed souls were following. Jumping in, he and Adam sped from the scene.

"What the fuck... Was that Scar?" Adam asked while staring at Clutch in disbelief.

Clutch again ignored Adam's question and continued focusing on their getaway.

"Clutch! Was that Scar?" Adam asked louder.

"Yeah... that was him," Clutch responded while

his eyes combed the roads.

"Bro, but how? I saw him die back at the bar!"

"Look, there is no death okay. You saw Scar's body die, not his essence. When the Ky genetically modified humans, they left a back door open. If the human gets stressed enough, they can get possessed. It's another reason why they keep everybody stressed and the planet is so fucked up," Clutch screamed, becoming more annoyed at Adam.

"Ohhh... shit. If they can do that, then how do I know you haven't been taken over? Or how do you know that I haven't been taken over?" Adam asked.

"I still don't know about you," Clutch yelled as he glared at Adam clearly irritated by his questions.

Calming himself, Clutch said, "Kojo and I are good. Thankfully, Scar modified our DNA so that they couldn't repossess our bodies. As for the rest of humans, the Ky can take them over whenever they become stressed enough, or have low consciousness or low spirituality. That is how Scar's essence was able to take over that guard's body. Now I'd imagine you are somewhat safe because of your evolved DNA, or they would have taken you over by now."

"Can Kano be taken over?" Adam asked.

"I'm sure he can, his DNA wasn't modified like

ours," Clutch responded with growing irritation.

"Ohhh... okay... okay," Adam said, nodding and appearing content with his understanding.

"But how sure..." Adam began.

"Kill the fuckin' questions. Now is not the time to explain all this shit to you! Kojo already went over this with you at the corn fields. We got other shit to worry about right now!" Clutch yelled at the top of his lungs, with fully dilated eyes.

Knowing Clutch was becoming unstable, Adam backed off. Besides, Clutch was right, Kojo did go over a bit of this with him. Adam remembered Kojo explaining how the Ky and their goons could bend and take over human minds. He thought it was theory, or at worst they could just insert light ideas into the mind. Never did he imagine that a possession was akin to a remote high jacking. Earlier, he'd telepathically read Clutch's subconscious and saw the guards attacking him in the auditorium. Now it all made even more sense to him. Possession was real. Over the next couple of minutes, Adam sat in silence, raking over the magnitude of the day's colossal events.

After a few seconds, Adam looked back and checked on Kojo.

"How is he doing?" asked Clutch.

Adam sighed before facing Clutch.

"He is unconscious. Looks like he's been shot but I think the bullet went in and back out. We have to get him help; he's bleeding badly. And the demons may still be feeding on his soul in the astral realm," Adam informed with great compassion.

Chapter 22

The getaway car was a 2000 silver Ford Taurus. While franticly driving, Clutch reached under the seat, then the visor and the car's travel compartments. He found nothing. Not being satisfied with an empty search, he turned his attention to the glove box. His eyes swiveled over and he hammered the glove box with his large fist, popping it open. His eyes widened on the discovery of a phone. Satisfied with his find, he immediately grabbed the phone and tossed it out of the car, hoping to lessen their chances of being tracked, despite the traceable Kojo conundrum.

Adam watched, in close observation of Clutch's getaway game. Clutch drove for two miles, during of which his head inspected every observable angle. Ensuring a clean getaway he looked frontward, backward, left, and right. After spotting an almost identical Ford Taurus, his eyes popped with delight at the rare jewel of an opportunity.

Perfect timing, just what I needed, Clutch thought at the sight of the car.

He turned the car into a small restaurant parking lot, screeching and scraping its undercarriage at the entrance, stopping behind the matching silver Taurus. He kept the engine going while he took a moment to study the new Taurus.

Nodding with a crocked half smile he mumbled, "Yeah, this will do."

He wheeled his vehicle into the parking space next to the silver Taurus. Slamming the car into park, Clutch flew out of the vehicle with it still rocking back and forth from the violent stop. He crept to the back of the similar Taurus, reached in his pocket, pulled out an all-purpose knife and began to loosen the license plate. He started with the look-alike Taurus, then he moved to the getaway Taurus. After switching both license plates, he slipped back into his car and called 9-1-1 on his secure phone.

Operator: "911 what's your emergency?"

Disguising his voice in a high pitched manner, Clutch said, "There is a silver Ford Taurus that I think was involved in that shooting in downtown Phoenix. The license plate number is Arizona RTY-456. Hurry

Hanif Burt

these guys have guns."

Clutch hung up the phone and focused his attention on his BioMod. His brow bent and his eyes narrowed as he checked the status. Eyeing twelve percent battery life left, Clutch glanced over at Adam's BioMod to check its status. Seeing ten percent left on Adam's device, Clutch altered one of the dials on the device. The BioMod flickered Adam's image into a completely different identity. Before he was a middle-aged white man with grey hair. His new identity was a younger Caucasian male, mid-twenties, with blue eyes and blonde hair. The change dropped Adam's BioMod battery life down to seven percent. Once Adam's transformation was complete, Clutch also changed his BioMod's appearance. He changed from an older Native American man into a Caucasian male. He went with a slightly older, mid-thirties male with black hair and hazel eyes. Next, he altered Kojo's image as well.

"That will buy us a bit of time until we can get to the safe house and recharge the BioMods," said Clutch.

He threw the car in reverse and sped out of the restaurant parking lot, driving south toward the safe house. Clutch's eyes bounced from the road to the rearview window and back to the road, checking to see if his distraction trick worked. He hoped the license plate switch would buy him at least five to ten minutes.

No heat as of yet. So far, so good, he thought.

He turned the rearview mirror semi-vertical so he could keep an eye on both Kojo and his rear view. Clutch's face bore the intensity of a focused brawling lion. Adam knew this wasn't the time to bother Clutch with questions about what to do. He also knew that Clutch was furious about all that had happened; he hadn't spoken a word to him. He knew that anything he may say could agitate and set Clutch off. Not to mention he could see Clutch's eyes were dilated, a sign of the modified adrenaline surging throughout his body. He'd better tread carefully. Adam sat silently, facing forward, while Clutch continued the getaway. Not quite sure of what to expect out of Clutch in this situation, Adam decided to settle his heart by staring at the distant South Mountain. No matter what was happening, constant staring at South Mountain could always settle Adam's nerves. He locked his eyes on nature's peaceful megalith and besieged himself with thoughts. He thought of the long, peaceful drive along the foot of the mountain before he met Kojo and Clutch.

Oh shit... Kojo, Adam thought while he snapped out of his lucid daydream.

He crawled in the back seat, took off his shirt, and

started putting pressure on Kojo's wound. He positioned the shirt between Kojo and the seat belt so that it applied constant pressure to the bullet's exit wound. He was still unresponsive. Adam checked Kojo's pulse and noticed it was still very strong. He knew his physical body was stable, but Adam got the eerie feeling that Kojo's astral body was weak.

The damn demons might still be on him, he thought.

Adam wanted to go back in the astral realm to make sure, but now was not the time, especially not being quite on the same page with Clutch. Nonetheless, Adam's caring and timely gesture cracked Clutch's angry shell. Clutch knew Adam's attentive nurturing of his bleeding brother was genuine and necessary. Clutch knew timely moves such as this were what made teams work well together. However, Adam would have to do much more to win over his affection.

Clutch torqued the mirror a bit to put Adam in his view. "Didn't I say this was a bad idea... huh... didn't I?" Clutch yelled while angrily cutting Adam from the corner of his eyes.

From Clutch's loud bark, Adam knew it wasn't the time to justify his wanting to meet with Mark Green. Ultimately, Nia drove his decision to meet Mark, something he was sure Clutch wouldn't give a shit about.

Trying to be as optimistic as possible, Adam said in a calm voice, "Yeah, you did say that, bro, you did, but at least we made contact with Scar. All may not be lost."

"At the possible expense of my brother?" Clutch questioned with a ragged frown. "Like I said, I'm not new to this, rookie. I said we should lay low and live to fight another day!"

He sighed, "I don't understand my brother's obsession with yo' punk ass. I bet we can go into any one of the wisdom cultures right now and pull someone else that has your skills and is more trustworthy than you—the Cherokees, the Yogis, hell even the Zulus."

Adam hissed and cracked an arrogant half smile, "Well, it's a good thing you're not in charge."

Double taking at Adam and shaking his head, Clutch bit his lip while his nostrils flared like a charging bull. He fought back his anger at Adam while pounding on the driver's side door. The pressure of the blow and his large fist split an eight-inch crack across the panel.

He gathered himself before he boastfully continued, "Let me make this clear, you fuckin' pussy, if something happens to my brother... we're fucked! And who is gonna synthesize the counter agent? Yo' dumb ass?"

Adam, trying to keep on the light side of things, said, "Kojo is going to be fine; the bullet went straight through. No vital organs were damaged and his pulse is still super strong. Plus, we reconnected with Scar and the other Ky will help us!"

"So, you're a fuckin' doctor now?" Clutch asked with a deep, low-toned sarcasm.

He banged his large fist against the dash. The brooding blow left a large, webbed imprint.

Not waiting for Adam to respond, Clutch continued with a firm tone, "You don't get it! Them Ky gives two fucks about us humans, they ain't like Scar. Scar was fighting to win his family's empire back; it made sense for him to fight this battle. Why would the other rogue Ky risk their necks for humans? They got nothin' to gain with us."

Adam's limited knowledge was no match for Clutch's insight. He might have gotten the better of Clutch back at the bar, but on political points he was getting his ass kicked. Not having an answer, Adam sighed and directed his vision back into South Mountain.

Clutch was right, attempting to connect with Mark Green was an altogether bad idea, Adam thought.

He would have to add this one to a long list of life's regrets.

Adding insult to injury, Clutch continued with narrowed eyes, "To be honest, the fucking Colony has fell all because of you. You showed up and everything went to hell. Scar, the Colony, and now my brother. I tell you what—something happens to my brother, you and I gonna touch hands."

Taking his eyes off the road to look at Adam, Clutch said with contorted anger, "Without my brother or the Colony, I have nothing else to live for but to beat yo' ass. Fuck the bar, homie, this time 'round I'm gonna go all in on that ass."

Adam drew silent, and started to stew in the backseat. He knew this wasn't just Clutch's anger talking. This was how he truly felt about him. However, at this point Adam didn't care. Clutch may have been right about the mission, but Adam felt he deserved more respect for trying to save Kojo. After all, he did risk his neck fighting malevolent demons to save Clutch's own brother. He didn't have to, but he tried to help, and this was the thanks he got? Adam replayed the supernatural astral realm events in his head. He thought of the fights with the demons, the leaches, the demons engulfing Kojo, the demons whispering into Mark's ear, and the audience members being unsuspectedly fed upon. The memory fueled an explosion of anger in the pit of Adam's stomach. Not to mention that threats never sat well with his soul. His brow crinkled at the reminiscent thoughts. His nostrils started to flare with each deep breath. Clutch was getting out of line, and he was going to let him know about it.

Adam's breathing picked up, a granite frown slid across his face before he said, "Number one, I went in trying to save your brother—risking my neck. I literally went through hell! You best respect that. Number two, I just about completed my part until I got pulled back into my body from yo' fucked up driving."

Adam knew this wasn't the time or place, but something about Clutch just rubbed him the wrong way. He felt it was time to set him straight and the more he thought about it the more angry he became.

To make matters worse, Clutch continued barking verbal assaults, "You went through hell? Like that is supposed to mean something to me. You went through hell because you made a fucked up choice in the first place. And now you want credit for going? Get the fuck out of here."

"You got one more time to threaten me..." Adam scolded while shaking his head and clenching his teeth.

Adam paused, "You know what, fuck that, we can get down on general principle, I'm 'bout sick of yo' big ass!" yelled Adam.

Before Clutch could respond he made an unexpected hard left turn. Adam's unbuckled body was thrown up against the backseat car door, causing him to bump his head against the window. Adam's eyes darted to Clutch to prepare for what may happen next. Clutch flew into an empty commercial business parking lot, chassis bottoming out at the entrance again. He headed for the back corner of the business park. Not slowing down, he rolled over speed bumps. He beelined the car to the back building. He brought the car to a violent stop, slamming it into park; so violent that the car again rocked with motion. He got out of the car and sprinted to Kojo's side of the car. Adam carefully and cautiously watched Clutch as his heart rate rose. Clutch opened Kojo's side door, unbuckled Kojo, and carefully took him out of the car. Carrying Kojo like a swaddled baby, he ran inside a building called Corequest Medical Research. Sitting wide-eyed in the back seat, Adam's eyes swiveled to follow Clutch.

Perhaps he is getting help for Kojo, Adam thought.

He slowly got out of the car, hesitant and unsure. He checked all directions to see if anybody was looking. Once clear, he began trotting inside the building to follow after Clutch. He walked into the building's waiting room and noticed an empty receptionist desk, no activity in the waiting room, and no sign of Clutch. The waiting room was well decorated with couches, chairs and magazines neatly placed on the coffee table. He walked to the coffee table and thumbed through a few of the magazines. The titles were all concerning genetic research. He walked to the receptionist desk and noticed the switchboard all lit up.

If all calls are routed to voicemail, it's after-hours; no one must be here, he thought.

Adam poked his head around the corner and could see one door that led to the back of the building.

Clutch must be in there, he thought.

He tried the door and found it locked. Adam raked his hand through his afro before he lightly knocked on the door. No answer. He nervously walked back toward the entrance door and looked outside. The parking lot was completely empty as far as he could see. Even in moments of crazy franticness, Clutch knew how to stay hidden. He was thankful for the muscle-bound oaf's ability in that sense. He must have found a way to get Kojo some help. Despite the stress of the situation at hand,

Adam sensed a good energy about the place. He couldn't quite place why, but he definitely felt relieved to be here. Was it because Kojo may be getting help, or that perhaps Clutch may have a handle on the situation? Or could it be the exposure to the Arizona setting sun? He truly didn't know, but whatever it was, it left him feeling complete and whole. His heart beat started to calm. He thought perhaps this was another stronghold of the Colony.

Maybe they have some super alien technology to fix up Kojo, he thought.

"I'll just take a seat and wait it out," Adam mumbled to himself.

He casually strolled to the waiting room and plopped down on the sofa. With nervous anxiety, he waited while thumbing through magazines. His thoughts drifted to Kojo, and how important he was to saving humanity. If Kojo didn't make it, he wondered if the Ky in the Grand Canyon would help. Or would they dismiss them like Clutch said? All that would be left to free humanity would be him and Clutch.

Fuck that, he's a son of a bitch to deal with, Adam thought.

Would that even be possible, given the heavy friction in their relationship, pondered Adam. Sure, he wanted to put Clutch's big mouth to rest, but who was he kidding? He needed Clutch, especially right now. Clutch was all he had.

He now knew why Winston Chase wanted him dead, and why he used him to flush out Kojo and Clutch. The CEO had no chance of finding the Colony with Scar secretly guiding the movement. The CEO knew with Adam's natural abilities, he'd have a much better chance of finding the Colony. And so Adam did, satisfying Winston Chase's agenda to kill two birds with one stone. Adam thought if the mission failed, then he helped make the CEO's plan successful. In a sense, Clutch was right. Adam was single handedly responsible for bringing down the Colony. From that perspective, he understood Clutch's anger toward him. He could understand why Clutch didn't trust him entirely. He had to do something incredible to ultimately convince Clutch he wasn't a spy.

"Whooomp, whooomp," Adam's deep thought was broken up by his BioMod blaring. It was warning him it had three percent battery life left. Ten minutes went by, and his BioMod was down to one percent. Adam got a bit more anxious, not knowing what to do if his cover got blown. His palms began to sweat and his throat began to thicken. Then Adam's attention was diverted to voices picking up inside the locked room. Easing off the couch, Adam began to scrunch and creep closer and closer to eavesdrop.

"Whomp, whomp, whoooooomp," suddenly his BioMod began to beep louder and louder before it finally failed all together. There stood Adam in his person. Knowing security cameras would be watching, he began to panic. He looked down at his BioMod to see if there was anything he could do.

"Crash!" Clutch kicked the locked door open, shattering its hinges. He bee lined straight to Adam and grabbed him by the throat. Clutch's highly dilated pupils dialed in on Adam. His lips tightly peeled back, showing his gritting teeth. With his large hand practically wrapped around Adam's entire neck, he lifted Adam's large frame effortlessly with one hand. Adam made a feeble attempt to kick Clutch in the groin, but Clutch batted down each kick with his free arm. Clutch continued to drive Adam into the wall.

"Now what was you saying in the car?" Clutch barked.

Adam gargled and gasped for air. The first time they fought, Clutch had a calm look in his eyes. This time the high-octane rage in his eyes was highly disturbing. He'd seen the calm level, but had no idea what this level would do. Not being able to match Clutch's strength, Adam began to call on his telepathic ability to save him. Adam pushed the pain away from Clutch's crushing grip in order to concentrate. The chairs, sofas, receptionist desk all started to vibrate with more intensity than what Adam was normally able to muster. The rumbling of the furniture began to get louder and louder. The furniture began to lift slightly. Even though Clutch was applying crushing pressure to his windpipe, Adam knew it wouldn't be long until he was free. He felt thunderous power surging through his veins, similar to the day he moved the earth against the CEO and his goons. He felt so much power. "Zap... zap," learning his lesson from their last bar brawl, the ever-so-prepared Clutch hit Adam with a stun gun; disrupting his telepathic powers. "Boom," all the furniture hit the ground.

"Not this time, you fuck!" Clutch screamed.

Adam fell limp and Clutch hit him with another round of electrical volts.

"You set us up, you fucking rat!" Clutch bellowed. Adam continued to gag for air in his paralyzed state.

"He is brain dead, you shit bag!" Clutch said with rising rage in his eyes.

Clutch drew back his fist as far as he could to deliver his mightiest blow to Adam's skull.

Suddenly, Adam heard, "Stop, Dr. Ridley, you are going to kill him!" Clutch halted his attack, quickly turned around, and dropped the paralyzed Adam to the ground. Adam fell helplessly to the ground and slid between Clutch's legs, gagging and drooling.

Clutch bent down over Adam's paralyzed body and whispered, "Bitch ass, I'll finish up with you later."

He turned around and headed back through the damaged door.

Adam, barely cognizant, heard Clutch say, "He is all yours Doc... for now!" When Clutch's large frame passed through the doorway, it cleared Adam's view to the voice. When Adam looked up, he was shocked into full consciousness—low and behold, it was Nia!

Chapter 23

Adam feebly tried to stand, despite his inoperable muscles. He awkwardly fell while trying to keep his eyes on Nia. His faulty tendons reduced him to waddling on the ground like a fish out of water. He layed on the floor, flailing, drooling, and gagging. Adam fantasized about meeting Nia his entire life. He'd dreamed about how romantic and powerful their first meeting would be. In a thousand years, Adam never would have imagined himself scrambling on the floor in front of Nia, hoping not to piss his pants. He tried to stand again only to flop back down clumsily. He gave up and decided to just let his aching muscles recover before he further made a fool of himself. Adam let out a long sigh, the damage was done. It wasn't going to be possible to salvage this moment with any cool points.

"Fuckin' asshole," Adam angrily slurred at Clutch

for robbing him of this life's opportunity for a dreamy reunion with Nia.

Nia cupped both hands over her nose and mouth at the sight of Adam's dazed, paralyzed body on the floor. Once Adam calmed, he felt power surging back into his muscles. He felt clarity in his thoughts, clarity in his memories, and a growing clairvoyance coursing through his mind. Nia began to walk toward him. The closer she got, the faster Adam's recovery began to accelerate. He no longer ached and he now had full control over every fiber in his body.

While marveling at Nia's walk, he thought, This must explain the good energy in the building I felt earlier. It was Nia all along.

He felt his telepathic powers were far stronger since entering this particular building; but until this moment, he wasn't sure why.

Without any doubt, Adam thought, *It all makes sense, she really is the key. The closer I am to her, the stronger I am.*

Nia's close proximity the day of the CEO's attack increased his power exponentially. That is how he was able to use his relationship with the earth to defend himself against the CEO and his goons. He felt that same power throbbing and coursing through his veins minutes ago, just after entering the building.

He noticed that Nia's face was slightly different than in their past lives, but her eyes were exactly the same. One deep gaze into Nia's eyes connected Adam back to her warming aura. The glowing soul behind her eyes was identical to the Nia he had always known. Her eyes had a liquid hazel brown tint. Adam instantly connected hundreds of lifetimes with those eyes, each vividly flashing before him. Her skin was a creamy shade of mocha, smooth and vibrant, making her age impossible to accurately tell. She was a young woman, no older than thirty perhaps, he thought. She had a sweet spring pheromone scent oozing through her pores that filled Adam's nostrils. Her hair was in long dark braids that comfortably rested past her shoulders. She had on a teal green business skirt that hugged her athletic frame well. Her breasts strained through the fabric of her shirt. She was drop-dead gorgeous. Nia continued trotting toward him, and Adam was magnetized by her firm breasts. The sight boosted an erection in Adam similar to a well pressurized fire hose. He slowly shook his head at the unbelievably beautiful sight. The rising endorphins brushed away his irritation with Clutch.

Fully recovered, Adam grinned at the gorgeous woman, blowing the earlier thought of embarrassment out of his mind like a spring breeze. She squatted down next to Adam and lifted his head. It was their first touch in this lifetime, and it instantly sent chills down Adam's spine, almost paralyzing him with overwhelming gratification. Nia's touch began a long parade of telepathic information rushing into his head. As always, she was still the warm, caring, loving, honest, devoted, and nurturing person he'd known. Her personality was still well attached to her soul. He caught a glimpse of her eyes again, and immediately felt the magnetic connection of the twin flame pouring in. As his heart rate picked up, he stopped thinking and bathed in the love he felt for her. His entire life he had felt alone with very little purpose. But at this moment, he felt complete, safe, and fulfilled. The world ending would be fine, just as long as he had a chance to experience this moment. By this time, Nia was also locked into a gaze of her own; Adam knew she felt the connection too. She looked at him with narrowed eyes, a tilted head, and a confused look. It's not every day that one gets to feel the energy of their twin flame. Most of her life, she lived with her soul closed off. To experience a stranger like Adam open her up with a single key, made just for her, was overwhelming. She pulled her braids behind her ear and gathered herself.

With a warm smile showcasing her milky white teeth, she asked, "Are you okay?"

Adam scooted up to one elbow, hid his erection, smiled again and said, "I am now."

While coughing and wiping saliva from his mouth, Adam eased the moment by jokingly saying, "Did you see what I did to the other guy?"

Grabbing Adam's arm, Nia smiled and softly said, "Come on, let's get you to the couch."

Holding onto Adam's arm, Nia stumbled back slightly from the sparking twin flame energy. Adam quickly and athletically jumped to his feet and caught her.

"Sorry, you'd think I'd been hit with a stun gun," said Nia, hiding the embarrassment of her clumsiness.

Adam just held her, staring deeper and deeper into her eyes with a grin of amazement. After a few seconds of his hypnotizing stare-down, he began to lead her to the couch.

Sitting next to her, Adam said softly, "Nia, I don't know how much time I have, but we have to talk."

Nia frowned with bit of confusion, "Wait, what did you call me?"

"Nia," responded Adam.

"Nobody calls me that, nobody even knows that is my real name. How did you know that?" she said, slightly tilting her head.

"That's what I want to talk to you about, but before I do, is Kojo really brain dead?" Adam asked.

Nia hesitantly paused, not sure if she should share any information with this strange man.

Against her better judgment, she continued, "I don't know anyone named Kojo, but if you are referring to Dr. Turner, I've stopped his bleeding and stitched his wounds. His vitals are good and he is stable, but at this point he has no brain activity. He is in some sort of coma. We need to get him to a hospital. This is just a research facility, we have limited equipment and staff here. Perhaps there we can get him the help that he needs. In fact, I don't understand why Dr. Ridley brought him here."

Then it dawned on Adam, Kojo's BioMod was still confusing Nia's brain chemistry. She was unaware of who she was actually helping. Clutch must have kept their identity from her in order to protect her. Therefore, Adam knew this wasn't a Colony strong hold, nor was Nia part of their group. To keep Kojo alive, and him and Clutch hidden, he'd have to explain everything: evolving DNA, twin flame, reincarnation, astral realm, psychic abilities, and the Ky—worst of all, the spiritual imprisonment of mankind. And he must do it in a timely fashion to keep the mission on course. They needed cover, needed to grab the weapons from the safe house, and connect with the other rouge Ky hiding in the Grand Canyon.

Adam sighed with a long breath and rested his face in his palms, searching for an approach. Waking someone up to reality was never easy.

Lifting his head up with a confident smile, Adam said, "I want to thank you for what you did in there for Dr. Turner. I know you did your best, you always do and always have."

Nia, squinting her eyes, said, "I'm sorry, but how would you know that? You are starting to scare me. Tell me how you know me by that name."

She grabbed a magazine from the table in front of her and showed it to Adam. He looked at the magazine and saw Nia's face on the front cover, but the name said Dr. Welsing.

With his customary smirk, Adam grabbed the magazine, slightly touching Nia's hand. In the process, his telepathic powers confirmed his hunch through their touch. Kojo and Clutch had been secretly interacting with her only through the aliases of their BioMods. She was working with Kojo, or as she knew him, Dr. Ridley, on several DNA and genetic research experiments. He momentarily stumbled on the fact that Clutch, of all people, convinced Nia he was also a doctor. A tinge of jealousy set in at the fact that a muscle-bound steroid head like Clutch had brains too. Nonetheless, Adam figured Clutch must have thought she was the only option he had at this point. Through all the turmoil, Clutch neglected to tell Adam she wasn't in the loop. Understandable, considering the gravity of the situation. It wasn't on his list of things to cover. No problem, thought Adam, with his powers he knew he could convince Mark Green, and certainly it would be no problem convincing his twin flame.

Adam set down the magazine, and a polite smile glided across his face before he answered Nia's question, "Because I know who you are and I've seen you before. In fact, I know everything about you."

Nia fidgeted and slid away from Adam on the couch, "Excuse me?"

Adam eagerly and excitingly continued, "I have seen your face before. I know you, I mean not in this lifetime, but in another..."

Nia interrupted, slowly shaking her head, "I'm sorry, Adam, but I don't believe I've ever seen or met you before."

"If you don't know me, then how did you know my name? Go ahead and I'll wait for you to answer," he said.

Nia's mouth popped open to spill her answer but

nothing came out. Knowing Clutch wouldn't have given out his name, Adam confidently let her wrestle with the question.

Adam knew that since this was their first meeting in this lifetime, Nia would likely have doubts. If she was like most people, she wouldn't be connected to her past lives. He also knew she felt the twin-flame attraction, and being armed with vivid memories of their past, he wouldn't be denied. Adam would bring her closer using the intoxicating lure of twin-flame energy.

Nia continued to stumble for an answer, "Uhm, I must have heard... uhh... because..."

Adam interrupted and slid closer to Nia. He softly took her hands and looked deeply into her eyes, "Nia, Nia, you became a doctor because you can't stand to see people suffering. I bet people, even strangers, still tell you their life stories because they can sense your loving heart. Taking it further, you've never liked eating meat because you could always sense the animal's energy from the inhumane way it was slaughtered. Routine disgust you, which is probably why you love to fly in your dreams. You root for the underdog because you despise authority. I bet you bought that dress because it's green. Green has always been your favorite color. You often have pains in your chest and you can't figure out why."

Adam hesitated, "But I'm a bit confused as why you live in Phoenix. I would have imagined you living in a place surrounded by water... flowing water and beaches calm your soul."

Nia stared, confused and dumbfounded, but Adam didn't stop.

"You love South African foods and have always preferred the night over the day. In fact you sometimes cry and become emotional when looking at the stars, and you've never known why, but I do!"

Adam's candor struck such a deep nerve in Nia that she had to hang on for more. His insight about her very soul, her very deepest thoughts and feelings, was much more than a coincidence. She thought the best stalkers could Google her to find her real name, but these things no one could know, at least not all of them together. Something intrigued her about this man. Something deep inside of her kept her wanting more of him. Her eyes bounced about Adam's face, trying to make logical sense of what she was feeling.

Adam confidently smirked, "This is more spiritual than physical. None of your degrees can help with this. Your rational mind can't explain it, but if you quiet your thoughts, your soul will explain everything."

He took a second, looked down, and slowly raised his head to Nia's face.

He reached and grabbed her hands again and said, "You are drawn to me, as I am to you. Confusing, I know, but I'm sure deep in your heart you know it to be true. There is no one out there that completes you like I do, no one willing to fight, or die, as I am to protect you—not only in this universe, but any others to come."

Nia sat in silence after being rocked by Adam's testament to her. With the twin-flame energy, Nia couldn't pull free from the moment. She started to pay more attention to Adam's strong chiseled jaw line, his dark liquid skin, and his sexy, seductive presence. She felt herself getting wet, and her nipples harder. Her body was yearning and urging her to get closer and closer to this man. In her mind, she was so distressed, but in her heart she was extremely comfortable. She felt her heart racing, flutters in her stomach, and chills down her spine. Her body had a mind of its own; she had to fight it back from wanting to press up against Adam's body. She knew he was right, but her rational mind couldn't explain it. She was an expert on the human body, yet none of her degrees could explain what was happening to her.

Nia looked deep into Adam's eyes. She leaned close to him and asked, "Who are you? How do you know these deep things about me?"

Adam stayed close and let the twin-flame energy

season Nia a little more before answering, "You and I are equal parts to the same soul. In layman's terms, we are twin flames. That is why we are drawn to each other."

Nia leaned back on the couch with her mouth agape and her eyes searching for understanding.

Adam continued, "Because of my DNA, I have the innate ability to recall my past lives. I have recalled these past lives as dreams my entire life. In these past lives, you and I were together many times, and I can recall these memories. That is how I know these things about you. I know your soul, and you know mine. In fact, ever since our souls have been on this planet, we have looked for one another. Meetings like this between us have happened thousands of times before. Nia, I love you in a way that no other soul in the universe can. You are part of me, and I am part of you. It's my business to love you. It's always been my business, and it always will be."

Nia was again speechless. She stared back and forth into Adam's eyes for what seemed like an eternity. Adam let her. He met her stare with increasing intensity. They each covered every possible corner of each other's eyes. Nia felt the soulful connection and Adam knew it. She began to feel the twin-flame energy dancing up and down her spine. Nothing in her lifetime had ever given her this feeling.   It was like spiraling tingles tickling and playing up and down her spinal column.

Adam thought in his mind, *She feels it.*

Nia replied, "I do."

Shocked at the telepathic connection, Nia again cupped her hands over her face and asked, "Oh my God! Did we just speak with our minds?"

"Yes, we did," said Adam grinning at the strengthening telepathic connection.

Adam moved closer, "There is a lot more I need to explain to you."

Trying to gather herself, Nia stuttered, "Well, shouldn't we get Dr. Turner to the hospital?"

Adam raked his hands through is afro, "Well, that is what I have to explain. Dr. Turner isn't who you think he is."

Blankly staring at Adam, Nia said, "I don't understand, who is he then?"

Adam heard Clutch and Kojo's BioMods blaring and warning from within the room.

While still sitting on the couch, he leaned his head forward to peer through the broken door and said, "You're about to find out."

He stood up, extended his hand to Nia, and motioned to the door with the other, "I can show you better than I can tell you. Shall we?"

Nia looked up, confused, but obliged his request by grabbing his hand and allowing him to lead her into the room. Adam walked into a windowless research room with lab equipment, pc monitors, dry erase boards, and desks centered against the walls. Toward the back left, there was a smaller room. Nia took the lead, and softly guided Adam to the back room. Adam trailed Nia while still holding her hand and basking in her beauty.

"He is in here," said Nia upon arriving to the back room's entrance.

Nia turned to Adam and in a soft voice said, "We have basic equipment to stabilize him, but without further staff, I can't promise anything."

The room was a cross between a high-end hospital room and a low-end surgery room. Kojo was lying on the bed, or as Nia would see it, Dr. Turner. He appeared to be in a peaceful slumber and was connected to an EEG machine and a heart rate monitor that was displayed on two flat-screen monitors encased on the wall. Clutch sat alongside Kojo's bed with his head down on Kojo's chest. Adam halted at the door at the sight of Clutch's presence, not sure of what to expect out of him. Clutch barely acknowledged his presence. Adam glanced at a dazed and somber Clutch, who displayed intense pain in his eyes—a rare sight. His entire life, Clutch defended Kojo and now he was helpless to protect him. For the first time, Clutch was facing life without his twin. Even though minutes ago Clutch was crushing Adam's windpipe, he still felt deep sorrow for him.

"Whomp whomp whooooomp," went Kojo's BioMod as its battery died. Kojo instantly transformed from middle-aged white man back to his compact self. Startled, Nia whisked back and gasped at the sight of Kojo's true identity. The sudden transformation was mentally too much for her to handle. She stiffened and stood motionless. Nia's mouth dropped open, with her hand covering it. Her eyes ignited with intensity that locked onto Kojo.

She tried to speak, slurring her words, before suddenly fainting, "Dr. Turnerrr!"

Adam glided in and caught her. Clutch was too grief stricken to move to Nia's aid. A few seconds later, Clutch's BioMod died while Nia was still unconscious. He still didn't flinch, uncaring that he was now exposed.

Seconds later, he finally looked up at Adam, helplessly shaking his head. Adam carried Nia over to one of the chairs next to Kojo, opposite Clutch. He softly placed her in the chair, carefully holding her close to him. He leaned her body against his and caressed the back of her neck to keep her head still. Now that Nia had seen Kojo, Adam worried what battle-hardened Clutch would do to further protect the Colony.

"Clutch, Nia can help us," Adam said while fanning Nia and still holding her close.

"Who?" asked Clutch. "You talking about Dr. Welsing?"

"That is her professional name, her first name is Nia," Adam clarified.

Clutch let out a long-winded sigh, "At this point I'd have to agree with you, we need her help."

Seconds later, Nia began to regain consciousness. Adam squatted in front of her to be the first image she connected with after her regaining consciousness.

When she fully awoke, Adam tenderly asked, "Are you okay?"

Looking at Adam first, then swiftly turning and staring at Kojo, Nia stuttered, "That... that is the guy that is...."

Then she spotted Clutch and screamed, "Oh my

God, oh my God... he is the other one, you guys are wanted terrorists. What happened to Dr. Ridley?"

Nia started to panic, shuddering and fidgeting with discomfort.

"Nia, Nia," Adam softly said, trying to calm her, to no avail. Nia continued to fidget and push away from Adam.

She screamed, "Please just..."

She stopped in mid-sentence, and her eyes darted away from Clutch and onto a toothpick slowly spinning in front of her face. Her eyes widened, fully exposing her irises. Nia's mouth gaped open and she fell silent, staring at the whirling toothpick. Once he had Nia's attention, Adam floated the toothpick into his mouth. Her eyes drew to him.

"Nia, sweetheart, try to calm down. We are not terrorists, things are not what you think they are," Adam said calmly.

He gently took her hands and said, "Everything you have been told is a lie."

Still shocked and silent, she stared at Adam, paralyzed and quiet for what felt like an eternity.

With her eyes slitted and brow scrunched, Nia asked in a low whisper, "Wha... what are you?"

"I'm human, baby," Adam said firmly.

Nia's eyes narrowed.

He continued, "I know this is scary, but I know you can handle what I'm about to tell you." Nia continued to fidget and squirm with discomfort.

Adam continued, while still rubbing Nia's hands, "We had a connection earlier. We both felt it... focus on that feeling. Trust that feeling, and you will know that what I'm about to tell you is the truth."

Adam saw the tension slowly vanishing from Nia's face. Her shoulders started to relax and she squeezed Adam's hands, letting him know that she was ready to listen.

He continued, "I am what you call an indigo child, one born with restored DNA. As such, I have psychic, telepathic, telekinetic abilities."

He paused and gave Nia a thin smile, "You may have experienced some of these abilities as well."

Nia slowly nodded.

Surprisingly, Clutch interjected, "Mankind is evolving to have these same abilities, and..."

Adam interrupted Clutch and said softly to Nia, "This is the part that you will need to prepare yourself for."

Adam nodded to Clutch to continue.

Clutch carried on, "A group of aliens called the Ky are trying to prevent this evolution in order to continue full enslavement of the human race. My brother, Kojo, or as you know him, Dr. Turner, was trying to synthesize a counter agent to help assist with this evolutionary process."

Adam cupped Nia's hands to his face and said, "So, you see Nia, they are not terrorists, they are freedom fighters."

Nia sighed and a numb expression fell over her face.

"We were getting help from one of the Ky's rogue scientists, Scar—that is, before he was killed," Clutch said, glaring at Adam.

Adam ignored Clutch's angry eye and said, "Of course, the Ky controls everything: governments, education, banking, media outlets, and information. They have brainwashed the world into thinking the Colony is a group of terrorists."

"Scar designed these devices that hid our identities. So, that is how you saw my brother as Dr. Turner, and me as Dr. Ridley. They allowed us complete anonymity. We were always able to outwit the Ky, but now that he is gone, we need your help," said Clutch.

Scooting away from Adam and toggling her glance between the two men, Nia said, "You expect me to really believe this? Why didn't you take those devices to the authorities to prove your point? Hell, why didn't this helper alien you are talking about just walk into a news station and let everybody see him as proof of these aliens? I'm sorry, but your story doesn't make sense to me."

Adam was stumped; Nia's point actually made him wonder the same thing. Why wasn't it attempted in the first place? He turned and looked to Clutch to field her questions. Clutch hissed and smirked at Nia.

Leaning off Kojo's bed, Clutch retorted with a deep voice, "Sweetheart, just because humans know about these aliens doesn't mean something is going to be done about them. Number one, everybody at that news station would have been either killed or re-cloned. Number two, if that message would have gotten out, it would have been played off as a hoax by the Ky-controlled media. Number three, if anybody still publicly preached that message... well, they would have been labeled as crazy—kooks or conspiracy theorists. That brings us to number four: if any person was still publicly persistent with this alien message... see number one again."

Nia squinted, "I'm sorry, but did you say... clone?"

"Yes, clone. Their technology is light years ahead of what we can even comprehend. So, yes, they have the ability to clone and replace an individual until the situation can be properly dealt with. This is only one trick among many they have to keep us humans in check," Clutch said.

Looking deep into Nia's eyes, Adam asked, "Nia, how else do you explain the technology you just witnessed here?"

Nia sighed while shaking her head, "I don't know, this is all too much. Helping you is illegal and endangers my research practice and...."

Adam interrupted, "In one of our past lives together, they ripped you apart... with our child inside of you. The memory was so painful it is forever recorded in your cosmic DNA as a pain body, and from time to time you feel it. That is why you have those excruciating pains in your chest."

Nia slowly touched her chest in amazement as she finally understood the pain that had plagued her for as long as she could remember.

Confused, Nia said, "This can't be real. Wait, how..."

Adam interrupted again, "I'm afraid it is real. Our village was attacked and many of us were slaughtered by the Ky that day."

Nia paused. Her eyes volleyed back and forth before welling up with tears, "Wait, I've dreamed of something horrible like that. You mean to tell me that really happened?"

Adam nodded while rubbing Nia's back.

A single tear trailed down her cheek. She rested her face in the palms of her hands and asked with a shaky voice," They arrived in silver oval wheels, didn't they?"

Again Adam nodded while soothing Nia and looking deeply into her tear-filled eyes.

"And for thousands of years they have plagued mankind, enslaving us, and feeding off of us, lifetime after lifetime," Adam added.

A tinge of jealousy fell over Clutch at the sight of Adam consoling Nia. He and Kojo had secretly worked with her from time to time, but under the circumstances, he could never get close to her. Clutch could only watch the beautiful Nia, but could never act on his crush for her. He simmered at the thought of Adam just waltzing in and fancying up to her.

Clutch fumed to himself. First he wins over Kojo, then practically gets him killed, and now he gets the girl?

He figured he'd better interrupt the building chemistry between the two, or he may never have a chance with Nia.

With a distinguishably hostile tone, he blurted out, "Look, now is not the time for you to distract her with your little reunions. We have to try to get my brother help and carry on with the mission. Nia and I will stay here, you go back to the safe house and get the weapons and Jolon."

Clutch succeeded at souring Adam's consoling moment with Nia, but little did Clutch know there was no way Adam would leave Nia's side. It took him a lifetime to find her and he wasn't going to let her out of his sight anytime soon.

Regarding Clutch through the slits in his eyes, Adam said, "Clutch, you're right about the mission, but I have to stay with Nia. I think it makes more sense for you to go."

With a voice wet with sarcasm, Clutch said, "So you can stay and try to continue hitting on the good doc? Yeah right, and I'm not leaving my brother. And plus, last time we used your judgment, shit got worse!"

After picking up on Clutch's jealous vibe, Adam

realized Clutch must have feelings for Nia. This crush on Nia could potentially add fuel to the fire. Adam now knew he was going to have to walk a fine line with Clutch concerning Nia. Although Nia's presence gave Adam an edge against Clutch's super-human strength, he couldn't afford to get into another scrimmage with him. He needed Clutch, so he had to find a productive way to work with him. More importantly to Adam, now that Nia was involved, her safety could be at risk as well.

Adam took a deep breath before responding, "Clutch, you have got to trust me on this one. I know..."

"Trust you?" Clutch interrupted sarcastically.

Adam cracked a small grin at Clutch's cynical comment, "Look, Kojo isn't dead, and because he is not dead, they can follow his silver cord here at any minute. Nia and I will stay here to protect him and keep him alive."

"Silver cord, what silver cord," Nia said looking around.

Coming to his feet, Clutch continued the sarcastic banter with Adam, "Protect him, you're the one who damn near got him killed in the first place! How the hell are you going to protect him with no weapons? I'm done listening to you. Go get the fuckin' weapons!"

Nia watched with discomfort as the two men verbally jabbed back and forth, trying to follow the ebb and flow of the conversation.

He spotted the dedicated rage in Clutch's eyes. However, Adam was staying with Nia, and that was final. If any issue was worth fighting Clutch over, this was the one he'd gladly take. However, he also knew Clutch was emotional, not to mention strong enough to lift a 500 pound Ky-ote off the ground with one arm. This made any battle with Clutch far more dangerous, for the mission as well as his safety. He knew he had to take a diplomatic approach with Clutch.

Taking the toothpick out of his mouth, Adam sighed and said, "You don't understand!"

He pointed at Nia and anxiously said to Clutch, "She can help more than you know. She is the key."

"What does she have to do with getting weapons?" Clutch asked with growing annoyance.

Adam turned back to Nia and said, "There were some men that were killed on 16th street across from the library about a year ago. You were there! I'm right, aren't I?"

Hesitantly, Nia said, "Yes... yes I was, but how did you know I was there? I didn't..."

Adam politely held up his finger, interrupting her, "I was there that day. That was me who moved the earth. I was able to do it because you were in the vicinity. Your presence drastically increases my abilities."

Adam turned back to Clutch, "Nia is my twin flame; with her, I can defend and protect Kojo against any assault they will bring."

"You were the one who killed all those men?" Nia asked hesitantly, with growing disgust on her face.

"Yes, I mean no... They were attacking me. Let me show you," Adam stuttered while pulling out his memory card from his phone and handing it to Clutch.

Clutch inserted the memory card into his phone and pulled up the surveillance footage of Adam's run-in with the CEO and his goons. For the first time, Clutch saw Nia's presence on the footage, proving Adam's point. Clutch let out a deep sigh and nodded before he handed the phone over for Nia to watch.

Nia watched, mouth open, at the rising stone and gravel in the surveillance footage. With utter shock, she gasped at the sight of the earth firing off and shredding through flesh and bones like wet paper. Cupping her hands over her mouth, she continued to watch as the SUV flew across the street from the impact of the flying gravel. She was aghast at the sight of the carnage, but as a scientist, she was intrigued by her influence on Adam. Nia looked at Adam in awe and disbelief when the footage came to an end. She was dazzled and aroused by his powerful abilities.

Despite how Clutch felt about Adam, he was always thoroughly impressed with Adam's crushing victory over the CEO's henchmen. Now, upon seeing Nia in the video for the first time, there was no denying that Nia's presence really was the key. He hated to admit it, but Adam was right. Clutch would have to concede this point to him. He knew he had no weapons and couldn't fight off any onslaught. Adam with Nia was a weapon in itself and probably stood a better chance of keeping Kojo safe. He had to put his crush for Nia aside for now.

"Nia, are you okay with this?" Clutch asked.

With genuine comfort, Nia smiled at Adam, then nodded in agreement at Clutch.

Deep inside it was painful for Clutch to see Nia's magnetic pull toward Adam. It didn't seem to make sense for two men to be fighting over a woman during the dawn of the biggest war mankind had ever faced, but one glance at Nia and it would make sense. Clutch realized that if Adam was right about this twin-flame connection, he surely would have to kiss goodbye any chances of ever having Nia. Even during his brother's crisis, his feelings for Nia were still in his thoughts.

Clutch pushed out a long sigh, "Okay, I'll go. Nia, may I take your car and park ours in the loading garage out back?"

"Yes, and take these," said Nia, handing Clutch a hat and glasses.

A sliver of a grin crossed his face at her feeble attempt to disguise him.

"Call me on the secure line if you need me, Nia. I will be gone for at least three or four hours."

He gave Nia a rare smile and handed her a stun gun, "If he tries anything, use this on him."

He wrapped his enormous arms around Nia and gave her a gentle hug before thanking her. He turned to Adam, leaned in close, and said with a slow, bitter tone, "Don't fuck up!"

Adam remained silent while tonguing his toothpick and flashing a thin, sarcastic smile back at Clutch. The face-off lasted for a couple of seconds, thickening the tension. Clutch turned and grabbed Kojo's hand. Knowing this might be the last time he saw his twin brother alive, he leaned in and softly kissed Kojo's forehead. In a flash, Clutch left.

Chapter 24

After Clutch left, the room was heavy with an uncomfortable silence.

Adam drifted into deep thought, not sure if he would ever see Clutch again. With no weapons, no team, and no cover, Adam knew Clutch could be a sitting duck for the Ky. Adam also knew that since he was not fully aware of all the Ky's capabilities, he was just as much of a sitting duck. Although their relationship was plagued with as much tension as two warring factions, Adam was still sad to see him go. Being at the mercy of his ignorance, Adam felt like a slave to the unknown.

Nia, on the other hand, was hesitant, nervous, shy, and giddy from Adam's presence, all uncustomary characteristics of her. Normally she was aggressive, thorough and persistent, traits that led her to owning her own practice and being a powerhouse in the field of genetic research. Her tingling nerves made her feel like a young school girl experiencing her first crush. Nia's heart fought to contain itself in her chest. Her eyes glazed and her skin became extra sensitive to every tingle tickling her body.

Nia took control over the fluttering butterflies in her stomach by returning to her normally aggressive self. She wiped her cold, clammy hands on her skirt and took a few deep breaths to calm her body and pounding heart.

She looked intently into Adam's face and broke the stretching silence, "So, would you like to catch me up on things?"

Nia's voice broke Adam's listless daze. Looking up, he drew strength from her very beauty.

Adam smiled and said, "I'd love to."

Smiling back, Nia said, "Let's go to the lab."

They both walked out of Kojo's room into the main lab and sat across from one another at one of the lab tables.

Adam went from worrying about Clutch to feeling anxious by Nia's presence. He hid his twirling and fiddling hands under the table and hoped like hell he could properly get his words out. Adam took a deep breath and drew on some of the meditative techniques he used to enter the astral realm.

Calmly smiling and looking at Nia, he said, "My DNA allows me to have extra abilities like moving things with my mind, seeing auras, and even reading your thoughts."

He unclasped his fidgeting hands from under the table and reached for Nia's. She anxiously lied her hands inside of his. The spark of the twin flame energy further ignited the tingling and butterflies in the pit of her stomach. She let out a low moan from the spark in energy.

"I'm going to read your mind. Take a second and think of anything you are comfortable with me knowing," Adam said.

Scrunching her brow at him, Nia nodded and said okay while her eyes rolled to the corner of their sockets. Coming back to Adam, she nodded giving him permission to proceed.

Adam paused and hesitantly said, "ZtyGymq1234yUr?"

Shaking his head and searching for words, he asked, "Is that some sort of... code or something?"

Before Nia could answer, Adam's lips spread into a full grin, "Yeah... yeah... I must be right 'cause now you are thinking that was amazing!"

Nia batted her eyes at Adam and her face slowly grew into a wide grin of awe at his accuracy.

Adam continued, "And you are thinking not only is this scientifically impossible, but it also feels amazing."

"I'm right, aren't I?" Adam asked confidently.

Nia giggled in wonder, "Oh my God. Wow... you are right, Mr. Adam."

The accuracy of his telepathic powers punched Nia in the stomach. Never before did she even think it was possible for someone to read her mind as accurately as Adam, and especially that it was possible to read which letters were capitalized.

Relieved that Nia was responding comfortably to him, Adam continued holding her hand, relaxing her and himself.

"Now that you are around, everything is so much more clear in my head. Scar taught me that human DNA was originally capable of gifts like this and much more until it was genetically removed by the Ky long ago," Adam said.

Nia leaned back in her chair and said with a straight face, "I see. So, that must explain junk DNA."

She jolted forward in her chair again, "Hmmm... so junk DNA are the modules that the Ky turned off... and yours has evolved to being turned on?"

"Yes, and I think the sun has something to do with my evolution. The sun's rays on my skin seems to somehow assist all this," Adam said while looking down at his hands.

He continued, "From time to time, human DNA evolves to show this ability. To keep us blind to it, they hid the truth. That is why they attacked me that day."

Nia again flopped backward in her chair. Her eyes rolled to the corner of the room in deep thought, connecting multiple dots of information.

Shaking her head, she said, "Wow, mainstream science argued that evolution has turned off those abilities. I'm going to guess the Ky have their hands in controlling mainstream science as well."

"From what Scar has told me, everything is controlled by the Ky one way or another," Adam confirmed.

After a few more moments of deep thought, Nia began to nod as if she had full understanding. She came forward out of her chair and reached for Adam's hands.

While shaking her head in astonishment, she said, "Wow, I've seen clairvoyants before in my research, but nothing, I mean nothing, like you before."

Adam grinned with confidence, "And you probably never will, baby."

He held Nia's hands tighter, "But it gets worse. Because of what they took from us, we are stuck here reincarnating over and over again. That is how you and I have had our many lives together."

Nia softly licked her lips and slid her braids behind her ear and asked in a soft, titillating voice, "So, you and I get to spend our lives together, over and over again?"

Adam smiled from ear to ear in response to Nia's flirtatious question. It warmed his heart to know she would adore spending lifetimes with him. The way she looked at him, the way she said it, he knew that no matter how many lives he lived, he'd always remember that moment.

Fighting down his smile in order to talk, Adam said, "I thought the same thing at first. It doesn't seem like a bad thing, spending lifetimes with you, except for the fact that we are much more powerful beings and are capable of a higher existence than what we've been told."

Over the next hour, Adam continued updating Nia on the entire story—the last year's education with Miles, Kano, Scar, the Colony, the CEO, Mark Green, and the events that led up to him meeting her. He dove deeper into the Ky's spiritual prison, the astral realm, and life after death.

"You know, I've felt things my entire life. But as a scientist, there exists no definitive explanation or proof for these feelings. It doesn't fit the mainstream scientific model, so I've always discarded them. Even when you entered the building, I sensed it. When you and Clutch were fighting, well when he was fighting you..." Nia laughed.

"Hey hey now, don't get it twisted... I can handle my own," Adam joked back in a confidently deep voice.

Playfully grinning, Nia continued, "The point is, I felt that you were in trouble and I knew I had to come to you."

Suddenly snapping her fingers, Nia blurted, "Oh, I have an idea! You mentioned you guys went to see Mark Green, right?"

Adam nodded, "Yeah, we did."

"Well, I know him personally. We went to school together at MIT. A lot of the research I do here comes from his funding. I can talk to him," wide-eyed Nia said eagerly.

"Damn, that is perfect, except I don't know if we can trust him. I saw demons attacking his astral body. He might be controlled by the Ky by now. How do you know if we can trust him?" Adam asked.

"I don't have to trust him, I trust what he is going to do with the information. Trust me, if he can stand to make a profit he will be interested. I'll just give him enough information to finance the counter agent. Once we know he is on our side, maybe then we can give him more information."

Nia took a deep breath, grabbed Adam's hands, and said sadly, "Adam, we will never know for sure who we can truly trust."

"I know, I know," Adam said raking his afro.

"If possession is real, like you say, then anybody at anytime can be a threat to the movement," Nia mused.

Adam took a big breath and slouched back into his chair.

Shaking his head he said, "Sometimes it just seems like an impossible war to win."

"No, impossible is finding your twin flame out of

seven billion people, yet here we are," Nia said, looking deep into Adam's eyes.

She slowly leaned forward and kissed Adam on the lips.

She gently pulled away, "Don't worry, you have me, I will help you. We will do this together."

Nia's kiss warmed his soul, but her words touched it. Those were some of her last words to him before the Ky attacked their village.

"Seems like I need to show doubt more often," Adam chuckled after their first kiss in this lifetime.

Nia blushed before continuing, "If Clutch gets more weapons, specifically the BioMods, you and he will be able to hide among the general population long enough to wake back up the Colony's fallen members. By that time, we will have the counter agent."

"Very impressive. You always grabbed on to this kind of stuff quick," said Adam.

"Well, duh... this is kind of what I do," she said jokingly.

"And of course we will run the Mark Green idea by Clutch to cover all of our angles, "Nia said, winking at Adam.

She continued, "Once the Colony members are

vaccinated, it will be a major win for us; it will unleash a whole new generation of free, liberated humans. That will be the catalyst to free us all."

"I don't know, Nia. I know the counter agent idea is the plan we have, but it just seems like that won't even make a dent," Adam said, second guessing the plan.

Confidently, Nia assured him, "Well, actually, it is a genius plan. It's subtle and indirect enough to stay hidden long enough to be effective. You don't need the whole population, just enough to make the human potential obvious to the masses. Think of it: three hundred evolved super humans similar to you, Kojo, and Clutch among the population, walking the earth. Once their evolved DNA propagates into the populace, it will continue to grow and be almost impossible to stop, completely turning the tables on the Ky's BioGrid."

Adam nodded, impressed and trusting of Nia's backing and understanding of Scar and Kojo's plan. He was the power, but it was becoming clear she was the brains.

"Don't worry your pretty little head about Mark, I can take care of him. You and Clutch need to re-establish the Colony and make connection with the Ky in the Grand Canyon," Nia continued.

Seeing Adam's face still canvassed with doubt, Nia grabbed his hands again.

Leaning forward and looking deeply into his eyes, she said, "After everything you've told me, this is not just some random event. There is something grandly intelligent at play here, guiding you, guiding me... something is favoring our success. And if it is true that a soul never dies, then you and I will continue this fight together through eternity."

She smiled and softly touched Adam's cheek to further reassure him, "So let's get started, shall we?"

Just like in their many lives before, Nia could always spark Adam by her supportive motivation. She could always pull the best out of him with her subtle nudge of reassurance. Truthfully, he knew Nia was the spark that had ignited this entire resistance in him. In fact, he knew that she was the reason why this war was winnable. Without her presence that very day, he wouldn't have had the power to fight off the CEO's men. In all likelihood, he'd be dead without her, and all chances of a counter agent being made would be destroyed with his death. Without Nia to fully activate Adam, the world may have never known the human potential. With Nia in his corner, he couldn't go wrong. Adam smiled and nodded to her direction. He'd gladly follow this woman into the bowels of hell, if necessary.

"We have to take your blood and do a complete medical workup on you," Nia said while putting on latex gloves.

Adam smirked, "So now you want to turn me into a lab rat?"

"You're my rat, I can do whatever I want with you," Nia smiled.

Loving the flirtatious banter, Adam conceded to her point. "You sho' can, baby girl," he said while flashing her his million-dollar smile.

Slowly dialing down the intensity of his pearly whites, Adam said, "But, Nia, they most likely will be coming here; they can be following Kojo's astral cord here now. They will destroy everything, all of your work... including your research facility. I can't let you risk..."

Nia interrupted, "Which is why we have to get it done quickly. It will take about an hour."

She confidently continued while grabbing lab equipment, "And relax. Does it look like I've gotten this far by thinking inside the box. I have my ways of getting things done against the odds."

Adam followed Nia around the lab while she prepared the exam. Her lean, fit body mesmerized him. The battle was lost against his rising libido. His eyes occasionally unclothed her, while his hormones stirred up his body's lust. Stoned by her intoxicating scent, he barely comprehended her instructions.

"Adam... Adam... this exam will be documented by those cameras," Nia said, pointing to cameras tucked around the lab.

"I am simultaneously streaming online the results to a partner I trust and also mailing the results to another one of my associates. That way, if they do follow Kojo's astral cord here, we at least have the information out. If something happens to me, they will know to contact Mark and go from there," she said.

She began her medical examination of Adam. She started with documenting Adam's telepathic and telekinetic abilities. She documented his heart and abdominal function. Next, she moved to testing his neurological functions. From there, she took his blood, body, and limb measurements. The entire time, their connection and chemistry grew stronger and stronger.

During the exam they flirtatiously fumbled and brushed across each other. Adam reminisced with her about their past lives together. They laughed at their immature former selves and selfish behaviors of the past. He gave Nia deep insights about herself that no one else could, insight that answered many questions in her current life. There was no learning curve or misunderstanding between them; their personalities gelled together like the rising and falling tides. They had comfortably reconnected inside of a couple of hours, a familiarity that took most couples decades to accomplish. Each of their flaws were perfectly compensated by the other's strength, molding them into one complete soul.

Nia knew it was an incredible story. It was the greatest honor possible to have a part in such a fascinating adventure. Adam renewed her, gave her a new vigor toward life. Her butterflies tickled her stomach and tingles danced up and down her spine with every glance at Adam. She didn't worry about the Ky or the daunting task of saving the world. She knew everything would be okay; she knew that Adam would see to it. For the first time in her life, she truly felt safe, understood, and, best of all, she felt complete. At this point, they could barely fight the urge to keep their hands off one another. They were in a drunken haze from recaptured love from hundreds of lifetimes. The magnetic pull of the twin-flame energy bonded them tighter and tighter as time went by.

"Okay, let's check your respiratory and lung function on the treadmill. Will you take your shirt off, please?" Nia asked.

"I thought you would never ask," Adam said with a confident half grin.

As Adam pulled the shirt over his head, Nia's eyes fell to Adam's rock hard wall of abs.

Biting her lips, she said, "Wow, I wasn't quite expecting that."

"Most aren't," Adam said with a confident smirk.

He playfully tossed his shirt to Nia and walked over to the treadmill with a sneaky smile. Nia stared, aroused at the sight of Adam's athletic, god-like ebony frame—his broad shoulders, herculean chest, and muscularly winged back. She shyly hooked him to the sensors on the treadmill, all the while fighting back her urges to caress his chest.

"Okay, a few minutes on here will give me everything I need to send off the package," Nia said.

Combing through Adam's exam results, Nia noticed Adam naturally had the strength of two or three men, the athletic ability of a jaguar and reflexes of a mongoose. His charged DNA kept his metabolism magnificently efficient, keeping his body fat percentage just above seven percent. All five of his senses were extremely enhanced, so much so that she didn't have the proper tools to test their full capabilities. It was clear to Nia that Adam had raised the definition of what it meant to be human. The code inside of him could make humans faster, stronger, telepathic, and telekinetic just to name a few characteristics humans long ago lost. An entire industry could spring up overnight, just around Adam's DNA. He would easily become the new Henrietta Lacks, having cells that live on infinitely, like the stuff of science fiction. To the world of science, he would be a god by the smallest of standards, and greed would see to it that his immortal cells would fetch billions.

In amazement, she watched Adam run on the treadmill. Each of his steps sent a flash of rippled muscle flexing across his body, and she snuck in a few extra peeks, purely for enjoyment.

"You're doing great, keep it up," she giggled.

After ten more minutes of fantasizing about him on the treadmill, Nia grabbed the lab report of Adam's respiratory functions and headed to the mail drop.

"Okay, we are all done. You can put your shirt back on. All I have to do is disguise your results so that no one will suspect anything," she said.

She appropriately mistitled the envelope to her confidant and dropped it into the mail slot. Nia turned around to a stunning view of Adam in full stride coming her way. He was still shirtless and his body was gleaming from the light workout on the treadmill. Her eyes tried to focus on his face, but the lure of Adam's hard-outlined muscular chest and rippled abs caused her to do multiple double takes. Nia's butterflies ignited again with a renewed energy, pounding away at the walls of her stomach with each of Adam's steps toward her.

Chapter 25

Pulled by his transcendent love of Nia, Adam made his way over to reunite his soul with hers. With each step closer, his body surged with tension and anticipation. She was technically a stranger by most terms, yet he felt lifetimes of love converging in his heart.

"Do you feel it?" he asked.

"Feel what?" she asked.

Searching for the right words, Adam said, "This energy between us?"

"Yes, I do. I felt it as soon as you walked in the building," she said.

"No, not that energy. I feel this push, uuhmm... a tether, a force drawing me to touch you," Adam said, coming closer.

Another step.

"I hate to be so blunt, but, baby, you are incredibly beautiful, on so many levels, in so many dimensions," he said.

He paused and raked through his afro.

"It's like my soul has had enough of being without you, and has decided on its own to come to you. You have been in my head, my heart, my bones, and my soul for so long."

Nia nervously blushed while fanning her rising flames, "Yes, I feel it too and it's beautiful. I feel everything you are feeling, and it scares me. I feel like I don't have control."

"But I do," Adam said while lightly grabbing both of her hands.

Nia met his gaze.

A comfortable silence ensued while the rising emotional tide took its toll. At the same point in time, they were both wrestling with the same problem: how to respectfully rip off each other's clothes. Adam towered his tall, athletic frame over Nia, slowly combing through her hair with one hand and embracing her with the other. He slid his hand gently to the nape of her neck and lightly caressed and massaged it. The touch of his fingers gave her an instant calmness and a parade of tingles throughout her body. She let out a long--awaited moan from the needed pleasure. From her neck, Adam began to gently trace the soft curves on her face with his hands, smoothly gliding the back of his fingers across her cheeks. Nia's eyes narrowed with erotic passion while slowly placing her hands on Adam's chest. She traced his hard, muscular curves softly with the tip of her fingers. Nia felt Adam's thunderous beating heart synchronizing itself with her own.

"Truly beautiful," Nia said softly in amazement at their hearts waltzing together.

Unknown to the couple, the twin flame energy was slowly syncing and binding them together. During their embrace, they telepathically unburdened their innermost love for each other. Their minds merged, making things much less clumsy between the two. Telepathically, they agreed this moment was necessary, bigger than saving the world, and far more important than any alien agenda. Neither was exactly sure why, but somehow they knew it was essential to their overall story.

Using their eyes as a gateway into the soul, they stared into one another's inner most essence. Neither of them had ever felt this type of energy before in this lifetime, but they both welcomed it. Adam slowly bowed his head, leaned in lightly and softly kissed Nia's lips. He wrapped his hands around her neck while his tongue gently parted her soft supple lips. He made his tongue join hers, while trailing his fingers slowly up and down her spine. His touch excited a stampede of dormant pent up energy that caused Nia to explode with her own passionate tongue exploration. The newly unlocked passion oozing out of Nia caused her to firmly press her body up against Adam, begging for more.

Adam activated her ascension into his blissful erotic chariot. Silence between the two was only interrupted by their heavy, synchronous breaths and wet sounds of their lips and tongues locking. Adam slowly pressed her against his rising manhood, giving in to the pulling vortex of energy between the two. He grazed the stubbles of his beard against her warm, ebony skin, igniting her nerves with streaking jolts of fire. Nia slowly closed her eyes, taking in a long, deep breath only to exhale it in a long-awaited moan. Her shoulders rounded, her spine curled, and she fell helplessly deeper into Adam's arms, nestling in his bosom for security. Adam took in a deep breath of his own, filling his nostrils with Nia's pheromones and minty breath. Their twirling tongues opened a flood gate of erotic spasms between the two. They both pulled and tugged at each other's clothes, wanting only to increase the skin-to-skin connection. While still locked in the kiss, Adam unbuttoned Nia's blouse. She rubbed and pressed her hand against his manhood, further exciting him. Once her blouse was off, with a flick of his thumb he freed her supple breasts from the prison of her strained bra. Her breasts sprung free and fell into Adam's other available hand. Beads of sweat lightly decorated Nia's jetting breasts. Adam lightly twirled and caressed them while Nia unzipped her skirt. Adam followed, fumbling out of his clothes. The flesh-to-flesh contact set off a new blaze of emotional fire down each of their nerves. Nia moaned, blowing her warm breath against Adam's neck. Hundreds of lifetimes of intimacy and lovemaking burned alive in their minds and throughout their bodies. Adam hardened further, and Nia's body tingled and serenaded itself with goose bumps. Adam slowly rubbed and traced her curves with his large hands, while Nia continued to caress his manhood. Rubbing from her back down to her firm, round, athletic ass, Adam covered every crack and crevice Nia's body had to offer. She continued to grind and press her vivacious body up against Adam's manhood. Nia's nipples enlarged, her hips gyrated, and her vagina oozed with sensual secretions. Her wetness, sliding against Adam, attracted the attention of his granite-like member. Adam gallantly swept Nia off her feet, picking her up and impaling her with his manhood. Nia's eyes widened and her heart fluttered as she adjusted to Adam's size. The two stayed locked and entangled in each other's gaze while Adam continued slowly sliding inside of her. Nia curled her thighs around Adam, bringing him and his manhood deeper inside of her while grabbing hold to the lean muscles in his back. Adam slid his arms under her thighs, cupping her ass with his large hands, and setting the pace for his long, deep thrust into her. With each stroke, her eyes rolled with slight orgasmic tingles of climax as Adam's shaft bottomed out against her. Like a powerful machine, he held still and slid in and out while flicking his tongue about her mouth. Nia coiled, twisted, and curled her clitoris against his rock hard pubic bone. He moved her to the wall and went deeper, supporting her by the back of her knees while he opened her wide. The power, control, and strength of Adam's move caused her erotic juices to drip, splash, and slide down Adam's thighs. Nia's neck fell limp, giving way to the pleasure rather than maintaining muscle control. Nia's vagina got tighter and tighter, hugging every crevice Adam's enhanced manhood had to offer. Occasionally, Adam traced her nipples with his tongue, tasting her sweat perspiration of passion. Nia wrapped her hands around Adam's neck, while squeezing and hugging Adam's manhood with her womb. She continued to look deep into Adam's eyes while her vagina hugged and greeted his stroking member. With each deep, slow stroke into

Nia, she fell deeper into spasms. As Adam continued to move and grind her body around his shaft, their separateness slowly began to disappear. The twin-flame energy bound their consciousness into a rising, twirling, growing entanglement of energy, granting them the ability to see each other's soul energy. More than just lusting at their humanoid forms, they now could see each other's astral bodies. Their bodies resembled millions of violet, jagged bolts of lightning, throbbing and flickering inside a human shell. Somewhere between the astral realm and normal reality, their energies gelled together while they continued to kiss in this newly built spiritual world. It was another one of Adams gifts, the ability to take another into his own consciousness. Nia's memories were seared with her own past life regression of her and Adam together. The combining of their energy and souls made way for an embolden cosmic download of information into both of their brain synapses, covering hundreds of lives together. As the intimate bond continued, the twin flame's energy further intensified their energy bodies in the spiritual realm. They could both see their entangled energies, intermingling, glowing, pulsating, and throbbing. The alignment of their bodies' energy centers produced a display similar to a lightning storm without sound; each of Adam's thrusts caused jolts of pleasure branching out in all directions. Adam could feel Nia's soul opening up, allowing her physical body to be keyed only for him. They both climaxed simultaneously, erupting into moans and groans of ecstasy. Their bond was now complete. Adam stumbled back to sit in a chair with Nia straddling him, careful to keep his seeds and himself inside of her. They held each other in the nude to savor the moment—skin to skin, panting feverishly. It was what Adam had been looking for his entire life. He now felt complete. Nia too. Still straddling Adam, Nia continued scooting and snuggling to bring herself as close as she could to him; careful to keep him inside of her.

Recapturing her breath, and with tears in her eyes, Nia telepathically mustered the strength to say, "My God... that was beautifully amazing."

Adam continued to enjoy every second of Nia cuddling him. Even though the odds may be against him and the Colony's success, what mattered most to him was Nia, and he had her. He now knew the burden was heavier than ever before. He also knew he needed a new kind of vigor if he wanted to keep her safe, thus keeping their relationship safe. Before he could go deeper into his thoughts, he noticed there was something different inside of him yet again. He recognized that he had been growing stronger and stronger with every moment after making love to Nia. He took inventory of the sensations in his body. He could feel his heart pumping blood through his veins, even down to the smallest of capillaries. Both of his brain hemispheres were active. The hum in his mind was more pronounced from the sensation of individual neurons acutely firing in his brain. He felt the interconnected relationship between trillions of cells and could account for every twitching muscle fiber. He felt his energy centers surging and throbbing, making the intimate connection with his body more remarkable. Adam had never been so alive before and he knew it had everything to do with his consummation with Nia. Bonding with his twin flame had made him more powerful than ever.

"Oh my God, Adam, look," Nia said with urgency while pointing to the flat screen TV in the far corner.

Shifting out of his deep thought, Adam rolled his head in the direction of the television. It was a news story running with Adam, Kojo, and Clutch's BioMod faces being broadcast as dangerous terrorists, wanted for questioning in the recent downtown Phoenix shooting.

"Breaking news... Police are on the lookout for three men who they say shot five security officers at the Hyatt Regency in downtown Phoenix just hours ago. We don't have many details, but Phoenix Police released this surveillance video showing the men who they say are responsible. They describe them as two white men, and one native American, all at least six

feet tall. One of the suspects has blonde hair, and we believe he may have been shot. At least three security officers are confirmed dead and authorities say the men you see here may be affiliated with the terrorist organization known as the Colony. Police released this photo of what they believe to be the getaway car: a 2000 silver Ford Taurus."

Chapter 26

A few minutes after the news story broke, Nia called to warn Clutch from the secure phone he gave her.

Clutch immediately asked, "Is Kojo okay, is Adam giving you problems?"

Nia stumbled a bit with her answer, "No, no, not at all, they are both fine, but they are looking for you... it's all over the news."

Clutch acknowledged her with a dull, apathetic tone, "Yes, yes, and all over the radio. We are okay, though. We just made it back. We're just about to enter your garage now."

Seconds later, Clutch and Jolon entered the lab while simultaneously deactivating their newly powered BioMods to save battery life. Still distracted with the taste of Nia in his mouth, Adam moved to greet Jolon. Like a long-lost brother, Adam embraced him with a big hug in an uncharacteristic fashion.

"Brooooo, back up, we don't hug," Jolon said jokingly.

"Who is that?" Jolon mumbled quietly to Adam.

After catching a view of Nia and Adam's googly eyes, Jolon quickly put the pieces together. A wide smile stretched across his face, "Ahhhh shit!"

Enthusiastically, he turned to Nia, "Hi, I'm Jolon, Adam's dad," he cracked.

Nia giggled, "Hello, Jolon, I'm Nia."

From the time Clutch walked into the lab, his enhanced senses told him what happened between Adam and Nia. He loathed smelling Nia's scent on Adam.

Carefully hiding the hurt in his eyes and barely making eye contact with Nia, Clutch asked, "Has Kojo made any signs of improvement?"

"No, sorry, he is still stable but no signs of improvement," she said sympathetically, consoling Clutch with a gentle rub on the back of his elbow. A temporary calming aura passed over Clutch at Nia's touch. Crude visions of Adam and her together wrecked his moment and brought him back to reality.

Clutch fidgeted from Nia's gesture and blurted, "We leave in five, get whatever you are taking." He turned and headed towards Kojo's room.

"Nia, can you disconnect Kojo from the equipment so I can take him?" Clutch asked while looking back over his shoulder at Nia.

Adam stepped in, "No!"

Clutch whipped around, glaring hard at Adam, and yelled, "What do you mean, no?"

Adam sensed Clutch's jealousy and knew he must choose his words wisely.

"I mean... I know how to save Kojo," he said.

"What the fuck are you talkin' about, man," Clutch said with a scrunched brow and confused gaze.

Adam strode toward Clutch, who eyed him with the intensity of a hawk eyeing its meal.

In a calm tone, Adam said, "He stopped having an aura after the downtown incident, and I haven't been able to feel his presence since. I couldn't put it together before, but now I know: his body is here, but the essence of him isn't. When I was in the astral realm before, I saw him being attacked and weakened. I think somehow they have managed to take his astral body."

"Okay, where they take him then?" Clutch asked irritably.

Adam hesitated and took a long sigh, "I have to go in the astral realm to find out."

Jolon's eyes widened with surprise, "Wha'?"

Nia gasped, bringing her hands to her mouth from the shock of Adam's announcement, "You can't be serious."

Nia and Jolon knew very little about the astral realm, but instinctively they knew this would be very dangerous.

"Awww, fuck nah, I'm not going through that shit again," Clutch yelled.

Adam retorted, "It's not about you, it's about freeing that man in there that took a chance to free me!"

Clutch, not sure of what to make of Adam's angle, stared at him in silence. He loved his brother, so he'd listen to any possibility to get him back, even the long shots. In many regards, this was akin to Adam committing suicide. Clutch saw what the Ky's minions did to Kojo in the astral realm, and he was an experienced astral combatant. Adam was barely trained. Being naively duped by Kano, surely he'd be a sitting duck wherever Kojo's astral body was taken.

"Look, you said it yourself, the Ky at the Grand Canyon may or may not help us, and the longer Kojo's essence is out of his body, the more likely it is he will never come back. I brought all this on him, it's only right I do this. From solider to solider, you can't expect me to live with knowing I caused all of this and not try to fix it," Adam said with a hard stare at Clutch.

Clutch scratched through the stubbles of his beard, weighing through the possibilities. He wasn't used to making such critical, consequential decisions. Kojo was much better suited for these types of strategic matters. Should he commit Adam to sudden death for the hopeful exchange of his brother? He couldn't help but wonder, what would Kojo do?

Adam continued, "Whoever took him won't be expecting me to come, so they won't be prepared. And if I fail, as a last ditch effort... you can still take him to the Ky at the Grand Canyon and try that route."

Clutch knew Adam had a point, and he respected him for stepping up. Looking into Adam's eyes, Clutch saw that this wasn't some kind of ploy. Adam was going to do this with or without him. There would be no stopping him.

"I'm all for you trying, but we can't stay, they are

probably already on their way here," Clutch said.

"It doesn't matter where we're at, they are going to keep Kojo alive as long as possible to be able to pinpoint us through his silver cord," Adam said.

He paused and dropped his head before looking somberly back up at Clutch, "And, honestly, taking him with you to the canyon won't work either, that will just expose the other rogue Ky and make matters worse."

"If Mark Green hasn't been turned, Nia has a direct connection to him. While you were gone she did a complete work up on my DNA and made arrangements to get it to some of the people she trusts. They will get it to Mark so the counter agent can be made," Adam said.

Adam walked closer to Clutch, reached his hand out to him, and said, "This is where we make our stand... so help us God."

Clutch let go a long sigh, he slowly nodded his head and shook Adam's hand. With the shake, Adam telepathically read that Clutch had temporarily put his grievances aside for the sake of his brother. He also sensed that Clutch was impressed by his courage and grateful for him putting his life on the line for Kojo. They both knew if they could get Kojo back, the Colony was back to becoming a major threat to the powerful Ky empire, powerful enough to put a major dent in their operations, bringing humans a step closer to being free beings.

"Alright, bro, any funny shit go down, I'm going to be the first to blow your noodles out the back of your head. You got twenty minutes. If you don't bring my brother back by then, we have no choice but to leave. Time is of the essence," Clutch noted sternly.

He turned to address everybody in his loud, direct voice, "I'm guessing they've known our location for more than three hours, so they can be here any minute. No time for speeches. We are outta here in twenty minutes or less... everybody... Nia, you too. So let's get prepared."

Everyone nodded quietly in agreement.

"Adam, you begin to set up. Jolon, let's unload everything we brought from the safe house and fortify in case of an attack. Nia, you stay with Adam and Kojo," Clutch ordered.

Adam turned to Jolon, "Bro, you don't have to be here..."

"Get outta here with that, bro, I'm not going anywhere. What do you think... I'm going back to work for Crow Corp Media and that dick of a CEO?" Jolon said with a firm voice.

Adam grinned. "I know, but do you understand what you're really saying?" Adam questioned.

"This isn't about me. It's about all my brothers and sisters out there getting screwed by the Ky. I'd die for them. This is my fight too! So I'm staying!" Jolon yelled.

What an honorable friend Jolon was, the world is lucky to have him Adam thought. He nodded and patted Jolon on the back.

"Don't start getting all mushy on me, bro. Go do your thing," Jolon said, flicking his arms to shoo Adam away.

"Oh, and Adam," Jolon whispered while pulling Adam close. Making sure no one caught his words or read his lips, he said, "I saw you two love birds lookin' at each other. After we save the world, you need to ask her out... dude, she is smooooookin'!"

"Yeah... I'm definitely going to do that," Adam said sarcastically, knowing Nia was already a kept woman.

He patted Jolon on the shoulder and headed with Nia into Kojo's room.

"I'll be there in a second, Nia," Adam said while guiding her with his arm into Kojo's room.

He turned to Clutch, "Can I get a second?"

"Make it quick," Clutch said.

"Now that this is all in the open, I need you to promise me that you will take care of Nia if something happens to me. Without you or me, she won't survive," Adam said.

Clutch stood speechless, peering back at Adam with tightening eyes.

"It's not just a favor for me. If Kojo doesn't come back she can finish this thing," Adam said, pointing to Nia in the room. "She is worth her weight in diamonds," Adam pleaded.

Clutch didn't need any convincing. He was going to take care of Nia despite Adam asking him. In the world of hardened men, those words meant, *I know you like my girl, and if something happens to me you have my blessing.*

With a heavy sigh, Clutch slowly nodded, "Okay... Okay."

Adam turned, headed to the room and greeted Nia standing at Kojo's bedside. Nia reached to embrace him.

With tears welling up, she said, "Adam... I'm afraid. I so badly want to stop you from doing this. There has to be another way. Are you sure about this?"

Adam sighed and kissed Nia's forehead, "No, I'm not, but I have to do it."

Nia clutched her chest and dropped her head, "The irony of our story... I've waited my entire life to find you and now you are leaving."

Tears slowly streaked down her face. Adam watched her silent tears drop to the ground. The sight of her tears falling on his shoes brought an indescribable pain to the core of his existence.

Adam stepped closer, and lifted her chin.

"Nia, it pains me to leave you for one second. I want so badly to be with you, but I realize that we can never be together in peace as long as the Ky are imprisoning mankind. They will haunt us and continue to fill each one of our lives with pain... as they have been. This is the only way," Adam said softly.

Nia continued to cry, falling into Adams chest for comfort.

Adam held her and repeated over and over again, "I love you."

Nia looked up, softly kissed Adam on his lips, wiped her eyes, smiled, and said, "I love you too. Just please, please come back to me."

Etching a half smile across his face, Adam

continued, "Okay, I'm going to go into a meditative state. Just stay near me, and continue to touch me. That will keep me at my strongest. No matter what happens, don't wake me... I have to finish this. And don't worry if something happens to me... I will find you!"

Nia cracked a painful smile, "I know, Love... you always do."

"And Nia, no matter what happens, today has been the best day of my life," he said while lightly brushing her tears away.

Adam borrowed Nia's phone and inserted his memory card. He brought up his favorite playlist to help spark his astral combat: "Rage Against the Machine." He put on his head phones and calmly sat while a focused and determined state engulfed him. Adam slowed his heart rate and began his mission into the astral realm.

Chapter 27

Adam's astral body rose out of his physical body, quickly ascending high above the lab and lingering close to Kojo's silver cord. Within minutes, the lab he once was inside was nothing more than a small square far beneath him. Next, the city of Phoenix turned into a grid of flat desert squares. As he continued to follow Kojo's cord, it wasn't long before he was out of the city and high above the north eastern Arizona desert. Kojo's cord took him to a large mesa rising out of the flat desert terrain. The mesa's base was decorated with scattered rock, cacti, and indiscriminate bushes. There were no roads, electrical towers, signs, or any trace of intelligent life. The land was desolate, minus an occasional trotting coyote or scrambling scorpion. Adam took a second to study the large mesa. The surroundings looked eerie, similar to the base where he was. Adam knew he could take his astral body through walls, but he wasn't sure about solid rock.

Only one way to find out, he thought as he dove into the belly of the mesa.

With ease, Adam's astral body penetrated deep into the mesa's structure. He continued flowing through the solid rock until he breeched into a hallway of some kind.

Holy shit, he thought as he quickly realized he was at the very base where he was trained, the very base he called home for a year.

Adam left this place just over a month ago, thinking it was the best thing that happened to him. What a twist of fate—not only may it be a place of Kojo's demise, but Adam's as well. For twelve months, he roamed these halls thinking of himself as some sort of hero as the scientists poked and prodded him for his DNA.

He continued downward, following Kojo's silver cord until he pierced the fourth floor of the base. He never knew the base had a fourth floor, and it looked dramatically different from the first three floors. The first three floors were polluted with scientists, military personnel, engineers, contractors, and subjects such as himself. The halls were usually bright and well lit with fluorescent lights. However, this floor was empty, no human to be found. It was dimly lit with a soft, low violet light. The concrete floors were almost perfect, like polished glass. Adam could see his astral body's reflection from the smooth craftsmanship. The walls were smooth and black, having a strange writing on them, similar to cuneiform. The writings looked oddly similar to the strange markings he saw on the walls of the silver oval wheels that day in his village.

Kojo's cord continued sweeping around the corridor. Gliding down the hall, Adam could see many empty rooms, possessing chairs with restraints. This gave Adam an eerie feeling for what this floor may have actually been used for. As Adam pondered the straps on the chairs, thudding sounds caught his attention, "Thump thump thump thump." Coming further around the corridor, Adam beheld two monstrous beasts pacing in front of a large security door. Having two arms and two legs, the hideous beasts stood well over eight feet. Their backs bore a muscular hump with jagged spikes down its center. Their color was dark grey, and they had large skeletal heads, similar to the grey aliens often talked about in popular UFO cultures. They weren't the small, frail, grey aliens, but more of a warrior class. Their arms were long and muscular, resembling that of a silver back gorilla. The beasts had upright hind legs and their bodies were retrofitted with some type of battle gear. Their unnatural build looked to Adam like they were another one of the Ky's genetic creations. The beasts carried large, metallic rifles for their security detail and were oblivious to Adam's astral presence. Days ago, the sight of such ghastly things may have overwhelmed him, but just hours ago in the astral realm, he'd seen worse. The fact that the beasts were unequipped to see Adam's astral body was reassuring, bettering his odds of not being detected.

Adam continued. Passing through the massive door, he came into a large lab with more security beasts roaming about. The room looked like it was originally part of an existing underground cave that was retrofitted into a lab. There were dozens of small, grey aliens with large heads performing experiments on a variety of caged chimpanzees. They too were oblivious to Adam's astral body. As Adam continued through the lab, he felt a presence. He cautiously continued, not sure of what this presence was. Combing the lab for the presence, he saw a large tank of water that ran the width of the lab far in the back of the room. In the tank, Adam spotted the presence—an alien-like amphibious creature. Its head was long and slender, carrying most of its bone outward versus under its skin like most animals on earth. Its body was long and thin, possessing four arms and webbed fingers. The creature's back birthed two large fins that stretched out like wings. Its fins allowed it to hover effortlessly in the water. Its body was decorated with a multitude of colors. Its head and back were hooked into probes that limited its freedom and mobility. To Adam, it looked completely alien in origin, yet oddly beautiful.

Its eyes locked on Adam's astral body and followed him as he glided through the lab.

"Helppppppp meeeee," Adam heard.

Is this some kind of trick? Is this creature really talking to me from the physical realm? Adam wondered. But how can it see me?

Adam didn't respond, not sure of what to make of the creature, not sure if it was a Ky trap. He continued following Kojo's silver cord while cautiously drifting along the outside of the tank.

"You must destroy this place... they will continue the suffering across many more worlds," the creature moaned.

"He caaaaan see me!" Adam confirmed. Not only could Adam feel its presence, it could feel his. Adam deeply wanted answers to how the creature could see his astral body from the physical world, but he knew he must quickly get to Kojo. A one second delay could put Nia, Clutch, Jolon, Kojo, and himself in deeper danger.

As Adam got closer to the creature, he could see

that it had been brutally experimented on. It was suffering and being held captive. With his astral senses, he could read the creature was very weak.

"They have taken over my home world. They have changed our species, we are no longer pure. Please help," the creature begged.

Adam's astral body flashed with jolts of sorrow at the creature's words, but still he continued ignoring it and following Kojo's cord.

"I've been a prisoner here for a long time, and I've seen what their BioGrid has done to your kind," the creature said. "If you have gotten this far, you must be the anti-body."

Anti-body? What the hell is this thing talking about, Adam thought.

"The creator designed all of its creatures with the means to defend themselves. Your planet is a living entity. Once a planet is out of balance, it produces anti-bodies to help combat its infestation. You must be one of earth's anti-bodies," the creature said.

Did that thing just read my thoughts? It must've, it answered my question. And the earth is a living entity? Adam pondered.

He couldn't ignore the creature any longer. His astral body started to change colors, turning from a bright violet to a dull red with anger. Adam slowed and stopped at the front of the large tank.

"What is this place?" Adam asked.

"Let me show you," the creature said.

In a flash, the creature projected to Adam the Ky's slaying of its home world, their painful genetic experiments, and their barbaric treatment of other species throughout the galaxy. Overwhelmingly brutal images poured into Adam's astral mind. He could temporarily feel the pain and suffering of the beings the Ky had massacred.

"They use this place to learn and study their enemy's genetic strengths and weaknesses before they attack them. I was an anti-body for my planet before I was used to find my species' weakness. They used the secrets they found in me to destroy my world. They purposely keep me alive so that I can suffer knowing what I did. Many other planets have and will be consumed this same way. You have to stop them!" the creature moaned.

"Glad you finally joined us, we've been waiting on you," Adam heard from a familiar voice.

He briskly turned his astral body around and was shocked to see Kano's astral body hovering a few yards away.

"If you can't beat them, join them... right?" Kano said arrogantly.

With his astral body glowing bright red, Adam said, "You're a trader, a fucking coward. I was off my game to let you get close to me, but now I can see your true colors. You's a bitch, worse than the Ky, at least they are down for each other..."

Kano interrupted while his astral body illuminated a bright red hue, showing his anger, "Spare me your condemnation boy, and open your bloody eyes. We are talking about beings intelligent enough to modify humanity and have mastered interstellar travel. Not only have they conquered worlds, but galaxies. And you think your little tea party movement is any threat to them?"

He drifted a bit closer to Adam, "Wake the fuck up! When you play the game right, you end up like me; resist and you end up in a fuckin' tank like that thing!" Kano said, pointing to the creature.

Calming his voice down, Kano said, "I tried to help you, save you, but no... you bought into Kojo's bullshit. You wanted to run off trying to save the world. And look where it has gotten you. You could have been a god on this planet, had you just cooperated."

"A god... you mean a slave! Package that shit up

and put a bow on it all you want! Bottom line, out of many there is always one born to be a sellout!" Adam scolded.

"Well, that's surprising," Kano said sarcastically.

Drifting even closer to Adam, "Intelligence was never your strong suit boy. You don't get it. I've struck a deal with the Ky to live like a king for each one of my lives here... and that ain't bad. I could have done the same for you. But you backed the wrong horse. Now you and your little girlfriend are going to live like pond scum," he added.

"What... what did you say?" Adam yelled, coming closer to Kano while his astral body blazed bright red.

Kano responded nonchalantly, "Nia, I think it is, isn't it? Had you just cooperated, I could have kept her and you safe..."

"Get the fuck outta here. I'd rather die a thousand more lives before I stain Nia's soul by aligning her with you devils!" Adam yelled.

"And pass up being a god? Package it up however you want, boy, but out of many there is always one born to be a sucker behind a bitch!" Kano taunted.

"So says the sellout," Adam yelled.

Kano's words were soul crushing, abandoned of compassion, and deep seeded with an evil only worthy for the bowels of hell. A clearer, less agitated Adam would have thought deeper about Kano's presence. He would have pondered how he arbitrarily found him, or the possibility of this being a setup. But Kano's words completely distracted Adam from his mission, and the possible likelihood he was lured to the base as a trap. Kano's words rattled Adam with his deepest rage yet. He could handle Kano's taunts, as long as Nia was left out. It was already an all-out war, but bringing Nia in made it something else.

Adam fashioned his astral weapons of choice: two double sided assegai spears. Enraged by Kano's words about Nia, he darted toward his former teacher. Kano laughed at Adam's approaching astral body while assembling his own sword in preparation for his battle with his apprentice. Adam struck with his spear. Kano formed an astral shield that deflected Adam's attack. Adam continued his onslaught, strike after strike, slash after slash, blow after blow, trying his best to weaken Kano's defense. While deflecting Adam's blows, Kano's astral body began to grow three times its normal size. Kano made a point to keep some of his best astral tricks secret, in the event he would one day have to battle his apprentice. Adam jolted back, halting his attack to analyze Kano's move. He looked at Kano with amazement, not knowing it was possible to do such a thing in the astral realm.

"What's wrong, boy? You look like you've seen a ghost!" Kano laughed.

Flippant with his response, Adam said, "Nah... I'm just looking at the same ol' coward, just a bigger one than before."

Kano, angered at the fact that he was unable to rattle Adam, switched his weapon, morphing his arms into razor-like blades that were double Adam's size. Then, with a ragged bitterness, Kano dashed toward Adam while he brutally took a swipe at him. Adam crouched and covered, shielding the blow. However, the sheer power of Kano's strike threw his astral body backwards. The force of the strike was felt throughout Adam's entire energy body. Kano continued strike after strike, laughing with each blow he delivered to Adam, who was taking a beating. In the physical world, Adam's body began to show the damage from Kano's razor-sharp claws. The damaging blows taken in the astral realm was transferred to his physical body. Nia cringed at the whelps on his face, neck, wrists, and blood trickling from his nose.

Nia continued to hold Adam tight, "Oh my God, baby, hang in there."

Adam's body continued to jerk and twitch, sending worrisome chills down Nia's spine.

"I don't know what to do," Nia cried while nervously rocking Adam back and forth.

"Boooommmm," a thunderous sound was heard throughout the lab that rattled Kojo's room. The lights and equipment flickered and shut off, plunging the lab into a deafening silence. Everything went dark—no emergency lights, not even a lit exit sign.

"Clutch... Jolon," Nia called in a panicky voice.

No answer.

"Clutch... Are you okay?" she questioned with an even shakier voice.

A few seconds of silence went by, seeming like eternity to Nia. Outside Kojo's room she saw a flash of light. She fell silent, clutching Adam tighter and tighter. The light appeared to be getting more defined, it was coming her way. Now she could hear approaching footsteps in the semi-darkness.

"Nia... they are here!" Clutch shouted from outside Kojo's room.

A second later, he entered Kojo's room with the light from his assault weapon leading the way.

Visually focused, he said, "They hit us with an electromagnetic pulse."

Nia quickly responded, "I have backup generators

that..."

Clutch cut Nia off with a firm voice, "No, all the switches are fried, so the generators are done too."

He pulled a cylindrical object with black fins around it from his duffle bag.

"This will keep Kojo's room temporarily powered for his safety," Clutch said, showing Nia the device.

He quickly slid the object under Kojo's bed. The device turned on and a blue hue engulfed Kojo's room. The electronic equipment in Kojo's room instantly powered up and began to work normally.

Clutch glanced at the welts developing over Adam's body. He turned to face Nia and spotted a dazed, and confused look in her eyes.

With a narrowed gaze, he handed her a weapon from his duffle bag, "Here, keep yourself and Adam safe with this... Anything comes through this door, blow its fucking head off, just point and pull."

The underlining stress in Clutch's words brought an explosion of nauseating jitters in her stomach. Keeping one hand wrapped around Adam, she slowly reached and grabbed the weapon. Unsteadily holding it, she brought the weapon in close. Nia wasn't a trained soldier, but in this moment Clutch needed her to be.

With a carefully constructed smile, Clutch said, "Knowing what must be done does away with fear. Find your desire for that, and you will be okay."

Nia swallowed and nodded, comprehending Clutch's words to her core. Clutch took a moment and filled his eyes with Nia's beauty, as if he was taking her in one last time.

"Jolon, switch on your OmegaScopes," Clutch demanded as he ran back into the lab with his assault rifle leading the way.

Both Clutch and Jolon switched on the OmegaScopes attached to their rifles. The scopes powered up, filling the lab with an electronic hum. They both swiveled about the lab, peering through their high-tech scopes. Another one of Scar's and Kojo's brilliant designs, the OmegaScopes allowed them to peer through the darkness and even through the lab's solid walls. The visual superiority always gave them the jump on their enemies' location, usually allowing them to stay a step ahead. However, the OmegaScopes revealed murky odds of an escape—Phoenix SWAT, Phoenix PD, and Maricopa county sheriffs had the building completely surrounded. Their high-tech weaponry even spotted a SWAT team seconds away from breaching the lab's back entrances.

"Jolon, activate the GammaField," Clutch

screamed, pointing to the device inside Jolon's duffle bag.

Just as Jolon opened the bag to activate the GammaField, two bright greenish plumes flashed inside the lab. Two of the large eight-foot security beasts materialized from the flashes. The beasts quickly jumped into action.

"Bam bam bam," fired the creatures as they laid down suppressing fire at Jolon. The booming sound from the beasts' high intensity rounds filled the lab with a deep, hostile thunder. The pulses from their guns engulfed the lab with blueish-green strobes of light. Unable to grab the duffle bag, Jolon was barely able to jump behind a lab table in time for cover. Clutch fired on the two beasts while diving for the duffle bag. The beasts absorbed Clutch's shots through their protective vests. The second beast swiveled and fired on Clutch, who grimaced as the beast's laser-like weapon tore through the flesh of his arm. He hit the ground with a thud. The fall jarred loose his weapon, putting it outside his reach. "Thump... thump... thump," stepped the eight-foot beast as it headed toward Clutch's position. Clutch continued to scoot back, in a trail of his own blood.

As the beast closed in on Clutch, Adam was still fighting for his life against Kano in the astral realm. Kano was much more powerful and advanced in the astral realm than Adam ever imagined. Most of Adam's attacks were deflected by Kano, and the others barely damaged him at all. Kano continued slicing Adam with his large talon-like claws. The slicing strikes scattered a painful ache throughout Adam's astral body. He knew there was only so much more he could take. Adam spiraled and tumbled deeper from the impact of Kano's attacks. Each slashing strike knocked Adam deeper down into the base, down to the fifth floor. It was a much larger floor, about football field in length and fifty feet in height.

Adam finally brought his astral body back under control. He probed his surroundings and observed another level of unimaginable horror. He saw banks and banks of human clones, none of which had auras—tying together the look alike aura-less men he met on the bus. They were soulless flesh, biological robots. The clones were of presidents, heads of state, entertainers, and wealthy businessmen. There appeared to be clones of other alien species as well. They were encased in large, vertical, blue, oval containers, filled with a gel-like liquid. The clones were kept in stasis sleep. In laymen's terms, it was a bank of vending machine clones, all dispersible at the Ky's will.

The captive amphibious creature he spoke with was right, this place was a hub of nightmarish proportions and needed to be destroyed. The horror temporarily distracted him from his battle with Kano. Just below, he could see cloning banks much different from the others. He took a closer look and was rocked to his core. He observed rows and rows of his genetic clones in different stages of development. They were plugged into a live audio-video programming feed, while their eyes were held open. They were being systematically programmed. Four of the clones were full term, ready for deployment to carry out whatever sick plans the Ky had imagined.

Kano glided in above Adam and interrupted his study of the cloning banks, "We couldn't let all that natural talent of yours go to waste, now could we?"

Adam never imagined Kano's betrayal could go this far. The former ache in Adam's astral body was now transformed into a raging fire of revenge, and it was going to start against Kano. His astral body detonated with jagged jolts of red lightning inside his astral shell. Fueled by the fire in the pit of his astral center, Adam threw one of his spears at Kano. Kano easily deflected Adam's spear attack and continued coming forward. Still fuming with anger, Adam darted in Kano's direction. Kano again effortlessly deflected Adam's attack and pounded him with another thunderous blow.

"Try something new, give me a challenge at

least," Kano laughed as he poked fun at Adam's feeble attacks.

Adam felt his aching astral body weaken further as he tumbled deeper down from Kano's strike. He came to rest, face to face, eye to eye with his clone as if it was mysteriously staring at him. He took a quick glance at his other clones in assembly line production and was hit with inspiration. Each clone reminded Adam of his multiple lives.

Perhaps Kano is right, I do need to try something new, Adam thought. If Kano is like Kojo and Clutch, he's enhanced, but not enough to have access to his past lives' knowledge. That means Kano only knows what he has learned in this lifetime, thought Adam.

On the other hand, Adam knew he had lifetimes of knowledge to pull from, including hundreds of martial arts, combat strategies, and techniques Kano had never seen and had no clue about. The combative advantage was clearly in his favor, not to mention he was at full capacity with Nia by his side.

There is no way he can deal with what I'm about to bring his ass, Adam thought.

This caused Adam's astral vibration to rise. His newfound confidence shifted his color to a bright violet, showcasing his rising strength. The shift in color began to disturb Kano's confidence.

"It's pointless, boy, give up," Kano taunted.

"Give up? I'm just getting started," Adam calmly said.

Kano's astral body began to throb with a deep red rage of anger at not being able to break Adam's iron will.

"I'm still trying to figure out if you are really this bloody stupid," Kano said as six goliath astral demons surrounded Adam.

The demons were similar to the beasts Adam fought in the astral realm during the downtown Phoenix clash, the shadow demons Kojo warned him about. They were at least four times his size, humanoid in form, with bulky, muscular shoulders and legs. The beasts had two large, sharp horns drifting back out of their heads, with slanted red eyes. Their faces were a grotesque mixture between goat and lion. The demons had no fingers, but large talons for claws. Attached to their wrists were long, soul-draining tentacles. Adam had felt their soul-draining power during the battle in downtown Phoenix and understood the danger they posed.

Still hearing music through his silver cord link, Adam was sparked by Rage Against the Machine's *Know Your Enemy*. Finding solace in the perfectly timed song, Adam chuckled and blurted a powerful quote, "If you know the enemy and know yourself, you need not fear the results of a hundred battles."

"Spare me your Sun Tzu quotes, boy. I'm done playing with you!" Kano screamed as he motioned for the astral beasts to attack Adam.

Unconcerned by their presence, Adam said, "You know, Kano, you only fooling yourself with all this tough talk and fake-ass witch doctor bit. I've looked into your eyes, and I know you... you're a coward... and once I turn this heat up on yo' ass, you gonna fall to fuckin' pieces!"

Adam's words infuriated the shadow goliaths and Kano. As the shadow demons charged, Adam braced himself for another intense battle. He created a shield and his favorite double-sided Zulu spear—and readied for war.

While Adam was immersed in the battle from hell, Clutch and Jolon scrambled for dear life in the physical realm. One of the eight-foot security beasts had Jolon pinned under heavy fire behind a desk. Jolon continued firing from behind cover, desperately trying to land a money shot against the freak of mutation. Unrelenting, the beast continued coming forward, determined to land a money shot of its own against Jolon.

The other security beast stalked Clutch, who was

exposed in plain sight. Still on the ground, Clutch continued scampering back, wincing with his wounded arm. To buy time, he tossed whatever he could find with his good arm to disrupt the beast—a chair, a keyboard, a microscope. The debris was flung at the marching mutant at high velocity, but the beast prevailed, continuing forward. When Clutch ran out of room and objects to throw, the beast finally cornered him. It raised its weapon and prepared to once and for all put an end to the mighty Clutch. Then, without warning, shots were fired, "Boom boom boom." The beast's head exploded. The headless mutant's body crashed to the ground with a loud thud. Clutch swiveled to see where the shots came from and saw Nia with clasped hands, holding the weapon he gave her earlier. She found the money shot of her own from the threshold of Kojo's room.

Instantly, a smash was heard. The SWAT team was breaching the front entrance and coming down the hallway. Wasting no time, Clutch rolled and grabbed his weapon. The first order of business was to address the beast firing at Jolon. Clutch swiveled his weapons and punched two laser-like pulses into the back of the beast's skull. The eight-foot mutant came crumbling down in a pool of its own grayish blood. Jolon collapsed, panting from the traumatic stress of the situation.

"Jolon, mount up, we got SWAT in the back!"

Clutch shouted.

He bolted to his duffle bag, while firing at the SWAT team approaching from the front entrance. His powerful assault weapon pierced through the team's shields and put down the first two members. While Clutch took cover, he caught a glimpse of Jolon still on the ground, gasping for air.

"Jolon, pull yourself together!" Clutch yelled while grabbing the GammaField out of his duffle bag.

Grimacing from the use of his wounded arm, he grabbed the device, activating and tossing it into the center of the room. The GammaField deployed a green force field, encompassing the entire lab. Two SWAT team agents attempted to pierce the GammaField and were immediately blown to bits. The power of the explosion rattled the lab and knocked the other swat team members unconscious. A couple more beasts attempted to be beamed into the room and were disintegrated on impact by the force field.

"Nia, stay with Adam, we need him at full power," Clutch screamed.

Reaching into his duffle bag with his undamaged arm, Clutch put a small, square device on his wound. The device turned on with a bright, white light and began repairing his ripped flesh. Clutch grunted with pain as he flopped down against the table, taking a moment to heal and rest.

"The rest is up to Adam. The GammaFields have enough energy to hold them off for twenty or thirty minutes tops," Clutch said, still wincing.

"Jolon, reload and grab me the MolGun. We are going to have to escape underground. We can tie into the sewers. We might even have to carry Kojo and Adam, so be ready! Once we are out, we can assume new identities with the BioMods," Clutch instructed while tending his wound.

Unbeknownst to Clutch, Jolon's face was beginning to contort. In the midst of all the action, and unknown to all, astral demons were present before the GammaField was deployed. Jolon's body was being taken over. The overwhelming fear of the situation caused Jolon's emotional state to drop low enough for his body to be compromised for a possession. The contortion and struggle on his face subsided, and his eyes went blank. His face fell glum, devoid of any emotion.

Clutch continued talking, unaware of Jolon's change, "These beasts dropping in means there is a cloaked Ky cruiser somewhere around here."

Jolon grabbed his assault rifle and slowly walked over toward the unsuspecting Clutch. While Clutch sat, oblivious to an armed and dangerous Jolon,

Adam had his hands full with six goliath astral demons. The shadow goliaths approached, surrounding Adam, cracking their soul-draining whips. Adam knew he was almost drained to the level of unconsciousness when battling two of the demons, trying to take on six would be suicide. In unison the demons attacked, lashing their whips at Adam. He dodged their attack by dropping under the whips. Adam plummeted deeper into the base, piercing down into the sixth floor. He drifted in on a busy, active scene that once again rocked him to his core. Like nothing he could imagine, the sixth floor was humongous, at least a couple of football fields in height and stretching a couple of miles in each direction. The great pyramids of Egypt would comfortably fit inside.

The base floor was split into two sections. The first section served as an airport with Ky ships docked, neatly hovering equal distance from one another. Adam estimated twenty or so ships with a low audible hum floating with some kind of magnetic lift technology. The smooth, metallic ships were similar to the large, silver oval wheels over his village that dreadful day of his death, with the exception of obvious technological improvements over time. Suddenly, Adam saw a large blue-violet cylindrical portal open. Quietly, a large Ky cruiser breached through and smoothly docked among the other ships.

Once through, the portal disappeared without a trace, another example of the Ky's technological brilliance. A small tinge of doubt crept into Adam as he took in the galactic might of the Ky. The other side of the base was separated by a bluish force field. This side of the base was active with many Ky scientists tending to rows and rows of captured alien beings and other experimental subjects. Adam cringed, knowing most likely the Ky had been abducting hundreds of intelligent beings from throughout the galaxy, brutishly keeping them captive and experimenting on them. The subjects were stacked in high-tempered glass containment units. The units were equally spaced, floating above the floor with some kind of magnetic lift energy, likely similar to the docked Ky ships. Most subjects couldn't see Adam, but the few who could begged to be freed. As Adam drifted past the units, he heard their moans, groans, and cries. Each murmur sent chaotic jolts of sadness inside of Adam's astral shell. As he approached, he could see that some of the captives were animal-human and human-alien hybrids. He wished he could help, but he knew now was not the time.

As Adam continued to descend deeper into the base, he surprisingly spotted Kojo's astral body. He was being held separate from the other containment units and was imprisoned inside of a small energy cell. Kojo was sitting peacefully in the center of his cell, routinely calming himself with his astral cigar—a good sign, all things considered. His astral body was very weak, though, as was evident by its dull, low-lit illumination of colors. Adam darted to Kojo, overjoyed and relieved. As he was just upon Kojo's cell, he felt his limbs and neck being wrapped and restrained. The immensity of the Ky ships, the captives, and Kojo completely sidetracked him, giving the ensuing demons an advantage. With a great force, he was yanked back by the whips of the three perusing goliath demons. With one whip latched firmly around his neck, and the other two around his arms, he felt an instant drain in his astral body. The demons gave a powerful tug, forcing Adam's astral body into a temporary crucifix pose. He felt as if his neck was being squeezed and his limbs were being torn and ripped from his body. The pain was immense, and he knew he couldn't stand to be held by the whips for long or they would drain his energy. Adam aggressively spun himself like a raging cyclone, drawing the demons closer with each revolution. While spinning, he extended his two spears and began to slice and lacerate the demons, lessening their grasp on him. Adam took advantage; with one powerful strike, he sheered through all three demons, sending them shrinking back into the aether. Free from the demons' whips, Adam darted back to Kojo. With the taste of victory pulsing through his astral veins, he got Kojo's attention. At the sight of Adam,

Kojo joyfully rose to the edge of his cell and dished out his normally arrogant smile.

"Are you okay? What do I have to do to get you out of here?" Adam asked while energetically patrolling around Kojo's cell.

Kojo attempted to communicate with Adam by mouthing instructions and pointing to the cell's energy modules above. Adam looked to understand but was unclear of Kojo's instructions. Normally communication was all telepathic in the astral realm; however, Adam noticed he was unable to communicate with Kojo. The nature of the cell was distorting all sound and telepathic communication. In desperation, Adam franticly began to punch and slice at the cell's energy modules. No matter how hard he hit them, he was unable to make any damage. Adam began to panic, driving his frustration higher.

"Think dude... think," he said aloud to himself.

He continued studying the cell's assembly, trying to comprehend Kojo's instructions.

There has to be a way to deactivate this thing, Adam mused.

It must have to be physically deactivated, he thought.

Kojo pulsated his astral body to get Adam's

attention. He pointed to warn Adam of what was coming behind him. Adam turned around and was jolted by the sight of Kano closing in with three more astral goliaths.

Still ripe with rage, Kano said, "Did you really think you could just walk in here and free Kojo?"

Walk... that's it, thaaaaas it... WALK, thought Adam.

The force field is too dense for an astral body to pierce through. This field's energy module must be controlled by some switch inside the base. And I bet I know who knows where that switch is, Adam pondered.

With that, Adam hatched his plan to free Kojo.

"You know, Kano, the supreme art of war is to subdue your enemy without fighting," Adam said.

"And what is that supposed to mean," Kano yelled, highly irritated.

"You're about to find out," Adam said as he zoomed past Kano and the goliath demons.

Kano grunted in annoyance, "Argggggg!"

He turned and raced after Adam; the goliath demons followed. Adam rose back to the third floor, closely following Kano's astral cord. Telepathically,

Adam could hear Kano, taunting and ripping him with profanities as he followed.

"Stand and fight, you bloody coward!" Kano shouted in his heightened rage.

Adam ignored his taunts. He continued with his plan, following Kano's silver cord back to his body. He saw Kano's body in his quarters, sitting in a meditative state. Kano was enraged, agitated, and distracted to the point that it sidetracked him enough to leave his physical body vulnerable to possession. Knowing that he was not immune from possession like Kojo and Clutch, Adam took advantage of the unsuspecting Kano and sat himself inside of Kano's body. The repossession began.

Adam woke up in Kano's physical body. He could feel Kano's heightened heart beat from the body's highly agitated state. The repossession gave him access to Kano's knowledge, including the base layout and the location of the switch to free Kojo. He also learned of the many astral tricks Kano purposely kept from him, including the all-powerful Merkaba. From Kano's quarters on the third floor, he had to get to the control room directly below. Although Kano knew where the switch was, he didn't have clearance to that level, so he would have to face armed guards if he was to get inside of the control room. He would also need the security lead's badge in order to gain entry into the security room. He'd have only one shot at it.

Adam continued probing Kano's mind. He learned that this was all a planned attack. Since they didn't find his body back at the bar, it was assumed he was still alive. The CEO's plan was to lure Adam's astral body to the base, capture it like Kojo, and attack the others in the physical world at the same time. Once they attacked and subdued the others, they would take Adam's physical body back and continue to study its enhanced evolution. Meanwhile, Kojo and Adam's astral bodies would be imprisoned indefinitely here at the base.

These bastards are relentless, they have no limits to the shit they do, Adam thought after learning the Ky plan.

Killing Adam and having him reincarnate again was no option either; the Ky wanted his soul trapped. He was getting more powerful and troublesome with each reincarnation and they could no longer take the risk of the world seeing Adam's abilities. This slip-up would certainly threaten their BioGrid and they weren't planning on losing their power source over one uppity slave. Adam now knew that if he failed he would be imprisoned indefinitely and he would never have a chance to see Nia again. He couldn't stomach that. The thought alone bore down on him like tonnage. He had to focus like never before if he was to be successful. His trepidation caused Kano's body to sweat, throat to swell, and tongue to become parched. Kano's thumping heart beat so loudly that it partially drowned Adam's own thoughts.

Hopefully Clutch and Jolon can hold them off long enough for me to free Kojo and get back, Adam thought.

He knew he needed to move Kano's body with lighting speed if he was to have any chance of getting back to help the others. He bolted out of Kano's quarters and headed into the elevator. Racing out of the elevator, Adam puppeted Kano's body down the hall to the security check point before the control room. After reading Kano's memories, he wasn't surprised to find the security check point heavily guarded. There were three men, heavily armed with assault rifles, hand guns, and bullet proof vests. One man was located inside a control booth, and the other two were guarding the large entry door to the control room hall. Adam, possessing Kano's body, approached the unsuspecting guards. They, of course, had no clue that Kano's body had been repossessed and was being driven by Adam.

Clueless, the first guard spoke, "Hello, Kano. May I see your credentials, please?"

"Sure, no problem," Adam said, reaching into

Kano's pouch.

When the guard's eyes drew down, Adam delivered a crushing upward palm strike to his nose. The guard stumbled back with blood gushing everywhere. Adam pinned the guard's assault weapon with one hand and took the guard's side arm. He raised and fired, "Boom boom," two shots to the head, and the second guard inside the control booth was dead. Knowing the guard had a bullet-proof vest, he quickly stepped behind the bloody-nosed security guard to shield himself. "Boom boom boom," fired the third security guard, sending high velocity rounds ripping into the body of the bloody-nosed security guard. Adam could feel the bullets hitting the vest and shredding through the bloodied security guard's flesh. Adam drove his human armor toward the firing guard. While coming forward, behind his human shield, Adam fired. "Boom boom," two shots to the head and the firing guard was put down.

Adam grabbed the guard's assault rifle and headed into the control booth. He snatched the guard's security badge and activated the security door. As soon as the door opened, Adam sprinted Kano's body down the hall to the control room. He noticed the difference between his DNA-enhanced body and Kano's. In Kano's body, he felt heavier, slower, and sluggish compared to his elite frame. Kano's persistent pipe smoking made the lungs inefficient. They screamed for more oxygen. The body had almost had enough. His vision, hearing, and reflexes were much worse. His astral body definitely didn't feel at home in Kano's body.

"Boom boom boom boom," automatic weapons sprayed from down the hall, hitting Kano's body in the leg, shoulder, and back. He fell, quickly flipping to his back and returning a spray of automatic fire of his own while scooting toward the control room. The bullets ripped through a main artery in Kano's leg, leaving the body inoperable from the waist down. From the spewage of blood, Adam knew the body would pass out soon. The ligaments in his shoulder were torn, and the blood seeping into Kano's lungs didn't make it much better. Adam made it to the control room door, leaving a trail of blood behind him. He fired more rounds to keep the guards off, simultaneously swiping the guard's ID badge to get into the control panel. A few of the engineers inside the control room nervously glanced at Kano's bloody body scooting into the room.

"Hands up and get away from the controls," Adam said with Kano's voice while coughing and spewing blood.

He fired a round in the ceiling to let the engineers know he was not playing.

"Kano, what are you doing? You know I can't do

that," one of the control room engineers said.

"Boom," a single shot to the head and the first engineer was dead. Adam didn't feel good about killing all these innocent men, but knowing that their souls would have a chance at redemption kept him sharp for the job.

The other engineers' eyes bucked at Kano, stunned at the behavior of the person they thought they knew.

Aiming his assault weapon at the guards, Adam said, "You two put your weapons on the ground and kick them toward me."

The engineers disarmed their side pieces and kicked them toward Kano's body. By this time, the alarm in the control room and throughout the base began to sound. The sound of thudding security doors closing could be heard throughout the distant halls. Kano's body was getting weaker and weaker; Adam knew he didn't have much time. He could barely breathe from exhaustion and the pooling blood in his borrowed lungs. The hemorrhaging blood was robbing his brain of vital oxygen. He could feel Kano's body losing consciousness.

"Now lock your fingers behind your head, get on your knees, and backs to the door—now!" Adam ordered, slurring Kano's voice.

The engineers once again complied.

His vision was getting blurry and he could taste Kano's blood reflexing up his throat. Coughing up blood and gasping for air, Adam forced Kano's body to the control panel. He struggled into a chair with Kano's one good arm. Once in the chair, he rolled himself in front of the control switch for Kojo's cell. He could hear the clamoring boots of soldiers running up the hall. He could feel Kano's soul fighting for repossession of his body. However, the damage to the body was too great; it was in shock and not responding well to Adam nor Kano. The trauma it was under was making it ill fitted to house a soul. Slumped in the chair, Adam found the strength to reach the lever.

"Still wondering if I'm stupid?" Adam said to Kano's lingering soul.

He pulled the lever to free Kojo and the other captives just in the nick of time. The thought of hundreds of alien captives set free to revenge their rage on the Ky and running about the base allowed Adam to force a pleasant smile across Kano's face. The security door flew open to reveal armed guards crouching behind their riot shields.

"Drop your weapon... drop your weapon!" one of the guards shouted.

Adam forced Kano's body to eke out a bloody laugh. His beating heart continued gushing blood into his lungs, making a mobile drowning eminent.

With blood gurgling up out of his throat, Adam chided Kano, "Buddy... this might hurt!"

In his head, he could hear Kano cursing, screaming, and panicking.

Adam raised his assault weapon to fire. The security guards unleashed a barrage of heavy shelling into Kano's body. The high velocity rounds pierced into his head, shoulders, and chest, sending Kano's body rolling back in the chair, pounding against the wall.

Adam joyfully exited Kano's bullet-riddled corpse in time to see Kano's astral body being pulled into the aether.

"This ain't bloody over... I'm coming for you... with hell as my army... " Kano shouted in his decent.

"Whateva, tramp!" Adam said dismissively.

Adam's victory was short lived. His astral body was surrounded by a gang of angry goliath shadow demons. No time to celebrate as Adam fashioned his Zulu weapons once more for battle.

During Adam's brawl with Kano, Jolon's

repossessed body walked toward Clutch with his loaded assault weapon. Preoccupied with his wounds, Clutch was unsuspecting and unaware of the repossession.

"I'll give this a few more minutes to heal then I'll go check on Adam. Get the next BioGrid ready," said Clutch.

Without notice, Jolon raised his weapon and fired on Clutch, 'Boom boom.' In the nick of time, Clutch caught Jolon's armed silhouette from the corner of his eye and rolled to dodge the shots. Jolon aimed and fired again, "Boom...boom." Instinctively, Clutch anticipated the second shots and heroically avoided them. To evade Jolon's deadly fire, he dove and scrambled, using his massive muscles to propel him out of harm's way. Clutch immediately knew what had happened to Jolon. He, Kojo, Adam and most likely Nia were immune to possession due to their enhanced DNA. However, Jolon was not, a minor detail Clutch left unturned and unaddressed. A costly mistake that Clutch now knew could ruin all chances of the mission's success.

"Jolon, I know you are in there," Clutch yelled, tactfully trying to reason with Jolon's humanistic side.

Unfazed, Jolon continued firing at Clutch with a blank gaze in his eyes, "Boom boom boom boom."

"Don't let that demon fuck control you!" Clutch yelled while jumping behind lab equipment and dodging Jolon's shots. Clutch continued tossing debris at Jolon, hoping to inch his way closer to disarming him. He ducked behind anything that could temporarily shield him. If Jolon's weapon was turned to full power, he would easily annihilate Clutch through any cover.

Peeking from cover, Clutch bellowed, "Jolon, you have to fight that demon and take back control of yourself, it doesn't belong in there."

"Boom boom," Jolon responded to Clutch's words with more fire.

Clutch would have normally blasted away a repossessed person by now, but at this point Jolon was gravely needed to help re-establish a Native American connection with the Colony. The next best option was to try to reason with the soul to oust the invading demon. However, at this point it was clear that there was no getting through to Jolon. Nor was there much time to continue trying.

Bracing himself behind a lab table for cover, Clutch dialed his weapon down to stun.

"This talking ain't workin'. Fuck it, I'll stun his ass and deal with him later," said Clutch anxiously.

From behind cover, Clutch punched two pulses into Jolon's torso. Jolon stumbled back and stiffly fell. He began to convulse and spasm. Clutch casually walked over to subdue him long enough for the demon to leave his body. He kicked Jolon's weapon away, squatted over him and grabbed plastic ties from his back pouch. Jolon layed on his back, still and motionless. Clutch checked his pulse and pupil dilation. Unnoticed by Clutch, a slow cruel smile grew across Jolon's face. Pretending to be stunned and paralyzed, Jolon pulled out his side pistol. He quickly raised his weapon and fired on the GammaField device. The shots pierced into the device, scattering its pieces everywhere. The green force field dissipated, plunging the lab back into darkness. The dosage on Clutch's weapon was set for a human, and not quite enough to completely subdue a human possessed by a demon. That simple difference in dosage left Clutch and his crew more vulnerable to attack.

"Shit," Clutch yelled.

He pumped more paralyzing pulses into Jolon before diving for cover. Preparing for what may come, Clutch turned his weapon to full power. With dilated eyes, he put his undivided attention behind his OmegaScope to search for attackers in the dark. Clutch slowed down his breathing to blend his location inside the sheets of darkness in the lab. The silence was deafening. He looked up, down, left, right, and behind himself. Only Clutch's careful footsteps over the broken glass on the floor was heard. He saw SWAT was preparing for another attack.

"Nia, stay sharp," Clutch yelled while reloading his weapon for the coming assault.

From behind, Clutch saw another greenish flash with a security beast materializing. Clutch swiveled and fired. He grimaced with each pull of the trigger, hitting the beast in the head. The beast dropped, spilling its brains on the lab floor. Another green flash directly behind Clutch. He turned to fire and greeted the eight-foot beast face to face. The beast knocked his weapon loose and grabbed him by the throat. It swiveled its weapon for a point-blank blast to Clutch's head. Clutch immediately jabbed the beast in the eye, throwing off its shot. The beast's crushing grasp around Clutch's throat loosened. Clutch grabbed the beast's wrist and bent it against the grain, snapping the bone through and through. The beast cried out in pain.

Clutch pulled out a knife from his shoulder harness and plunged it deep in the beast's throat, "Eye for eye, and throat for throat, muthafucka!"

The mutant beast dropped to the ground, kicking and screaming, eventually losing the battle to death. Clutch reached down and picked up his assault weapon. More members of SWAT breeched in from the back entrance, laying down heavy fire toward Clutch. The lab flickered from their heavy storm of bullets. He quickly rolled to take cover behind a metal lab table. From behind cover, Clutch used his OmegaScope to pinpoint the SWAT team's exact location. He fired, punching a hole through the table. Still behind cover, he let go a barrage of pin-point shots from the table's hole. His gun's pulses penetrated their shields and vest, causing the first two members of SWAT to drop. Their shields and vests were of no match for Clutch's high-caliber pulse gun.

The next two agents tossed flash bang grenades in Clutch's direction. Reactively, Clutch tossed his own pulse grenades. He braced for the impact. "Booom," sounded Clutch's grenade, denoting first. Clutch's grenades exploded with a dark green flicker, disintegrating all biological material in its path, taking out all of the SWAT team. Clutch eyed his duffle bag across the room. He knew he must get to it and deploy their last GamaFeild before more security beasts materialized and SWAT entered. He sprinted toward it. A second later the flash grenades blew, "Bang Bang." The loud sound of the flash bang grenade disoriented him, sending him stumbling awkwardly into lab equipment. Clutch got up, ears ringing, vision blurry and balance wobbly. He clumsily stumbled to his duffle bag while still feeling disoriented and concussed. He reached and grabbed the last GammaField device. He armed the GammaField and tossed it to the center of the lab. Before the field could completely deploy, two more security beasts beamed into the lab. The first beast fired and destroyed the GammaField device, ruining any chance of Clutch shielding his crew from further attacks.

While the two beasts closed in on Clutch, Adam was surrounded from top to bottom with raging goliaths in the astral realm. One whip latched around his neck, another around his torso. Once again, the drain on his strength was immediate. He spun the first two off, only to be met with more shadow goliath whips subduing and draining him. More goliaths joined in on the astral feast and continued latching and pulling at his astral body. He felt immense pain, as if he was being ripped apart.

Fight, Adam, fight! Don't give up, he said to himself.

He tried to muster his strength to unleash another attack, but the goliath frenzy was too great.

Fuck! fight these bastards, Adam said to himself.

Who was he kidding? The thought faded away as quickly as the fleeting sensation in his arms and legs. Doubt began to set in. He knew he was meeting his fate. He could feel his consciousness slowly slipping away and knew he hadn't much time left. Easing into his doomed fate, Adam knew what he was going to do with his last bit of time, he was going to spend it in deep thought of Nia. He ignored the pain and the marauding goliaths aggressively trying to rip him apart. They could have his astral body, but he wouldn't let them ruin his last moments of Nia. He diverted all available resources to her memory. He thought of her sexy walk, her hair, her bright smile, her intoxicating smell, her warm breath, her sweet taste, her full lips, her voluptuous curves, but most of all how heartbroken she would be if he didn't come back to her. The thought of not seeing her saddened him to no end. Death was nothing compared to the betrayal he felt for not honoring his promise to return to her. He let her down. He pushed through those horrible emotions and thought of their last time together. He thought of her alluring eyes staring back at him while she caressed the back of his head. To Adam, the memory was so clear that it was almost as if her eyes were right in front of him. He would recognize those eyes anywhere.

Those eyes, he thought peacefully.

"Those beautiful eyes," Adam said drifting further out of consciousness.

He murmured the last words he said to her while

preparing for his death, "My business is loving you; that is why I'll always come back!"

He somehow knew that way back at the lab, Nia would feel him go. Now the visual of Nia's eyes started to fade. A calming darkness began to set in as if his soul was fading into the abyss.

"Adam, you have to stay conscious," yelled a familiar voice.

Fading in and out, Adam saw a sword striking and slashing at the shadow goliaths.

"If you lose consciousness, you will be separated from your physical body," said the voice.

Adam drifted a bit more before the words started to register. The words stay conscious echoed over and over in his mind. Drifting back in, he saw a blurred humanoid image.

"Koooojo?" questioned Adam, not sure if he was hallucinating.

"Adam, stay conscious!" the voice shouted again.

He felt the goliaths' drain on him slowly ease and his strength returning. Coming to, Adam got a clearer picture of what was going on. Kojo had come to his rescue, mounting a surprise attack while the goliaths were distracted with Adam. Kojo continued to take advantage of his blind attack by moving with lightning speed, dishing out strikes and slashes to the goliaths. His surprise attack continued to weaken the goliath's hold on Adam. Their whips slowly started to subside around his astral body. One by one, Adam felt the tension in the whips slacken. His power slowly started to return. Adam knew he must enter into the fight or Kojo wouldn't be able to hold off the goliaths for long. He also knew the sooner he finished the fight, the sooner he could get back to his Nia. The thought sent bolts of power surging throughout his astral body. His strength continued to rise, and he felt pulsating tingles as his astral body came online. Eventually his torso was free. Now his arms were free. He felt an invigorating surge of freedom coursing through his body. He quickly created his double-sided spear and joined Kojo in the fight at once. Adam ripped, shredded, and sliced as Kojo chopped, cut, and stabbed. They both put on an incredible display of astral combat. When the last goliath was put down, they embraced.

"I see you have connected with some of your past life techniques... very impressive," Kojo said with his famed arrogant smile.

Floating closer and staring intently at Adam, Kojo said with a firm voice, "But our work is not done here. We have to get back to the sixth floor."

"What do you mean? We have to get back to the others. I saw the Ky's plan and they are probably being attacked right this second!"

"We have to destroy this place first," Kojo said while diving deeper into the base.

Adam followed, pleading his case to Kojo, "Why? We have what we need. Mark Green is covered. We have a way to make the counter agent. If we don't leave now, the others may be in danger."

Kojo stopped his decent and swooped closer to Adam, "That cell I was in can hold souls, Adam. That means no more reincarnation; we could spend eternity there. At some point or another, that is where we will end up if we don't destroy it now... while the time is right. They are completely distracted by the prison break. We won't have this opportunity again."

Without waiting for an answer or comment, Kojo continued his downward dash to level six.

While plummeting deeper, Kojo said, "Adam, you can go, but I must do this."

Fuck, Adam thought.

He hated the idea of Nia and the crew being at risk any longer. For all he knew, the Ky could be torturing her right this very minute. Kojo's clever and keen insight was right again, of course. They must stay.

"Alright... what do we need to do," Adam asked.

Flying down to the sixth floor, Kojo explained, "Those cells produce an energy field denser than the vibration frequency of a soul. It's so dense that a soul can't pass through its barriers. It takes an incredible amount of energy to do that. They have to be using some kind of ultra-high gamma reactors to power it. If we can bring that reactor down, we can cut the head off the snake!" Kojo said as he pierced into the sixth floor.

"But how do we do that from the astral realm?" Adam asked, still trailing Kojo.

Arriving back on the sixth floor, Adam saw a monumental scene of hellish proportion unfolding before him. The floor was engulfed in a small war, with blotches of battles occurring throughout. There was chaos everywhere, and he helped cause it. The Ky staff were being ravaged by the newly freed captives. Many Ky were dead already. Several of the Ky soldiers and the security beast were in heated gun battles with the prisoners. Some of the captives were firing on the docked Ky ships, bringing them crashing down into the others. The ships exploded with loud concussing sounds and fireballs billowed up into the cave ceilings. The blast caused some of the cavern's ceilings to fall and break apart. The crumbling rocks further damaged equipment and set off another round of rippling detonations throughout the base floor. The chain reactions of the explosions continued ripping into the ceilings, bringing down the floors above. The debris plummeted to the base floor, passing through Adam and Kojo's astral bodies.

"This way," Kojo said, nudging Adam's attention away from the chaos.

Adam followed behind.

"What we have to do is vibrate our astral bodies at the resonance frequency of the cell. This will raise its temperature and transfer the heat to the gamma reactor. Once we bring the core temperature up on the reactor, it will ignite, taking everything with it for miles," Kojo said.

With little confidence, Adam said, "I don't know how to..."

"Just vibrate your astral body as fast as you can. It will heat up the molecules," Kojo instructed.

Adam began sending millions of pulsating vibrations from his astral body into the cell that once imprisoned Kojo. He could feel his atoms affecting the atoms of the gamma reactor.

"Faster, Adam, we need more energy!" Kojo yelled.

Adam continued as hard as he could, giving it everything he had.

"It's working, just a bit more!" Kojo screamed.

The unit began to fall apart, breaking down bit by bit, piece by piece.

"Just a bit more," Kojo said excitingly.

Suddenly, without warning, Kojo and Adam were pulled back into their physical bodies.

Chapter 28

Adam returned to his body suspended in the air, hovering a foot above the ground in a dark room. Still groggy from his astral battle, he tried to understand his circumstances.

Where the fuck am I? he pondered. *I can feel my own body weight, so I'm definitely not in the astral realm.*

He noticed a strange smell in the air, similar to the scent given off by burned electrical equipment. The temperature was oddly cold for Arizona. No defining sounds could be heard, just a low audible hum.

I must be either still at the base or on a Ky cruiser, he gathered from the low-pitched sound.

A rising stampede of panic took him over. He tried to study his hands in the darkness, flipping them over back and forth. He probed his body for feeling. His movements were difficult, laborious, almost as if his body was immersed in quicksand.

Alarmed, Adam pondered to himself, *Am I dead?*

He franticly called out in the dark, "Kojo! Kojo!"

An eerie gut feeling took hold throughout his body, raising the hairs on his neck.

"Welcome back!" said a spine-chilling voice from inside of the darkness.

Immediately recognizing the voice, "Show yourself!" Adam demanded while feverishly trying to see in the darkness.

A light above Adam turned on. Enough light bounced off Adam to show the CEO, Winston Chase, standing before him, eerily peering at his face. He had an even more threatening and sinister presence about himself than at the news station. Fire and rage flashed in the CEO's eyes, while begrudging a cold, dark stare into Adam's soul. They were exactly the same eyes as in Adam's past life regression, boldly peering down at him before his gruesome death on the large silver wheels. That same day he had another familiar run-in with those devilish eyes at the news station. In a flash, Adam connected those sinister eyes with many other troubled encounters from his past lives.

Same eyes, just different forms, Adam thought bitterly while straining his arms to reach the CEO's neck.

Moving at the speed of molasses, however, put the CEO in no real danger. More lights turned on in the room, exposing two heavily-armed security beasts behind the CEO, similar to the ones he saw at the Ky base in the astral realm. The room appeared empty, circular in origin, with black, smooth walls having a polished glass finish, similar to the underground levels at the Ky base.

One at a time, soft, low violet lights turned on like spotlights above, revealing his gang. Nia was to Adam's left, and Kojo, Clutch, and Jolon were to his right. All were suspended in the air; their dazed eyes looked forward while their bodies dangled lifelessly, paralyzed by a similar weapon that froze Adam months before on the bus.

Adam struggled feverishly, trying to twist and turn his way closer to Nia. "Nia, Nia are you okay? Did he hurt you? Nia!" Adam cried.

"Please, baby, speak to me... please," Adam begged.

She didn't answer. Stiffly looking forward at first,

her eyes slowly swiveled over to Adam. She was unable to speak, but her eyes showed her misery. Tears began streaming down her face the more Adam called out to her. Every tear that Nia shed was like a dagger to his soul.

Angrily turning to Winston Chase, Adam yelled, "If you hurt her, I swear you will see a side of me that you never thought possible. I will follow you beyond the depths of hell!" Adam screamed.

The CEO stepped closer to Adam, "No need to follow me, I will gladly take you there myself."

Adam again struggled to grab the CEO, despite his immovable state. He urgently looked over and checked on Clutch.

"Clutch... wake up Clutch," Adam called.

No response. Clutch dangled lifelessly. Adam continued to wiggle and flounder. He realized he was the only one who had the ability to move, if only slightly.

But why? Why can I move and the others can't? Why haven't they all been killed? What is he up to? Adam panicked.

"Where are we damnit?" Adam demanded.

"The gates of hell," coldly said the CEO with a

villainous smirk. The evil smirk gave off that all-too-familiar giddy spark in the CEO's eyes, similar to the day he had Adam's body ripped apart inside the silver wheels.

The CEO walked over close to Nia and smelled her. Adam could see Nia blinking her eyes frantically, panicking for help. Adam continued trying to wiggle himself free, but the more he tried, the slower his body moved, as though the quick sand was thickening. He could see Nia fighting to turn her head; the cords in her neck were straining to get as far away from the CEO as possible. She was clearly reacting to him and not the situation. Adam's mind raced a thousand miles an hour wondering what the CEO had done to instill such fear into her.

Adam learned from Scar that the Ky fed off of human's emotions. The emotion of choice is fear, and Adam was witnessing the phenomenon right before his eyes. The more fear Nia gave off, the closer the CEO got to ingest it.

"Leave her alone. Your business is with me!" Adam yelled.

He started to take bigger breaths, his chest stretching the threads of his shirt. He felt a raging, familiar energy stampeding throughout his body. His face snarled, his lips peeled back over his teeth, and the room began to rumble and shake. The security beasts nervously looked around.

The CEO calmly walked up to Adam, "Nothing in here for you to play with or throw around. We've taken the necessary precautions in the event you'd have one of your little tantrums."

He was right. With nothing in the room to throw, Adam's telekinetic powers were useless. Adam closed his eyes and tried harder.

I'll connect with the earth's minerals underneath the floor and rip this bastard to shreds, Adam strained.

Nothing.

Fuck... the walls then. Okay, concentrate on the shit in the walls, Adam thought.

Once again nothing. He felt no connection with the earth whatsoever, bettering the odds that he was high above the ground on a Ky cruiser.

"You fuck, face me... quit hiding behind your technology," Adam yelled while erupting into a useless tantrum.

The CEO walked closer to Adam, resting his dark, cold gaze on him. He studied every inch of Adam's face, every pore on his skin. He and Adam were locked into an eye-to-eye battle without breaking the stare. Adam hacked up a giant ball of mucus and spit in the CEO's face. It hit with a loud spat, landing on the upper left side of the CEO's forehead. Still locked in their gaze, the CEO stretched his long, slithery tongue and licked clean the ball of mucus from his face. With Adam's mucus still stuck and dangling from his tongue, the CEO dropped it into his mouth and devoured it.

Smacking his lips together and savoring the taste, he paused before saying, "Mmmm tasty. Did you know human saliva is a delicacy among my kind?"

Pacing in front of Adam the CEO said, "Now let me tell you a fun fact about your kind. When we were modifying you humans to serve us, we wondered what characteristics you should have. Our scientists toiled with this for quite a while, but the answer was right in front of us the whole time. Oddly, it came from some of earth's animals. For safety, herd animals willingly forgo their rights, independence, and individualism just to... fall in. They will even perform irresponsible actions just to fit into their social groups. Ultimately, we programmed into humans a few DNA sequences from earth's herd animals to make you more subservient. That's why the only way you humans feel safe is if you are following. So you see, Adam, like herd animals, it is in a human's nature to be led. To you humans, it just feeeeeeels right to be a mindless slave. You crave it. This is in your DNA."

"So you thought, muthafucka! I'm not one of your little science projects. I guess It seems something else in the universe has bigger plans than you. You can never stop what powers me inside. I'm coming for you!"

"And every time you try I make you pay. Have any chest pains lately?" chuckled the CEO.

Adam stared back at the CEO, wide-eyed and mouth agape—shocked that he knew about this past life experience.

"Ahhh, you do remember then. Every so often one of you pathetic humans wants to challenge your creators' authority. In your case, your entire South African Zulu village paid the price for your transgressions against us. It brought me great joy to break your spirit then. Watching your flesh ooze down the drain was so very rewarding for me. That day was most memorable; you should take pride that you and your little girlfriend here contributed to one of the Ky's greatest feasts."

Up to this point, Adam never knew what the massacre of his village was about. Now he found out that they were food—ground into a soup and drunk for a royal feast. To make matters worse, it was his fault. Standing up against the Ky cost him his village, dooming Nia, his unborn child, and his entire family to the most gruesome death imaginable. Worse yet,

Winston Chase had been living for centuries, plaguing other families.

Still fighting the CEO with his words, Adam responded to the Ky's feast remark by barking, "Yet here I am again. You can't kill me; you can't get rid of my soul..."

Interrupting, the CEO said, "Oh, on the contrary. I can get rid of your soul and that is exactly what I have planned for you! You have killed thousands of my kind over the centuries. You have heavily damaged my base and caused hundreds more to die with you and your buddy's charade. And that incident of you flipping over my SUV—didn't make things easier for me. It's only fair that your behavior gets rewarded. So now you have my complete and undivided attention."

Shifting into his original Ky body, he said, "So you and I are going to play together for a loooooong time."

Unlike Scar's frail frame, the CEO's physique was bulky, lean, sturdy, and muscular-esque. His skin wasn't transparent like Scar's, but light grey, scaly, and twitching feverishly, feeding on the misery in the air. His head was much wider than Scar's, having a large cranium, similar to the worker grey aliens Adam saw at the base. Like Scar, he had no eyelashes or visible hair. He had a ridge present for his nose, with two small, barely visible holes. His mouth was much larger than Scar's, apparently much more active from eating flesh. He also had reddish tribal tattooing on his face and body. An altogether different breed than Scar, possibly belonging to a warrior clan within the Ky species.

The CEO stepped closer, letting his daunting appearance evoke more fear and suffering in Adam. His eyes kept in line with their usual cruel stare, rich with hatred.

"Fuck you and your BioGrid. I ain't scared of you. I know where you live, muthafucka. Now your shit's never gonna be safe!" Adam screamed, showing no signs of shrinking in the presence of the monster before him.

"Ahh, so that brings us to you. I must admit you are an interesting specimen. There is something extraordinary about your Kode-X. You have been a growing splinter in my side for quite some time now, approximately three hundred years. So here is what we are going to do... You will no longer get the option of death and starting over. Those days are gone. Your soul will spend eternity imprisoned in a plasma cell. But don't worry, there will be plenty of entertainment for you to ensure you won't get bored."

"What the fuck are you talking about," Adam yelled, still fighting to get free.

The CEO turned to Nia. While sniffing her, he

licked her face with his long, slithery tongue and said, "You get to watch as we run every beast in the universe into her."

He quickly turned to Adam, "We are going to fuck her over and over again... and you are going to watch while we stretch and rip her womb to shreds!"

Adam violently flailed away once again, trying to free himself. He screamed, his pulse sped up, and his muscles grew tense with rage.

"Oh, I'm not stopping there, Mr. Adam. You have killed way too many of my kind for me to just stop there."

Chuckling, the CEO circled back to Nia and groped her breast and crotch.

"Mmmmm, nothing like the taste of fresh flesh suffering. It's something so very few of you would understand," he said.

Tears continued to pour down Nia's face.

"Keep your fucking hands off her," Adam yelled with a voice cracking from the sorrow in his heart.

"You know, another delicacy among my people is the flesh of a well-suffered woman. Suffering adds the right amount of seasoning to the flesh," the CEO said with the most maniacal of smirks.

"Did you know we have the ability to re-grow human limbs? Sometimes when we find a human with good flesh we keep them around for... what's the word... ah yes ...dessert! From the looks of it, your girl here is going to be quite the dish," he added.

Adam flung his body around as violently as he could, screaming and yelling. The thought of his precious Nia being devoured by the CEO carved away any wholeness left in his heart.

Adam dropped his head from the emotional agony. Whimpering he cried, "God no. Oh God no!"

The CEO left Nia's side and rushed over to Adam. Lifting Adam's bowed head, he yelled, "I'mmmm your fucking god!"

Coming closer to Adam, inches from his face, "We are going to eat her alive, then slowly re-grow what we ate and continue eating her again and again. I'm going to feed her best parts to my children... all while you watch!"

Now tears streamed down Adam's face. He fought through his paralyzing state to reach for Nia's hand.

"There is more. I've saved the best for last. Your little girlfriend here was pregnant. But don't worry, we have already taken care of it. We have some great things planned for your female offspring," the CEO said.

These maniacal words and actions gave Adam the rage and strength necessary to partially overcome his paralysis. He grabbed Nia's hands. Adam was met with a slew of telepathic information. Minutes before he came back into his body, he saw Nia's womb being stripped of their child, and Nia screaming at the top of her lungs in pain. He saw the embryo, his daughter, put into a container and jettisoned from the ship. Adam looked over to Nia, and her eyes gave him a clear reminder of that day in their Zulu village when her eyes had begged for his help—for her, their unborn child, and their families. As a Zulu warrior, he had failed her, a punishing blow to his psyche, and it was happening all over again.

While holding Nia's hand, Adam's emotions continued to swirl and spew like a newly erupting volcano. His fists and jaw clenched as the data poured into his head. His face contorted, his nostrils flared, his eyes closed into tight slits, his mouth quivered. He felt his temperature rising. He could almost feel his blood boiling in his veins. The anger inside of him surfed its way up and down every nerve ending and blood vessel in his body. It was as if a new circuit of rage had been tripped. Now lifetimes of emotions started to collide inside of his head. His Zulu village, Vietnam, Nia, the Colony, and the other billion damned souls came to mind—and the Ky behind it all. The overwhelming urge to take Nia away from this miserable fate ignited an electrical spark at the base of his spine. The only possible way he could help her was to activate his Merkaba. Remembering what his Master Zulu taught him, he channeled the immense spark of emotions up his spine. Holding Nia's hand tighter caused the spark to throb and crawl upward. As the spark rose, it picked up momentum from each of Adam's chakras. With each pass, it gathered more energy and began to transform itself into an electrical rumble. Midway up Adam's spine, it started to form a circular bulge of violet energy, expanding outward. The bulge of energy was living and seemed to respond to his soul's intention to be free. He didn't know how to explain this phenomenon, but the thought of them both being free from all the misery seemed to be somehow possible. Adam began to tremor, his veins started to pulsate, and his glare at the CEO became stronger. The security beasts next to the CEO stepped back and drew their weapons.

"He is helpless, let him try," said the CEO arrogantly waving off the beasts.

Little did he know, the rising electrical rumble was the activation of Adam's Merkaba.

The bulge of energy continued to rise pass his third eye chakra. His pineal gland, a single point slightly above his eyebrows in the middle of the forehead, began to swell. A single trail of blood trickled out of Adam's nose and his eyes rolled back. Adam's body continued to vibrate and convulse. From deep inside Adam's chest came a small, circular, violet geometric aura. The shape resembled two pyramids spinning inside of themselves; one vertical and the other upside down. The two pyramids started to spin faster and faster in opposite directions. Instantly, Adam's eyes rolled forward and directly locked in on the CEO.

The CEO stepped back, eyes wide, now aware of what was happening.

"Fire... Fire... Fire!" he yelled to the security beasts.

The bulge of energy continued to rise. Adam cracked a sneaky smile while the electric rumble closed in on his crown chakra. The security beasts stepped forward to fire, but it was already too late. When the rumble hit Adam's crown chakra, the Merkaba fully activated and engulfed Adam's crew. It sent shockwaves throughout the room. The shockwave blew the security beasts and the CEO backward, shattering the walls of the room. Shards of black glass exploded everywhere. Parts of the ship started to combust and ignite. Pressure valves exploded and liquid spewed about the room. With alarms blaring, the pitch of the craft changed, and the hum of its engine became labored. More security guards ran to the area and began firing on the circular protective aura, energy pulse after energy pulse. The beasts' weapons were harmless, bouncing off the Merkaba and ricocheting throughout the room. Heavily wounded from the blast, the CEO picked himself up, snatched a weapon from a beast, and opened fire at Adam's Merkaba. He walked as close as he could, firing head shots at Adam and trying his best to penetrate the field.

Staring directly at the CEO, Adam said, "You just fucked up... it's beyond personal now!"

With more blood trickling from Adam's nose, he gleamed at the CEO with a crinkled brow and said, "I'm coming back for my daughter first, then I'm coming back for you and your BioGrid."

Adam's Merkaba started to rotate faster and faster.

Instantly, with the force of hundreds of jet rockets, Adam's Merkaba blasted upward, propelling through the room's ceiling and taking his paralyzed crew with him. It ripped through the top of the Ky ship, shredding through its structure like butter.

They continued to rise higher and higher with blazing speed, reaching the outer atmosphere within seconds. Nia slowly recaptured her body's control first and drew close to Adam. Kojo, Clutch, and Jolon slowly regained control of their limbs as well and looked in amazement at the incredible scene: flying out of a Ky ship, rising high above the desert landscape, mountains, roads, and buildings—all shrinking within seconds. Nia drew even closer to Adam. Less impressed by the amazing scene and more impressed by Adam, Nia's eyes stayed locked on him. Kojo arrogantly smiled while inserting his cigar in his mouth. Clutch proudly nodded, no longer questioning Adam's loyalty. Jolon was back to his old self, jovial and free from possession. In awe, he hugged the edge of the Merkaba and screamed, "Fuuuuuuuuuuuuuuuuuck!"

Adam and his crew noticed other beings peering in at them from what must have been another dimension. The activation of the Merkaba had caught the attention of higher dimensional entities—friendly entities, entities that could not be perceived with the typical five senses. The entities surrounded Adam with their own Merkabas. Their forms were humanoid, similar to a human's astral body. Much larger in size, they were roughly twenty feet in height. Their facial features were blurred by the extreme light of their bodies. The crew could feel the warm, loving energy given off by the entities.

One of the entities began to speak telepathically

to Adam.

Adam alerted his crew that the entity was communicating.

"Welcome back, Operative. We thought we lost you."

"Operative? What do you mean, lost me?" Adam responded in confusion.

"You volunteered to incarnate into the physical in order to destabilize the Ky BioGrid and free your twin flame," said the entity.

"Incarnate in the physical?" Adam questioned.

"Yes, Operative, you are one of us. As all souls are on earth, we are pure energy, forms of consciousness that don't need a physical shell to exist. A gift from the creator. As an Operative, you gave up your spiritual existence to serve this purpose."

Adam's mouth gapped open, as he became more intrigued by the message. Adam held Nia closer.

The entity continued, "At the time of your incarnation, we underestimated the strength of the Ky BioGrid. The Ky manipulated your human shell to block your purpose and upon your incarnation you forgot who you were and became disconnected from us. You have been trapped on earth ever since."

Then it dawned on Adam, he actually did remember his incarnation. That is what his dream was about that morning at the safe house. He remembered seeing the earth peacefully rotating in the darkness, and the rumbling thunder storms. He even recalled the moment of seating himself inside the fetus being prepared in his mother's womb. This explained so much about why he excelled in the astral realm; he was back to his true self. This also proved the longevity of a soul's life.

"We have tried to awaken you through your dreams, and by putting *intentional coincidences* on your path. However, we were unable to reach you without starting an all-out war with the Ky. We have lost all of our operatives this way. You are the first to come back. Your awakening became complete once we received cooperation from your mother earth Gaia. It was she along with the sun that helped evolve your kind's DNA to assist in the awakening," the entity explained.

Adam remembered Kojo scolding Clutch about his presence being an *intentional coincidence*. Even the alien-like amphibious creature imprisoned at the Ky underground base told Adam that he must have been an antibody raised up by his planet to fight off the Ky infestation.

Adam continued processing and making sense of the incredible story. He'd been stuck on earth for centuries, fighting the Ky and looking for Nia on a prison planet, and the desire to find her only got stronger as the years passed. He found her, and he'd gladly risk spending another eternity looking for her. After all, he had no choice in the matter, his completion was only through her.

Adam gazed into Nia's eyes with centuries of love and admiration. She returned the same euphoric glance. There wasn't anything they needed to tell each other; their matching glances showed more than words could say. The couple gripped each other tighter, clambering to bring their souls as close as possible.

"More will come back to you now that you have activated your Merkaba, and even more will be remembered once you shed your physical form," another one of the entities said.

An unbelievable story, but who was he to question it? After all, he was rising above the earth in a force field he created.

"So who are you?" asked Adam.

"You may call me Eroke. We are from the United Alliance for Justice, Freedom and Equality."

Another one of the entities came forward and telepathically communicated to the entire group, "I am Wanu. I want to welcome you all to your true freedom, your true reality, your true selves. This meeting tells us there is hope for the human souls trapped on earth; it is possible to escape the BioGrid. The Ky are formidable foes, too great to attack directly, but we now have reason to commit resources to the human cause. We will rejoin the struggle and help free and liberate the human prison of consciousness."

Meanwhile, the Ky ship had became severely damaged by Adam's Merkaba. The ship's ability to remain cloaked was lost. Over the Phoenix skies, a large, mile-long, V-shaped vessel materialized into existence. The sight was witnessed by thousands. Fires and plumes of smoke billowed from the craft as it fought to maintain its altitude. The craft began a slow decent, crashing into South Mountain. The night sky lit up with a retina-burning fireball, followed by a deep, thunderous sound. Small shards of debris and fireballs spewed into the night sky for all the residents of Phoenix to witness. The Ky had now been fully exposed.

Over the next twenty four hours, the world plunged into chaos. News and media outlets around the world covered the crash 24-7. Citizens became outraged, as world governments scrambled to hide their involvement with the Ky. Protests, looting, and riots broke out while world markets plunged. Internet blogs, search engines, and social media sites heated up in hysterical craze over the conformation of the foreign presence. Various Colony hives resurrected with triple the members as before. Religious institutions struggled to explain the events with their doctrines. All major wars and offensive strikes around the world halted temporarily in order to assess the foreign threat. The world waited on pins and needles to learn how the Ky would respond to exposure.

Forty eight hours after the South Mountain crash, Adam, Nia, Kojo, Clutch, and Jolon had still not been seen, and the Colony anxiously awaited their return. A new war was coming, with a new weapon of hope to battle against it.

Made in the USA
Charleston, SC
12 December 2015